The Five Facets of Murder

Salema Nazzal

PNEUMA SPRINGS PUBLISHING UK

First Published in 2017 by:
Pneuma Springs Publishing

The Five Facets of Murder
Copyright © 2017   Salema Nazzal
ISBN13: 9781782284277

Salema Nazzal has asserted her right under the Copyright, Designs and Patents Act, 1988, to be identified as Author of this Work

British Library Cataloguing in Publication Data. A catalogue record for this book is available from the British Library.

Cover design by Richard Johnston of www.rjfilmdesign.com

Pneuma Springs Publishing
A Subsidiary of Pneuma Springs Ltd.
7 Groveherst Road, Dartford Kent, DA1 5JD.
E: admin@pneumasprings.co.uk
W: www.pneumasprings.co.uk

Published in the United Kingdom. All rights reserved under International Copyright Law. Contents and/or cover may not be reproduced in whole or in part without the express written consent of the publisher.

This is a work of fiction. Names, characters, places and incidents are either products of the author's imagination or are used fictitiously. Any resemblance to actual events or locales or persons, living or dead, save those clearly in the public domain, is purely coincidental.

To Jessica Stroud, my sister,
for being the best sister anyone could wish for
and
a big thank you to Polly for her help in the editing process

Prologue

Helen Porter crept about downstairs with only the light of the moon to guide her. She focussed on the one thing that had to be done and completed the task quickly before groping her way over to the library.

Slipping inside, and taking a few deep breaths, she tried to push down the irrational feelings of irritability and restlessness that were gnawing at her insides. However, despite her best efforts, a very real sensation of foreboding kept rising remorselessly to the surface.

Seconds passed before a wave of nausea rolled up and began to wrap itself around the young woman with force. As her hot forehead began to drip, a blinding dizziness assailed her and, trembling, she fumbled at the sodden collar of the blue shimmery dress put on for the occasion.

Helen knew she was in trouble. Blindly grabbing at the shelves of a large bookcase, she fell forward onto it, a few of the larger tomes tumbling out onto the floor.

Confused and disorientated, she sank to the floor, the blood roaring in her ears.

"Help me, someone help me," she croaked in a weak voice, but no one answered her call.

Chapter 1

The 10.32 pulled in to the station with a series of loud grinding squeals, its smoke billowed out onto the platform making the waiting passengers cough.

Mary Percival hastily took her handkerchief out of her handbag and clamped it over her mouth, the other hand fanning around her face in disgust. Once the smoke began to clear, Mary stuffed her handkerchief back into her handbag and shut the clasp with a snap. She grabbed her trunk and made her way to the nearest door, pushing determinedly past the arriving passengers who were jostling and clamouring their way to the exit.

Independent as ever, she waved the waiting porter out of the way and pulled the heavy trunk up onto the train herself. Finding an empty compartment, she slid the door shut behind her and hauled the trunk up onto the overhead luggage rack with difficulty, sending a plume of dust through the corded construction and making her sneeze. Eyes streaming, she placed her handkerchief over the faded seat, sat down on it gingerly and placed her handbag on the floor beside the comfortable flat-heeled shoes that were her constant companions.

At a glance, to anyone who didn't know her, Mary looked older than her middle years. She wore an old-fashioned grey suit, fit for someone of a more mature generation, and had a prim straight-backed way of holding herself. Her dark hair, flecked with silver, was thick and wiry and seemed to hold no definable style.

The compartment door slid back and a young woman came in, a cigarette dangling nonchalantly from her bright red lips. The woman nodded at Mary and sat down on the opposite seat, placing her handbag on her lap and removing her cloche hat to shake out her pale gold hair. She had no other luggage with her and was dressed in the latest fashion with shoulder pads and a fur slung over her shoulder.

Mary looked at the pretty face opposite her, took in the fact that the woman's lips and nails were the exact same shade of red, and felt irritated by it. Hadn't she seen this woman somewhere before? Mind you, all the young people seemed to look the same these days; blonde hair from a bottle, pale skin, and the brightest coloured lips possible.

The door opened again and admitted a middle-aged man with a serious face and hair greying at the temples. He raised his hat politely to the two women, put his briefcase and holdall on the luggage rack above his head and sat down on the furthest seat away from them, opening up his newspaper.

Mary shut her eyes, trying to conjure up the emotions experienced when last heading to Oakmere. She had been an excited child then and was visiting relatives with her father. It was such a long time ago and now her father was dead, and her mother was too. In fact, the only relatives left were the ones still living at Oakmere Hall.

The train whistled piercingly and the door to the compartment slid open for a third time admitting a young man wearing a brown plaid suit and holding the handle of a rather battered trunk that seemed to be covered in faded and torn luggage labels, suggesting a well-travelled salesman. He sported short dark brown hair and a handsome, if not cheeky, face that looked ready for fun. Freckles danced across his nose, and dimples came and went as if playing peek-a-boo with a child.

"Morning one and all," he said cheerfully and swung his trunk up onto the rack next to Mary's.

"Good morning," smiled the lady with the red lipstick while the middle-aged man looked over the top of his newspaper and nodded in a dismissive manner.

Mary said nothing. Brushing an imaginary piece of dust off her coat sleeve she sniffed, something she was prone to do when in the company of strangers, and pushed her handbag further underneath her seat, turning her thoughts back to Oakmere Hall.

She remembered her second cousin Elsie well as they were a similar age and had played together during the summer of her last visit. Mary remembered them playing hide and seek in the big old house and running rings round Elsie's twin brother William.

Mary tried to recall why there was no more contact after that visit, but could only vaguely recollect her father taking her away in a hurry. Unable to say goodbye, she had cried bitter tears. Her father, angry and upset, pursed his lips together and never told her why, and now it was too late to ask him.

With any luck Elsie and William would be able to put her in the picture now. It was nice of them to send the invitation after all these years, for at least thirty, if not forty, summers had passed since their last meeting.

The train moved out of the station and people prepared themselves to settle down and enjoy the journey.

"Oh dear, do excuse me!" The compartment door slid back and a tall, rotund man with wispy grey hair haphazardly combed over the top of a balding head entered. He was wearing a white dog collar and was trying to steady himself and carry his small leather suitcase at the same time. The train picked up speed, and the vicar lurched forward onto the seat between Mary and the cheerful young man.

"Oops-a-daisy, careful how you go there!" The young man grinned and grabbed at the vicar's suitcase as it bounced off the edge of the seat.

"Why thank you young man," smiled the vicar, showing a lot of horse-like teeth as he smoothed his hair across his balding pate. "Thank you. This is so like me, always late, always making a nuisance of myself. My wife despairs sometimes!" He laughed, reminding Mary of a braying donkey.

"You're more than welcome." The young man stood up and placed the vicar's suitcase up onto the overhead rack. More dust floated down, and the vicar let out an enormous sneeze making everyone jump.

"Wahh CHOO!" He dived for his pocket and brought out a large white handkerchief and sneezed again, blowing his nose as if it were a trumpet doing its first valiant solo in the church band.

"I'm Reverend Bird, by the way." He stuffed his handkerchief back into his pocket and held out a large hand to shake the young man's.

"Oh, nice to meet you Rev. I'm Frederick Adams, Fred to my friends."

"Well, lovely to meet you Fred," bellowed the vicar, his teeth gleaming. "I shall certainly include myself as one of the fortunate ones! So where are we all bound for today then?"

"All the way to the end of the line for me, and then I'll change trains again," said Fred. "I'm off to stay with some old friends of the family for the weekend."

"How hospitable of them young man, er I mean Fred. I'm headed for my vicarage in the country, and I must say I'm looking forward to it. Can't beat my wife's steak and kidney pudding!" He wheezed with laughter and slapped Fred on the arm.

"My goodness Rev, that's a strong back-hander you've got there."

"Don't know my own strength, young man, don't know my own strength! That's what my wife always says. She says, 'Bobby Bird, you don't know your own strength.' She's always saying that."

"Yes, I'm sure," grinned Fred. He looked across at the young woman. "Where are you bound for?"

"A house-party in the country," she said, giving him the benefit of one of her most alluring smiles. "I was only there the other week, but have been invited again."

"You must be a sought-after guest. For me, I introduced myself to the host only recently. Our parents were friends. We got chatting, found we got along well together, and he invited me over."

"Maybe it's the same people!" interrupted Reverend Bird with a laugh that was followed by a snort.

"I'm Flora James, by the way." The young woman reached across and shook Fred's hand and then shook the hand thrust forward by Reverend Bird.

Mary dreaded being dragged into the conversation and kept her eyes firmly shut in the hope that they would think her asleep, but the vicar suddenly dug her in the ribs, making her gasp.

"Oh do excuse me," he said. "Always the clumsy one, that's me. Always putting my foot in it although that happened to be my elbow and not my foot this time." He slapped his knee and chortled loudly.

"That's quite alright," sniffed Mary.

"And what is your name?" beamed the vicar as if talking to a young child. "I'm Reverend Bird, this is Freddie Adams, and this here is Flora James."

"Yes, quite. I did hear the introductions." She looked up and briefly caught the eye of the man who was trying to remain hidden behind his newspaper. He gave her a sympathetic look and then retreated back behind his publication.

"I'm Mary Percival," bristled Mary.

"How marvellous!" The vicar was oblivious to any kind of hostility. "Pleased to make your acquaintance Mary Percival." He glanced over towards the newspaper, and prodded at it with a sausage-like finger.

"Hello there, anyone in?" he whinnied.

The man put his paper down and glared.

"Yes, what is it?" he said.

"Just introducing ourselves, what?"

"I'm afraid I'm not one for small talk," said the man rudely and raised his newspaper again. Mary smiled to herself.

At that moment the train gave an ear-splitting shriek of a whistle and disappeared into a long dark tunnel, stunning everyone into silence.

"Peace at last," thought Mary, and shut her eyes.

Chapter 2

Oakmere Hall was a large imposing building with formal gardens, a maze and an ancient apple orchard. It perched on the top of a remote cliff and stood haughtily above the village that nestled in the valley below. The vast gardens stretched down to the edge of a rocky precipice, steep and sheer, and then plunged into the sea beneath it where angry foaming white waves would rise and smash back down on the large black jagged rocks. Generations before, steps had been hewn out of the rock to make a way down to the bottom where an old boathouse had sat and braved the elements. However, it no longer existed, having long since made its home at the bottom of the sea, and the steps were too dangerous to descend. Only a rather weathered and brittle-looking fence prevented any unwarranted accidents though few people ever went that far down the property anyway.

In the far distance an old red and white striped lighthouse stood at the edge of one of the cliff protrusions. It had once been lit up by an old-fashioned gas lamp, but electricity was now the order of the day. Ships didn't often skirt that piece of coastline anyway, but on stormy nights the lamp would faithfully shine out and sweep across the sea to warn any wayward sailors of imminent danger.

The estate had been in the Percival family for generations and currently housed brother and sister William and Elsie. William, tall and athletically built, sported short reddish brown hair with distinguished grey temples. His face was pleasant and full of fun, his mouth always quick to smile. Elsie's hair also erred on the darker side of red and looked striking when loose but, more often than not, found itself scraped back in a loose bun at the nape of her neck. Her face, unlined and pretty, shone with humour. Neither of them had married, and they spent their time enjoying the lavish wealth passed down from their parents on leisurely pursuits and extravagant parties. They lived for fun, and were not often serious, unless necessity enforced it.

Now both approaching middle age they looked down and found maturity biting at their ankles and realised that partying their lives away could not continue forever. The twins' money was beginning to dwindle and, after a series of bad investments, they had buried their proverbial heads in the sand and continued to splash out in defiance.

At their last house-party an hilarious game of hide-and-seek carried them through to the early hours of the morning, much to the consternation of the prim butler who had been forced to stay up all night replenishing drinks while guests leapt about the place whooping and making a lot of undignified noise.

William and Elsie, fleeing to the vast attics in the east wing to hide, discovered a large trunk full of old photographs, letters and other keepsakes that their parents had hidden away up there many years before. In surprise, they dragged the trunk down to the drawing room and shoved it in the corner to investigate later. Once the house-party concluded and the guests sleepily despatched to their homes the next morning, they had gone through it.

"Look Wills," said Elsie, producing a photograph and showing it to her brother. "Remember her? That's cousin Mary. That was her name wasn't it?"

William nodded sombrely. "I remember her alright," he said gruffly. "You and her were beastly to me when she came to stay here last time. I was never allowed to join in with anything you did."

"Oh, don't be so dramatic," laughed Elsie. She carelessly ran her hand through her wavy hair and looked at her brother with her cat-like green eyes. "We weren't that bad! Do you remember her sleepwalking?"

"Indeed I do, and it wasn't sleepwalking alone, but sleep talking too! She apparently always did it when stressed, though I can't imagine what made her feel like that in our house. Cook found her fast asleep in the larder one morning amidst the pots and pans, and she couldn't say how she got there, though she was rabbiting on about having been chased in by an intruder. Then another morning she woke up and found herself lying in the bath in her clothes. Lucky for her the water hadn't been added! I wonder why her photograph is in here." He thrust his hand down into the trunk and produced a bundle of letters tied up with string. "I wonder what these are. Surely not love letters?"

"Unlikely," said Elsie, taking them and flicking through the envelopes. "I recognise the writing, and think this lot is correspondence between our father and Mary's father. Here, take a look."

William took the bundle of letters, unfolded one and began to read.

Elsie sighed and put her head in her hands. "You know what Wills, I don't think I want any more parties, my head is in agony. We've been much too spoilt having all this money and now we're paying the price. Still, I guess we haven't married and produced heirs to pass it all on to, so we may as well carry on spending until it has all gone!"

"There isn't anything much left to spend. I suppose we'll need to talk about what we're going to do about it."

"Oh not now, darling. I simply can't think about it today." She looked at her tall and handsome brother with a weary expression on her face, pulled the hair tie out of her hair and redid her bun.

"I know the feeling, but we will need to have a conversation soon whether we like it or not. I've sold most of the paintings in the long gallery to fund your lifestyle, my girl…"

"Hey! It's your lifestyle too, Wills," protested Elsie.

"Well not for much longer I'm afraid. Neither of us has behaved very responsibly."

"What do you expect me to do? Go and get a job? Would I suit being a charwoman?"

"Let's hope we don't have to find out."

"Maybe we'll find money stashed away in here, or even the elusive Percival diamond!" Elsie turned her attention back and scrabbled about in the depths of the trunk. "What's this? Looks like a receipt of some kind." She thrust a piece of paper under her brother's nose.

"Yes, it's a receipt alright but I can't make out this faded writing very well. What does it say?"

Elsie squinted her eyes and looked again at the piece of paper, then gave a gasp.

"Wills, talk of the devil. This looks like a receipt for the Percival diamond! How strange. Father told us the jewel had been stolen when we were tiny. When's this receipt dated? It looks like... no surely it can't be?" She looked at her brother, a look of confusion slowly passing across her face.

"Not...?"

"Yes, the summer that cousin Mary was here," said Elsie using her fingers to calculate the years. "What do you think it means? We were told the diamond had gone missing years before this date."

"That's exactly what we were told, you're right. I remember seeing an old newspaper clipping about it in a drawer somewhere. Maybe we'll find the answer in this trunk. Keep looking, while I read through these letters."

For a few minutes a silence hung between them before Elsie spoke. "Found anything interesting yet?"

"Plenty. Hush a minute Elsie, this is intriguing," said William, his eyes wide.

"What do you mean?"

"Hush a minute."

"William Percival! Stop lording it over me and tell me what you've found."

William looked over at his sister and passed one of the letters over to her.

"You'd better read this." Snatching up another letter from the pile he deftly slipped the paper out of its envelope and began to read.

A short space of time passed before another word passed between the siblings, and then Elsie looked at her brother who seemed rather shell-shocked.

"Perhaps I do have one more house party in me, Wills," she said in a quiet voice.

"I think you're right, sister dear."

Chapter 3

Mary Percival was feeling irritable. Fred Adams was talking to Flora James above the rattling noise of the train carriage, with the Reverend butting in now and then, his voice sounding like a honking goose. Her head started to ache, and she rubbed at her temples.

The guard came by and knocked on the door.

"There's tea in the dining car," he called out.

Mary jumped up and stepped over Reverend Bird's large feet, making her way swiftly to the door.

"Going for a drink, my dear?" The Reverend drew his long legs back out of the way and beamed up at her. "Perhaps I'll join you. I'm a bit parched myself."

"No, no. I'm just getting some air." Mary left the carriage in haste and slid the door shut behind her before he could follow. She made her way to the dining car and sat down. Honestly, those people were insufferable.

With a sinking heart she realised that she'd left her bag in the carriage. She rudely waved away the waiter who was looming in her direction and busied herself looking at the menu to buy a bit of time.

"Excuse me, may I join you?"

Mary wearily looked up into the face of the man who had been hiding behind his newspaper.

"Well, I'm afraid the whole social situation of a train journey doesn't really appeal to me. I came in here to escape the non-stop drivel of shallow conversation in the carriage."

"I wholeheartedly agree," smiled the man, not taking offence. "Why do you think I was hiding behind my newspaper? They're still talking a lot of bunkum in there, and the only voice I took notice of was the one coming from the cup of tea and the toasted teacake that I heard calling out to me. It was the only option of escape!"

Mary said nothing, but gave a weak smile and gestured to the seat opposite her.

"We don't have to talk if you don't want to, but the tea is on me. I'm Peter Moore by the way."

"Mary Percival."

"Yes, I heard you introduce yourself earlier in such a delightful way!" The man smiled again as he sat down and Mary returned it, despite herself. "So what are you doing travelling on this train, Miss Percival? Or is it Mrs?"

"Miss. I'm going to Oakmere to visit relatives."

Peter gave a little start. "Did you say Oakmere?"

"Yes, why?" Mary looked at him with enquiring eyes.

"Oh, nothing, just that I'm headed that way myself. I'm a solicitor, and have been summoned by some clients that my late father used to look after. They annoyingly insisted on my going there immediately."

A tea tray was put down on the table and Mary picked up the teapot at once, pouring out two hot, steaming cups, and passing one across the table to the solicitor.

"I wouldn't like to be summoned. Do you enjoy your work?" she asked curiously, spooning sugar into her cup.

"I do, mostly. I just wish that more of it could be done over a round or two of golf!"

Mary laughed and offered Peter the plate. "Teacake?"

Back in the carriage Fred was telling jokes and making Reverend Bird hoot with laughter. He rocked from side to side with mirth and slapped his hand down on Mary's vacant seat. More dust rose up into the air and he reached for his large creased handkerchief, sneezing into it.

"Well really, who would have thought a man of the cloth would have such a sense of humour?" grinned Fred as he winked at Flora. "And look at that handkerchief, it's enormous. It quite reminds me of my mother's old picnic blanket!"

"I was imagining more of a ship's sail," smiled Flora. She took her lipstick out of her bag and reapplied it in her little powder compact mirror.

"Religion doesn't stifle humour, you know. We can see the funny side of things just the same as the heathen." Reverend Bird wiped his eyes with his crinkled up handkerchief and let out a big sigh. "I enjoyed that laugh, I must say. It's a pity more young people don't go out of their way to bring cheer. Right, I'm off to the dining car to get myself a drink and some seed cake. Would anyone care to join me? No? Right, I'll leave you two young things in peace."

He got up and nearly fell back down onto Fred's lap as the train's motion unsteadied him. Righting himself he reeled out of the door and went off in search of sustenance.

Mary was enjoying her conversation with Peter, although she found the tea rather too strong, and the teacake a little on the stale side. Her headache disappeared as if it had never been there. As she was replying to one of the solicitor's questions, a shadow fell across the table and the large form of Reverend Bird loomed into view.

"Ah, there you are. I thought I'd come and join you for a bite to eat." The Reverend sat down heavily next to the solicitor, dwarfing the chair with his size.

"Actually, I've just finished and am going back now. Thank you for the tea." Smiling an apology at Peter, Mary got up and left the dining car. She squashed down the feeling of guilt at leaving the solicitor alone with the reverend, but told herself that he was old enough to fend for himself. She arrived back at the compartment and, stepping over Fred's feet, took her seat and reached down underneath to get her bag but it wasn't there.

"Something wrong, Miss Percival?" asked Flora looking at her.

"My bag, it doesn't appear to be here." She groped further under the seat but the bag had disappeared.

"Here it is." Fred pulled it out from underneath his own seat and handed it across. "It must have slid over when we went round a corner or something."

The journey seemed interminable and Mary took solace in watching the dramatic coastline appear as the train wound its way nearer to the sea. How vast it was, and how lonely it seemed. Swathes of green spread out over the sheep-flung hills, and the winter sun seemed to melt the line where sea and sky met.

The chatter in the carriage didn't let up for even one minute and gave its best impression of a babbling brook, but at long last the train puffed into its final destination at Oakvale station. Everyone said hasty goodbyes and departed.

Another train, on the opposite platform, was patiently waiting to take passengers along the coastal route to Oakmere but Mary had a car waiting for her, and within seconds she was being whisked off towards Oakmere Hall. She gazed at the shrieking seagulls rising up and floating on the breeze with outstretched wings, enjoying the wild scenery out of the window and noted that it was as beautiful as it had been all those years ago. There was the old lighthouse over there, and the familiar rocky landmarks. Slumbering in its blue robe, the sea nuzzled up to the coastline, and Mary finally began to relax.

At Oakmere Hall Elsie was straightening ornaments in the hall and calling out to her brother. "William where are you? She'll be here soon."

William ambled out of the drawing room. "Calm down Elsie, she's not royalty."

"Well I know that of course silly," retorted his sister. "We need to make a good impression on her, though. Goodness, can you see this dust?" She picked up the china dog from the shelf above the hall fireplace and frowned. "I need to speak to the maid."

"I'm sure Mary won't notice a bit of dust! You always were one for the histrionics, weren't you?" William grinned at his sister and decided to stop teasing her when he noticed the expression on her face. "Just be yourself. If our cousin sees the pickle we're in she may just offer us a share of that diamond." He picked up the poker and began to prod haphazardly at the fire. "If she's sold it, she'll be a rich woman."

"Oh William, do you think she will help us? She must still own the thing. If there had been a sale we would have known about it. The Percival diamond, and its disappearance has been well documented over the years."

"We don't know for sure that she does have it. All we do know is that her father gave our father a receipt for it. Why were we told it had been stolen? I'm sure we'll find out before the weekend is over so calm yourself down and be patient. Look, here she comes now. Smile."

The chauffeur drew up in front of the house and went round to open Mary's door for her.

"Thank you." Mary got out and stood for a moment looking up at the house. Winter-flowering clematis climbed all over the front, its stunning white flowers hanging down in soft clusters. The building hadn't changed at all and for a second she could have been the young girl that had run around here all those years ago. Sighing in a contented fashion she turned around and gave a start of recognition at the artistic topiary peacocks that sat nodding with pride in the breeze at the edge of the front lawn as if in welcome.

Just then the front door was flung open wide and Elsie came out, her arms open wide in greeting. "Mary, you're here at last!"

"Hello Elsie. My, you do look wonderful." Mary made her way up the steps and took the outstretched hands of her cousin, looking appraisingly at her.

"Are you still known as Mary? I recall you only wanting to be called by your first name of Diane when we were small."

"Oh my, I'd forgotten how adamant I was about that. Unfortunately, no one took any notice of my wants, and I've always been called Mary."

Suddenly William appeared at the door. "Cousin Mary! Remember me? Annoying little William at your service." He gave a mock bow and grinned broadly.

"Hello William," said Mary warmly, turning towards him. "Of course I remember you, although I don't recall you being annoying. I expect it was myself and your dear sister here that were the annoying ones, always running off and leaving you somewhere."

"So we did!" interrupted Elsie. "Didn't we leave him in the maze one time?"

"Oh golly, yes I'm afraid so. We could hear him crying behind the hedges as we ran off. How awful."

William smiled. "Well, I don't hold it against you. Mind you, I've never liked that maze since. Come on in, it's bracing out here. I expect you've had quite a long journey."

"It wasn't so much the journey, but the people on the train that I found exhausting. None of them seemed to know quite when to stop talking."

The twins laughed.

"Well, they've gone now and you're unlikely to see them again so put them behind you and let's look forward to a wonderful time together. We've a lot to catch up on. I'll show you to your room so you can rest and freshen up a bit." Elsie led the way across the hall to the stairs.

Mary sat down on her bed for a second and looked around at the room. It was the same one she'd occupied when last visiting, and the orange rosebud wallpaper transported her straight back through the years with a rush. The curtains were new, a floral print replacing the old heavy brocade, but the gloomy dark Victorian furniture remained. Someone had thoughtfully put a small pot of fragrant hyacinths on the bedside table. How pretty it all was. She took her gloves off and leaned back on the pillow, enjoying the smell of the flowers and the nostalgic feelings that kept bubbling up to the surface.

Rousing herself, she got up and crossed the room to peer out of the window, which overlooked the tree-lined driveway. Purple crocuses waved in the breeze and nodded up at her in a friendly fashion. The chauffeur who had just driven up again with presumably another guest, opened the car door and Mary frowned. Surely that wasn't the young woman from the train? What was her name again, Flora something or other? Flora James, that was it. No, it couldn't be. Mary looked in horror as Elsie ran down the steps and embraced the woman. Oh no, it looked like they knew each other.

Downstairs Elsie was leading her friend into the house. "I'm glad you didn't bring any more luggage with you, Flora. We still have your trunk from the other week. Honestly, that party surpassed itself."

"The best fun ever, Elsie. I don't think I slept for the whole time I stayed here so it's no surprise I forgot to take my luggage away with me."

"You did seem to leave in rather a hurry, I half wondered if something had happened. Anyway, how was your journey?"

"Dreary. Talk about a boring carriage I got stuck in. Well, apart from one nice young gentleman, that is. Fred was quite handsome and a bit of fun too."

"Fred? Fred who? William invited the son of an old friend of our parents here this weekend with that name and it's possible he could have been on your train. How funny if it were the same man."

"That would be a bit coincidental. His name happened to be Fred Adams and he said a house party in the country was his destination." Flora looked dreamily off into the distance.

"William," called Elsie. "What's the last name of the Fred who is coming here this weekend?"

William appeared out of the drawing room into the hall. "Oh hello Flora. I hope you've recovered from the last trip?" he turned to his sister, looking amused. "It's Fred Adams. Why?"

"It looks like Flo here met him on the train. What a small world!"

Flora gave a little gasp. "Really? Well, that is funny, isn't it? Still, I can't say I'm upset, he was great company."

Just then Mary appeared at the bottom of the stairs looking a little distracted.

Elsie beckoned her over. "Mary, this is my friend Flora. Poor Flora was telling us how frightful her travelling companions were on the train today."

Mary glowered.

"Why it's Miss Percival isn't it?" Flora looked Mary up and down in surprise. "Goodness me. First Fred, and now you!"

"Ah, Miss James," replied Mary dryly. "What a coincidence. What do you mean about Fred, er Mr Adams? He's not here too is he?"

"He will be soon I expect," said William wandering over and handing her a cocktail.

Mary looked weary. "Oh, no thank you William. I'd like a cup of tea, please."

"How funny," said Elsie with her tinkling laugh. "So the three of you were in the same carriage, but none of you knew you were coming here?" She laughed again and went to the sideboard to get a drink as Flora began to sip the cocktail that Mary had refused.

"Who else was on your train?" asked William with a wink. "Perhaps they'll all be coming here."

"A reverend somebody or other," said Flora holding out her glass for a refill. "A solicitor travelled with us too."

Elsie and William exchanged glances.

"Solicitor?" enquired William casually. "Actually we do have our solicitor coming later on this evening. Haven't met him before as it used to be his father that dealt with us. His name is Moore."

Mary held onto the back of the chair that stood in front of her and swayed. "Peter Moore," she said faintly. "He travelled with us too."

William let out a loud guffaw. "Well of all the strange things. You'll be pleased to know that we haven't invited a reverend so not quite a full house!"

Mary shuddered at the thought of spending any more time in Reverend Bird's company.

They were all still standing in the large hall, which housed a number of comfortable chairs, a sideboard stacked with drinks, and a roaring fire. The staircase led up from the back of the hall and veered off in two directions to the east and west wings. All the rooms on the ground floor led off from the vast hallway.

Just then a tap sounded at the front door and they all wheeled round to view the next visitor.

"It's only old Jonty," said William.

They could see a man through the window in the door. He was quite short in stature, had thin slick back hair and a moustache like a weasel's tail.

William threw open the door and the two men shook hands.

"'allo William," said Jonty. He looked round at the women in the hall and smiled pensively. "'ow do you do?"

William clapped him on the back and ushered him over to the others.

"This is Jonty Carshalton. I don't suppose he was on your train today as he lives in the village. Jonty, you've met Flora James before, but not Mary Percival. Mary is mine and Elsie's second cousin."

"Nice to meet you both," oozed Jonty not looking as if he meant it, and not quite meeting anyone's eyes.

Mary disliked him immediately and began to long for the cosy cottage she lived in, where no one bothered her and there were no distractions. Why had her cousins invited other guests if they'd wanted to reacquaint themselves with her?

The maid brought Mary some tea, with a puzzled smile.

Mary looked at her with a haughty expression on her face. "Is something the matter?"

"Oh no, ma'am, forgive me. I thought I recognised you from somewhere, that's all. When I showed you to your room earlier I thought the same too. Have you been in the village recently?"

"I'm afraid not, I haven't been in Oakmere for rather a few decades."

"My mistake, I am sorry." She handed the cup and saucer over with a smile, and scuttled out. Mary took her drink and went to sit down in one of the deep buttoned chairs, leaving the others to talk.

Chapter 4

By the time Mary had finished her cup of tea, her cousins and Flora James had consumed at least two cocktails each and were still standing around in the middle of the hall talking and laughing. Jonty was shuffling from one foot to the other, looking out of place and uncomfortable.

There was another knock at the door and the grinning face of Frederick Adams appeared at the glass. William raced over to let him in.

"Fred, welcome to Oakmere Hall. Come in, won't you?"

"Thanks William. What a great place Oakmere Hall is." The two men shook hands heartily. "Hello, you must be Elsie. You and your brother are very alike." He took Elsie's hand and kissed it, his eyes roving over towards Flora.

"This is hilarious," said Flora with a giggle. "I had no idea we were headed for the same place. We could have shared the car here."

"Miss James," smiled Fred. "How spiffing, I can't take it in either! The car would have been nice, but some business needed taking care of in the village before I came so I walked up. My word, it certainly is steep, but the sea views are fine. That isn't...? It is, isn't it? Miss Percival!"

Mary looked tired. "Yes, it is me. What a strange coincidence."

"Is the Rev here too?"

"I don't think a man of the cloth would approve of our house parties," said Elsie with a laugh, as Mary inwardly groaned.

"And this," interrupted William, seeing Mary's face. "This is Jonty Carshalton. Jonty, this is Frederick Adams. We've only met once before but his parents were friends of my parents."

"How do you do?" Jonty took Fred's outstretched hand in his and shook it in a weak boneless clench. William tried to conceal his involuntary shudder and backed away as soon as he could.

"Why don't you all go and freshen up and meet back down here for more cocktails?" suggested Elsie. "The maid will show you where you're sleeping."

William crossed the room and sat down next to Mary as the other guests left the hall and began to ascend the staircase behind the housemaid.

"Is this all a bit much for you?" he asked in a kind voice.

"No, no it is quite alright," said Mary, her smile faltering for a second.

"I guess in hindsight we should have asked you down alone this weekend but I always think a house party is fun. Elsie and I are very sociable creatures I'm afraid!"

"And there's nothing wrong with that," replied Mary quickly. "I myself, however, am a bit of a loner. It's not often I spend long periods of time with people, but I'm sure it will be a lovely weekend," she added as she saw William's worried expression.

"We'll make sure it is!" Elsie crossed the room and sat down next to her brother, patting her bun into place where the hair was struggling to escape.

"To be perfectly honest, I needed the break. The invitation couldn't have come at a better time."

"Oh? Why's that?" asked William and Elsie in unison.

"I don't want to burden you with my woes so soon after we've found each other again, however something happened recently that was most disquieting."

The siblings leaned forward slightly, questioning looks on their faces.

"My little cottage was burgled recently; quite horrible. It happened when I visited an old lady who lives nearby. She's losing her sight, bless her, and so I went to help with her knitting and fetch her shopping. If I hadn't gone to her that day I would have been at home when he'd come." She shuddered.

"How awful for you, Mary," said Elsie putting her hand over Mary's hands. She felt them trembling and gave a quick reassuring squeeze.

"What makes you think a man did it?" piped up William with interest. "What about children, or even a woman? People seem to stop at nothing these days."

Elsie looked at her brother pityingly. "William, what a ridiculous thing to say."

"It isn't such a silly thing," said Mary. "He's right, it could have been anyone. However, I saw a strange man coming down the road from the direction of my house when I was on my way back home."

William sat up a bit straighter. "You did? Did you get a good look at him?"

"Not really, although I noticed him for two reasons. He happened to be a stranger and we don't often get people we don't know down my road."

Elsie nodded. "What was the second reason?"

"Second reason? Oh yes, well I noticed that he was rather hirsute."

William let out a sudden loud laugh and then stopped himself, seeing Mary's shocked face. "I'm sorry," he said apologetically. "That just sounded so comical. Hirsute, you say?"

"Yes. He had a big beard and unkempt moustache, and rather bushy eyebrows."

"A disguise, do you think? Gosh, how exciting." Elsie exchanged glances with her brother and stammered out, "I don't mean exciting in a good way Mary."

"That's perfectly alright. I suppose he could have been in disguise."

"Did the police ask your neighbours about him?" asked Elsie.

"They did, and he hadn't been visiting any of them."

"Looks like he was your man then," said William.

"Probably, although he still could have just been a walker or visitor to the area having a look around. The thing is, my cottage is small and a bit tatty," said Mary. "What on earth would anyone want to burgle it for? There's no ostentatious display of wealth about my home. I can't make sense of it."

"I would guess it was an opportunist. Maybe he saw you leave and decided in an instant to break in."

Mary shivered. "Saw me go? That's horrible."

Elsie nudged her brother in warning. "No, that's unlikely, although I agree it was probably just a chancer. It happens all the time Mary. I know that doesn't make you feel better, but these are the times we're living in. Did he take anything valuable?"

"Nothing of monetary value. A box of letters and effects belonging to my father was taken. He, if it was the man I saw, made a terrible mess though. All the drawers were pulled right out and everything was on the floor in every room, almost as if he had been looking for something in particular."

The twins exchanged a brief glance.

"A box of your father's things?" queried William with a puzzled expression on his face. "Why would they be taken?"

"I can't answer that. The box was in my attic. I'd never even read through the letters or looked at anything, to be honest. It was always something I'd decided I'd do when I could face it, but I never got that far. I guess the burglar thought there might be hidden treasures in there. Well, more fool him."

"Let's hope the thief gets caught and your box returned," said Elsie. "Try not to dwell on it, Mary. It's happened now and you can't put the clock back. I don't mean to sound callous but you should move on and try to forget."

"You're right of course. Still, I don't know how these people sleep at night, their consciences must trouble them terribly." Mary shook her head. "It's taken me days to put everything right and now I'm going to have a lovely break with you. Seeing family again after all these years is already a tonic, and I plan to enjoy it and get the courage to go back and face my home again."

"Good for you!" beamed Elsie. "You always came across as brave. I remember when we were playing in the orchard down near the cliff and we heard a terrible sound coming out from behind the trees. I wanted to run away but you courageously marched round to see what it was."

William's face lit up with a smile. "And what was it? Surely not our father, bellowing because he'd lost another round of golf?"

"No silly," giggled Elsie, nudging him. "A poor deer was in great distress. It was caught in the fence, a little too near the edge of the cliff, and Mary here freed it."

Mary's voice was quiet. "I'd forgotten that. The poor beast was quite upset. Well, that's a nice thing for you to have said, but I never put myself down as the courageous type in particular."

Elsie had a faraway expression on her face. "We never really know what we're like until a crisis comes along to reveal our innermost workings."

Mary looked at her. "Is everything alright with you both? I was too busy thinking about myself then and haven't even asked how life has treated you all these years."

"We're fine, both in good health," said William, his face not quite carrying the conviction it should have.

"If something is wrong, please tell me."

Elsie hesitated. "Well, it's as William says. We are fine, we have our health, which is the important thing."

"And the unimportant thing?"

"It is nothing, Mary. Just a spot of financial trouble that's all. We seem to have got through practically all of our inheritance, and the house is about all that's left." She softened her statement with a laugh.

"Money, it can be a worry can't it? I live a very frugal existence myself, so don't own very much of it either. I wish I could help you."

"No, no, we wouldn't dream of it anyway." Elsie stood up and went back over to the sideboard to start mixing more cocktails.

"Hey slow down sister of mine," laughed William. "You've already had a couple, and the weekend is in its infancy!" He got up and went over to her, leaving Mary with her thoughts.

As the other guests began to filter back down the stairs into the hall, another tap sounded at the front door and Mary saw the butler coming from his pantry to let them in.

"Don't worry Jenkins," said William, bounding over to the door. "I've got it covered." The butler turned round and immediately disappeared back through the door he'd come from.

"Helen! Terence! Come in won't you?" He ushered the couple into the hall and announced them to the room. "Everyone, this is Terrence and Helen Porter. They live a stone's throw from Oakmere Hall, so we've not been hospitable enough to ask them to stay the night. However, falling for their hints we *have* been kind enough to ask them to dinner!"

The woman looked at her host. "You old silly, William! Hello everyone."

The couple raised their hands in a half-wave and made their way over to the sideboard, obviously at home with their surroundings.

"We'll just help ourselves," said Terence with a wink. Tall and smartly dressed, he seemed at home in his expensive-looking clothes. His dark curly hair seemed rather too long and hung in loose tendrils over his collar, and an air of superiority hung over him. His wife Helen appeared to be dripping with sparkling jewellery. She was also tall and had an angular jaw and a close-cropped brunette bob that shone as if it had been brushed at least one hundred times a day. Mary imagined that it probably was. She thought there was something altogether too polished about the couple, almost as if they were two characters acting in a play.

As she was staring, Helen turned round and fixed Mary with a beady eye. "Well, well, if it isn't Mary Percival. Elsie told me you were going to be here."

"It's been a long time, Helen," came Mary's curt reply. She unblinkingly held the gaze of the woman in front of her for a few seconds.

"You remember each other then?" smiled Elsie. "That's good."

"Oh, we've bought you a little something to replace what we consumed last time!" Terence brandished a bottle of gin and one of bitters. "Bottles of booze for our buddies."

"Well thank you both," said Elsie, her laugh tinkling out across the room. "This is going to be a good weekend."

Chapter 5

Dinner that evening turned out to be quite a trial for Mary as she was unused to much company apart from her own. Her evenings were usually spent knitting and reading large tomes by authors with unpronounceable foreign names, or playing whist with some of the ladies from her church.

Glancing at her, Elsie thought how Mary seemed old before her time and decided to liven her up a bit. She leaned over and poured some wine in to her glass.

"Thank you Elsie, but I prefer plain water, I'm afraid. I am a woman of abstemious habits."

"You should have a sip at least, it's medicinal!"

"Well it certainly helps me," shouted Terence Porter across the table. "My wife and I drink like fish and have never had a day off work!"

"That's because you don't work," grinned William raising his glass to him.

"You've got me there! I'll drink to that." Terence raised his glass back and the two men downed their drinks in one swallow. "Drink a double a day, keep the doctor away."

Mary grimaced. She was sitting next to William and on the other side of her was the weasel-like figure of Jonty Carshalton. He was ignoring everyone and eating loudly with his mouth open and his napkin tucked into the top of his shirt. Mary noticed him shooting occasional black looks in Terrence Porter's direction and wondered if they had a history. They obviously knew each other as they were from the same small village down in the valley. On the other side of Jonty sat Flora, then Fred and then Helen and Terence Porter. Next to Terence was Elsie and then back again to William. It was a round table so they could all join in with the conversation easily.

"We are hosting the annual wassail event tomorrow night," said Elsie conversationally. "It starts a few villages away and always ends up in our orchard, which is fun."

"Forgive my ignorance, but what is a wassail?" asked Fred.

"Oh, well it's great fun Fred, an ancient tradition that has been going for hundreds of years. A queen is chosen each year, and she goes from orchard to orchard blessing the apple trees followed by a crowd of dancing villagers collected along the way."

Fred chuckled. "Well that sounds like a lot of fun. How exactly do they bless the trees?"

"Well," said William, picking up from where his sister had left off. "The queen is lifted up high into the boughs of a tree and she offers up some wassail-soaked bread to the tree spirits while an incantation is recited and shots fired up into the air. It hasn't failed us so far, we always have an enormous crop of fruit!"

"We do indeed," said Elsie. "So much so that we don't know what to do with all the apples. Cook always makes the tastiest wassail for miles around, which is basically a hot mulled cider. Everyone wants to come up here to sample it, even though they have such a long hike up the hill! She makes it with the apples stored from the last harvest."

"So that explains why the house smells so deliciously of fruit, I did wonder!" Flora smiled and then turned to Fred, knife and fork in hand. "It sounds exciting! I wonder if your parents ever came to a wassail here. How did they come to be friends with the parents of William and Elsie anyway?"

"Mr Percival and my father used to go to the same club up in town and hit it off as soon as they met by all accounts. Both my mother and my father spent a lot of time here at Oakmere Hall."

"But you never came here before today? How come?"

"I think it was a case of children should be seen and not heard back then. I was tiny, and back at home with the nanny!"

"Isn't that a shame?" interposed William. "We could have had a lot of fun together, couldn't we? Me and Elsie used to sit at the top of the stairs and spy on the parties down below!"

"How did you meet each other?' persisted Flora, tucking into her food.

"Well, actually I happened to run into William in town, in a bank queue of all places. I had seen his and Elsie's photograph in the newspaper where they were being interviewed about the Percival diamond, and recognised him straight away. I remember my parents talking to me about the missing diamond, and I introduced myself."

"Percival diamond?" asked Flora with a puzzled expression on her face.

"Don't tell me you've never heard of the infamous Percival diamond?" teased Fred.

"No, I haven't, I'm afraid but I'm intrigued now. Elsie has never mentioned it to me."

"The Percival diamond was allegedly extremely old and rare. Do you want to pick up on the story," he added, looking at William.

"It went missing when we were tiny children and has never been seen since. The police got involved, and the house searched high and low, and a lot was written about it in the press but nothing came to light. Our parents were completely devastated. The insurance covered the loss, of course, but that wasn't the point."

"So what was the interview about, the one Fred recognised you from?"

"We decided to renew interest in the jewel, and we thought someone might recall information that they may not have wanted to share at the time. We went to the Daily News, and they interviewed us."

"I see. Did your article help?"

"Not so far," said Elsie, joining in the conversation. "We hope the picture may jog someone's memory though. It's the only picture we have of it. Did you see the newspaper article, Mary?"

"No, I didn't. If you have a copy I'd like to look, though."

"I'm sure we have a copy somewhere. How I wish I knew what happened to the diamond. Did you ever see it yourself?"

"Well, I think I was probably too young to remember if so."

"Oh how strange, I imagined you would have. Did your father ever mention anything?"

"Father? Well, I do recall him telling me how beautiful it was, but that's about all really."

William and Elsie avoided looking at each other.

"This is interesting," said Flora. "Perhaps one of us will find it hidden away in one of our bedrooms later on! There could be a nook or cranny that hasn't been explored properly."

"Feel free to explore," laughed William. "All help gratefully received."

"So anyway," continued Flora. "You and Fred met in the bank?"

"Indeed we did, and then we went for a drink at my club," said William. "I thought it would be nice for him to come over and see the place his parents spent so many weekends at."

"Is it how you imagined it would be?" asked Helen as she smoothed her shiny hair over her diamond spangled ears.

"Even better, Mrs Porter. It's a beautiful house, not that I've seen much of it yet. I'm looking forward to exploring the grounds too, especially the maze," Fred smiled. "And I hear that you and your husband live nearby?"

"Call me Helen. Yes, just down the hill at the edge of the village. We spend so much time up here that Elsie says we may as well move in!" She smiled in a self-satisfied way. The light bounced off her earring, dazzling Fred and making him blink. "Isn't that true, Elsie?"

"We've already prepared your rooms," joked Elsie.

Terrence laughed and his curly hair bounced up and down, drawing Mary's attention to a scar on his cheek. She stared at it for a second, wondering how he had got it, perhaps the remnants of his previous life.

"Don't tempt us, Elsie," Terrence was saying in a loud voice. "Ask us enough times and you might wake up one morning to see your servants carrying our belongings in!"

Elsie smiled broadly and then turned back to Fred. "Anyway, I'm glad to be meeting you at last, Fred. Wills was telling me what a top man you were."

"Very kind of him too," said Fred with a grin. "He's quite the top man himself."

Mary decided she ought to make more of an effort at conversation. Looking at Jonty shovelling food into his mouth still, she shuddered and ruled him out. She hadn't liked Helen as a child and could think of nothing to say to her, so instead she looked across to Flora.

"So, Miss Adams, I mean Flora. How did you get to meet my cousins?"

"I met Elsie at another house party, quite some way from here. We got chatting and found we had a lot in common. Suffice to say we became firm friends."

Mary's back was stiff. "How lovely," she replied. "And what did you find you had in common exactly?"

"Oh well, the usual things," said Flora vaguely.

"She means alcohol and gossip," interrupted William with a laugh. Elsie nudged him and gave him a look.

"Only joking," he said looking at Mary. "They have plenty of shared high brow interests such as, such as, er…"

"Oh, do stop teasing you beastly brother, you!" Elsie nudged her brother. "They know nothing at all about us do they, Flo?"

"Absolutely nothing indeed!" Flora put her napkin down and smiled prettily at her friend. "They'd be surprised if they did."

Noticing Mary's knitting bag on the sideboard Elsie decided to change the subject.

"Er, that's a nice knitting bag," she began, unsure of what else to say. She wasn't used to people coming for the weekend and doing crafts. "I almost think I recognise it."

"You probably do," smiled Mary. "Father gave this bag to me when I was small and I've always used it to keep my yarns and needles in. It hardly ever leaves my side."

"How quaint. Yes, now you say it, I do remember. You were batty on knitting back then. I recall you having a particularly large pair of needles that had a secret screw top so you could hide things inside."

"Yes that is so, how funny that you recall that. They're so big I never use them, but they're still in the bag. I think we hid some of William's small toys inside to tease him. Some might call us mean."

Jonty fidgeted with his napkin and an undecipherable look crossed his face for a second.

After dinner the women left the men to their port and went to the drawing room. Trying to stifle her yawns Mary opened up her knitting bag, got out her work and began to knit.

Helen wandered around the room with her glass, her tall and slim figure swaying elegantly across the rug.

"Darling, where's your wedding ring?" Elsie pointed to her friend's left hand.

Helen's eyes clouded over for a second. "Oh, I must have taken the thing off when I was washing up a cup earlier. I expect I left it by the sink in the kitchen."

"You were washing up?" said Elsie. "What were your servants doing?"

"It was only a cup, Elsie, and it's only right to help them out sometimes."

"Doesn't sound like you, darling! How come you remembered to put your ruby back on?"

Before Helen could answer, there was a knock at the front door and Elsie poked her head out into the hall to see Jenkins letting someone in.

"It must be the solicitor," she said to the ladies in a whisper. "I won't be a minute."

Mary sat up a little straighter in her chair and tried not to appear too interested. At first, she'd been peeved that most of the members of the train carriage seemed to have arrived at her destination, but Peter Moore was a gentleman.

A few minutes later Elsie came back in. "He's gone to join the men," she said. "He was in the village all afternoon going through our notes, silly man. He should have sat in our library if he'd wanted peace and quiet. No one ever goes in there! Still, seems like a nice enough man, although I can't imagine why he insisted on coming over at the weekend. Monday would have been more convenient."

Mary gave a little start. "He insisted on coming this weekend?"

Elsie gave her an enquiring glance. "Yes, why do you ask?"

"Oh, it's nothing. I thought he told me that it was you and William that had been insistent that he should come at once. We spoke on the train."

"Good heavens no, in the middle of a party? You must have heard him wrong."

"Yes, I must have. How very strange." Mary continued knitting, her brow furrowed.

William was handing glasses of port around the table in the dining room.

"Thank you William," said Fred taking his with an endearing grin. "So, Terence, tell me a bit about yourself. All I know is that you are married to Helen and live down below in that lovely village at the foot of the cliff."

Terence took a sip of his port, swept his curls out of his eyes, and nodded across the table at Fred, his cufflinks glittering in the light.

"Well, there isn't much to tell I'm afraid, I'm rather boring. I'm known as the vapid varmint from the village!"

William's eyes twinkled. "Come now Terry," he interposed. "That's not true. You tell everyone your story and they all find it fascinating, let's hear it."

Jonty looked at Terrence with a knowing expression but remained quiet.

"Well if you insist," said Terrence, enjoying the limelight. He pulled his shoulders back and thrust his chin up in a thespian manner. "In a nutshell, I have to admit to being a bit of a down and out before I met my wife. The company I kept was not exactly on the level and I got lead astray, leaping from one unfavourable scheme to the next. Well, skipping a bit, I met Helen at the races and we fell in love. She metaphorically picked me up, dusted me down and the rest is history. Suffice to say I became a changed man. We live in a lovely little lean-to and enjoy a life of luxury!"

"You're rather fond of alliteration, aren't you?" muttered Jonty.

"From rags to riches eh?" Fred spoke hastily. "I congratulate you!"

"I always knew I'd end up doing well for myself one way or

another. And what is your background, might I ask?" Terrence looked across at Fred.

"Oh, I drift around doing this and that," said Fred with a wink. "No wife, no particular place to call home. My base is the house I grew up in, but I tend to travel quite a bit. What about you, Mr Carshalton?"

Jonty looked up in surprise. "Me? Well, my story ain't very interestin', I'm afraid. I come from the village, I'm not married, and I live on my own. I don't have many interests, but I like readin', and that's about all there is to say."

With that he drained his glass, glared in Terrence's direction and stood up. "Talking of which, I think I shall go to the library if you don't mind?"

"Not at all old boy." William got up and clapped him on the back. "You wouldn't think Jonty was an avid reader, would you? He often comes up here just to spend time in our library, in fact he's the only one that really goes in there. Makes me smile. Elsie and I don't read so we're glad someone gets some enjoyment out of our books."

"What shall we have to drink?" Helen Porter was quite fed up with the conversation around her and wanted to liven up the proceedings. She tucked her hair behind her ears, highlighting her square jaw, then went to the table and picked up the cut glass decanter. Moving it to the back of the sideboard, she drew the more interesting glass bottles forward instead.

"What's this? It looks delicious."

Elsie grinned. "Vermouth," She moved into the light and it highlighted her youthful looking skin. "You usually like your gin, don't you darling?" She poured another glass and handed it to Flora who was flipping through the records that were all stacked up next to the gramophone in the corner.

"Thanks Elsie," she said taking it and having a large gulp. "Shall we put some music on? I quite fancy a little dance."

Mary groaned inwardly, not for the first time that day. As the music began to pump out of the gramophone and fill the room her head began to pound and she wondered how much longer she could leave it before making her excuses. Looking glum, she put her knitting back in the bag and watched as the three women kicked off their shoes and began to dance on the carpet, glasses in hand.

"Come on Mary, come and dance with us. The night is young!" Elsie beckoned to her cousin but Mary shook her head at once.

"I'm afraid I have two left feet so I shall decline. Actually, I'm a bit tired from the journey so would you mind if I went up to bed?"

Elsie tried not to look relieved. "Not at all. Do you need anything?"

"No, no I shall be quite alright. Goodnight one and all."

"Goodnight," said Elsie, Helen and Flora collectively. "Sleep well."

Leaving the room with her knitting bag, Mary padded up the stairs and along the east wing to her bedroom. She was just passing the bathroom when a door on the opposite side opened and Peter Moore stepped out into the corridor.

"Miss Percival! I half wondered if we were going to end up at the same place." He put his hand out to shake hers.

"Good evening Mr Moore what a pleasant surprise and please do call me Mary."

"Well, only if you call me Peter. Are you retiring for the evening?"

"I am, I'm afraid. I have a bit of a headache. Would you believe that the young people from our carriage are here too? Flora James and Fred Adams."

Peter laughed. "Well I never, what a small world. Don't tell me Reverend Bird is here too?"

"Thankfully not. Are you going downstairs to talk business? I recall you telling me you had been summoned for the weekend."

"And so I was, but I think William Percival may have had rather a few drinks and may not be quite in the mood to talk shop tonight. Perhaps I should have come tomorrow and got a round of golf in today," said Peter good-naturedly. "Ah well, never mind."

"Well, if you'll excuse me, I'll be off to bed but will no doubt see you tomorrow at breakfast." Puzzled, Mary went off to her bedroom and began to get ready for bed, trying to work out the confusion she was feeling.

Chapter 6

A couple of hours later Mary awoke with a jolt. She listened to the distant music trilling out from the gramophone downstairs, but that couldn't possibly have disturbed her. Was that a shadow over by the window? Feeling the hairs on the back of her neck begin to stand up Mary slowly reached out her hand to find the switch on the bedside lamp. The shadow began to move slowly towards her and Mary stifled a scream, snapping the light switch on.

The lamp illuminated the room and startled both of the people in the bedroom, Mary herself and the unwelcome intruder. It was Jonty Carshalton.

Mary spoke in a bold voice. "What on earth are you doing in my bedroom?" She sat up abruptly, holding the blanket up to her chin with both hands.

Jonty, momentarily stunned by the sudden brightness, shook himself and tried not to appear too startled. "I'm very sorry, please forgive me Miss Percival. I appear to 'ave stumbled into the wrong bedroom. It's late and I'm afraid I don't know the 'ouse as well as I thought I did." His voice petered out.

"I was under the impression you are here often."

"That's right, but I don't usually wander about in the dark. An easy mistake, I'm sure you'll agree."

Mary spoke with an edge to her voice. "I suggest you go and find the right bedroom then, Mr Carshalton."

"Yes, straight away, an' again I apologise." Jonty slunk quickly out of the room and Mary shuddered. What a horrible little man.

She sat up and waited for her rapid heartbeat to slow down to a normal rate, then climbed out of bed. What had he been after? Anyone going to their bedroom would have put the light on, so his words failed to ring true. Over by the window, where she had seen the shadow there was nothing but her old knitting bag sitting on a table, a glass of water, and a small potted plant. Well, if Jonty Carshalton had been about to steal something from her, he would only have found a pair of pink booties that she was knitting for a friend's granddaughter. A slow rage began to grow and bubble up inside Mary. Being robbed once was bad enough; she wasn't about to put up with it again, even if it only happened to be wool and a collection of vintage knitting needles.

She put her hands up to her temples and felt her head pounding painfully. Where was her headache powder? Reaching under the bed, Mary hauled her handbag out and rummaged around in it until she found a packet, then pulled it out. There was no way she was going to mix it up in her water, the taste was too bitter. She'd have to go and get a different drink.

Donning her dressing gown, Mary slipped her feet into the comfortable slippers she'd bought with her, picked up her water glass and opened her bedroom door. No one was about so she made her way down the east wing and went downstairs to the hallway, placing her glass of water on the sideboard. Sounds of revelry and merriment came from the other side of the doorway leading into the drawing room, and Mary hoped no one would come out. She just wanted to get a drink and slip quietly back upstairs without seeing anyone. Just then, the butler came out of the kitchen door.

"Can I help you with anything, Miss Percival?"

"I was after a drink to mix my headache powder in. I'm afraid water doesn't take the taste away."

Jenkins gave a small bow. "May I suggest a tomato juice, or some orange juice?"

"Tomato juice would be lovely, thank you."

The butler opened the sideboard door and got out a glass. He poured out her drink and handed it to her.

Thanking him again, Mary took the drink and went back up to her room.

Back downstairs the party was in full swing. Terrence Porter was dancing with Elsie, and his wife Helen was dancing with

William. Fred and Flora were also taking a turn around the carpet, both of them laughing.

"I believe we're going to wear your carpet out soon," said Helen as the music stopped. "I'm getting quite worn out myself."

"But the night is still young." Replied William as he led Helen back to her chair. "Let me fix you another cocktail."

"Oh no, not for me thanks William. I'm not normally one to turn down a drink, but I think I've had enough for one night. Haven't you, Terrence?"

Terrence collapsed onto the chair next to his wife and loosened his tie. "Actually, I imagine you're right my dear. I'm too drained to dance on the deck anymore! I'm almost too tired to trail my way back to our turf, and I twisted my ankle a bit on that last dance. Look, can you see it beginning to swell up?"

"Are you alright Terry?" said Elsie coming over to them. "I noticed your ankle turning over as we went over the edge of the rug."

"I'm fine thanks Elsie, but this ankle doesn't seem happy. Not sure how I'm going to get back down the hill on it."

"Oh goodness, that isn't good, you poor man."

"No, but don't worry, we can take our time and I can lean on Helen for support."

"I can't let you do that. Why don't you both stay the night for once? Save you struggling back. Do you need a doctor, I am happy to call one?" Elsie looked doubtfully at the clock.

"No, no, it isn't anything serious. It'll be fine after a good night's rest, I'm certain of it."

"Well, if you're sure. William and I would be more than happy to wake up and have breakfast with you!"

"Thanks Elsie that would be great, if that is okay with you Helen?" He turned to his wife who nodded sleepily but said nothing. "I'm beat, and near as we are, I guess it would take me until morning to hobble back to our humble homestead."

"Then that's settled," said William. "The blue room in the west wing is all yours. One more drink for the road? Or a game of cards? I think I'd like one more dance."

Mary couldn't sleep. Her head was still pounding and the tinkling of laughter down below was annoying. Finding Jonty in the room had bothered her quite a bit, and thoughts of the burglary at her house came to mind with a rush. Perhaps she should go and talk to Elsie about it. She tentatively opened up her door and looked out onto the dimly lit passage, half expecting to see Jonty Carshalton crouching in the shadows and waiting for her to go back to sleep, but thankfully nobody was about.

Wrapping her dressing gown around herself, and tying the belt up tightly she shut her door and crept past the rooms along the passage holding her handbag firmly over her arm. Mary arrived at the top of the staircase and heard the sounds of the party downstairs drifting up and, steeling herself, she crept down and paused outside the door before rapping on it with her knuckles.

Fred and Flora were dancing together as were William and Elsie. Terrence had his foot up on a chair resting, and Helen was sitting next to him. They all turned around guiltily as they noticed Mary standing in the doorway.

Elsie looked concerned. "Oh Mary, are we making too much noise?"

"The noise is the least of my worries. Could I have a quiet word with you? It is rather too loud to talk to you in here."

"What on earth is the problem?" asked William. He took Mary's arm and guided her out of the room, Elsie following closely behind. "Let's sit in the hall. The fire is still glowing in the grate, let's gather round it." William dragged some chairs behind him and arranged them by the hearth before gesturing for the two women to sit down.

"I wanted to ask you about Jonty Carshalton."

William looked surprised. "Jonty, what about him?"

"I was fast asleep but woke up suddenly to find him skulking about in my room. As soon as I put the light on and confronted him he came up with a silly excuse about being in the wrong room."

"His room is near yours so it is quite possible. Still, that must have given you a bit of a fright." Elsie patted Mary on her arm.

"If he thought it was his room why didn't he put the light on? No one would creep about in the dark in their own bedroom would they? I just wondered how much you knew about him."

"Well, he's always in our library, and has been to a few parties here over the last couple of years. He isn't married so is good at making up the numbers when needed." Elsie looked at her brother as she spoke.

"Yes, he's pretty harmless I'd say," said William returning her look. The fire illuminated his hair as if jealously trying to match the colour. "He doesn't talk much, but he's never done anything to deliberately upset anyone here before. I'd say, if you feel in any way uncomfortable, to lock your door when you go back up. However, I'm sure it was, as he said, a simple mistake."

At that moment the drawing room door opened and the other guests filed out looking sleepy.

"Night one and all," yawned Terrence waving his hand. "My ankle's quite painful so there's no more dancing for me tonight. This dawn dancer has deceased! Come on Helen."

"I have some painkillers in my bag, let me get some water." Helen grabbed a glass, took her husband's arm and helped him slowly hobble upstairs.

"I'm off too. See you all in the morning." Flora smiled and walked unsteadily towards the stairs. "I may well miss breakfast I'm so tired. You'll have to put the breakfast gong right by my pillow to wake me up!"

Fred followed her up. "Let me escort you to your room, mademoiselle," he said.

"I guess I had better go back to bed myself," sniffed Mary.

"I'll see you up," said Elsie getting to her feet. "Come on."

The two women walked slowly up the stairs together and headed down the passage to Mary's room. As they got nearer, Mary stiffened.

"My door, it's ajar. I distinctly remember shutting it behind me."

"Do you think someone's in there? Not Jonty again? How exciting! Come on, let's find out what's going on." Elsie reached out for the door handle but Mary held her back.

"Elsie, this isn't a game. Someone obviously wants something that is in that room. What if they're violent?"

Elsie looked at her cousin. "Mary, you're being very dramatic. There isn't anyone violent around here, and nothing of interest is in that room. Remember the courage you used to have, come on, let's get to the bottom of this mystery."

She pushed the door open and snapped the light switch down. Mary cringed, but the room was empty.

"There you go, nothing to worry about. Shall I double check the wardrobe and under the bed for you?"

"No, it's quite alright," replied Mary feeling a little silly. She realised her shoulders were tensed up and tried to relax them. "I shall just try to go to sleep now, thank you Elsie."

Elsie gave her a quick hug and disappeared out of the room and back down the passage. Mary shut the door feeling a bit foolish but Jonty had definitely been up to no good and she would have to keep an eye on him. She put her dressing gown over the end of the bed, pushed her handbag under the bed, and got under the covers.

Elsie had gone to William's room in the west wing and was sitting at the end of his bed chatting. "Honestly Wills, she seemed terrified. I suppose the burglary at her home must have shaken her up quite a bit, and she's become paranoid."

"You're probably right, but it does seem strange that Jonty was creeping about her room in the dark like that. I'll ask him about it tomorrow."

"Do you think it can be true that she's never seen the Percival diamond before? Why would her father take the jewel and not bequeath it to her?'

"It doesn't make sense does it? We need to keep subtly pressing her on the subject to see if we can find anything else out. I don't want her to think we've only asked her here to help us out of a tight spot, but if she's denying having ever seen it we'll need to be clever."

"Do you think it was in her father's box of things, and she wasn't aware of the fact?"

"Quite possibly," replied William looking thoughtful. "In that case, who did know? I wonder if it's true that she lives a frugal existence and has hardly anything in the way of money. Anyway, I can't get my thoughts straight now. Tomorrow is a new day, we'll see what we can find out then."

"Have a good sleep and I'll see you tomorrow." Elsie got up and left the room, yawning loudly.

William lay back on his pillow contemplating his cousin. He hoped she would be more forthcoming as she came to trust himself and his sister. They would be able to butter her up, no problem. He fell asleep as a shaft of moonlight struggled through the gap in the curtains and streaked the eiderdown with a thread of gold.

Terrence and Helen Porter were in the blue room getting ready for bed.

"Nice room this, isn't it Terry?" Helen was wandering about taking everything in. "Beautiful shade of blue on the wallpaper."

"Not really to my taste, but if you like it then I like it my sweet," said Terrence, his eyes narrowing as he watched his wife cross the room and sit down at the dressing table. "I'm more enamoured with the view out of the window. The moon's out and I can just make out the sea in the distance. My preference would be to peep at this panorama from our place."

"Doesn't it seem strange sleeping here?" said Helen swinging her slender legs round to the front and brushing her sleek hair whilst peering at Terrence in the mirror.

"Yes, but I appreciate being asked and look at these fancy nightclothes!" Terrence ran his fingers through his curly hair as he spoke, the tendrils bouncing back into place at once.

"So why are we staying here, Terry? What are you up to?"

Terrence smirked. "What kind of question is that to ask your husband? Obviously my foot is painful, so I'm keeping off it, to give it some rest."

"If you say so. Don't forget that I know you well, and you can't pull the wool over my eyes."

"I wasn't trying to, my dear."

Helen frowned. "I think I might nip down to the library and see if there's anything to read."

"Read?" replied Terrence. "When did you last read anything, apart from the bank statement?"

"I shall ignore that remark Terrence," said Helen in annoyance. "Elsie has rather a large collection of fashion magazines as it happens, so I'm going to go and grab a couple."

"Fashion for the first lady of fine frocks?"

"I wish you'd stop talking like that, it has begun to grate somewhat."

"Tiresome Terrence triumphs again."

Ignoring him, Helen got up, drank the water that she had brought up for her husband, and slipped into the dressing gown that had been put at the end of the bed.

"Hey, wasn't that was the water for my painkillers?"

"I'll bring some more back with me." She quietly opened the bedroom door and a moment later she had gone.

Chapter 7

It was very late but Peter Moore was sitting at the desk in his bedroom looking through his file once again. He held an old newspaper clipping up to the lamp and read the article yellowing with age and looking well thumbed. Peter had perused it many times over the years, ever since his father had spoken to him about the Percival diamond when he was a young lad. The beautiful sparkling stone coupled with the delicious mystery of disappearance captured the schoolboy imagination and it had never left him, causing him to listen with pricked up ears if anyone ever mentioned it. He wondered for the hundredth time what had happened to the jewel.

Placing the clipping carefully back in an aged brown envelope, Peter picked up the more recent newspaper article in which William and Elsie had been interviewed and began to read, concentrating hard.

William hadn't been asleep for long before being woken up with a jolt. He listened carefully but couldn't hear anything. He sat upright, stretched his arms up in the air and yawned. Well, whatever it was, sleep had run away and hidden from him, and he was now wide awake so may as well go and investigate. He made his way to the door, opened it and went out into the passage.

No one was about in the west wing, although a faint light glowed from under one of the bedroom doors further along. Was that Fred's room, or Flora's? It was too dark to make out from where he stood. With another yawn, William decided that all must be well and returned to bed. Silence wrapped itself around him like a warm blanket and he drifted off to sleep in its peaceful embrace.

Mary couldn't sleep at all. Jonty Carshalton's presence in her room had upset her more than she cared to admit and she tossed and turned for a long time before giving up. Getting out of bed she felt her way across the cold floor in her bare feet and went to the window where she drew the curtains back to let the moonlight stream in and make its best effort at swallowing up the utter blackness in the room.

She gazed out for a few minutes, enjoying the shadowy shapes of the oak trees that lined both sides of the driveway and then returned to the warm bed. Sitting up against the propped up pillows, she looked around the room, becoming accustomed to the light and then had her second shock of the night. The door handle was slowly being turned. Mary felt the chill of stone cold fright moving up her back like icy fingers. She blinked rapidly a few times and looked again, stifling the cry that was threatening to come out of her mouth. Yes, it was definitely turning downwards.

Remembering Elsie's reminder of her courage, fear began to thaw, and the overpowering paralysis that had held Mary in a vice-like grip melted away and was replaced with indignation. She gave a loud cough to alert the would-be intruder to the fact that she was awake, and noticed the handle slowly going back up again to its normal position. Feeling braver, Mary got out of bed and removed a knitting needle from her knitting bag, then quietly moved the chair to a position behind the door. She would find out what that Carshalton character wanted, for it must surely be him again.

Terrence Porter sat up with a start. He found himself lying on the bed and still wearing his evening clothes. Helen was nowhere to be seen. Yawning, he stretched languidly and began to remove the gold cufflinks from the cuffs of his shirt. He placed them on the bedside table and picked up the silk pyjamas that were sitting neatly at the end of the bed. It must be ever so late, where on earth was his wife? Perhaps he should go and find her. With another yawn, he stood up and made his way to the door.

It was dark but a dim light coming in from a window at the end of the corridor showed him the stairs, and he tripped cat-like down them to the bottom. Hadn't Helen said she was going to the library? In seconds he reached the door and grappled for the handle, still seeing everything in a sleepy haze. The door opened at his touch and Terrence realised that the room was in darkness. Where had the moon got to? He was sure that Helen had said she was going to find some reading matter? Flicking the light on, his eyes surveyed the room, before he gave a startled yelp and rushed in. Helen was lying prone on the floor at the foot of a large open bookcase, a lot of the books having spilled out onto the carpet next to her.

"Helen," he said. "What on earth are you doing? Helen, wake up!"

There was no movement or sound.

"My goodness, Helen," said Terrence in a louder voice. "Is this some kind of a joke?" He reached out to shake her shoulders and realised that she was cold.

"Is anything wrong down there?" called a voice from the top of the staircase, and Flora began to descend to the hall.

"It's my wife," said Terrence appearing at the library door and looking up at her. "There's something terribly wrong with her."

"What do you mean?" Flora pushed past him and rushed over to Helen. "Let me see her, I know first aid."

She knelt down and felt for a pulse on Helen's wrist.

"Her pulse is very weak. Go and get William, he'll call a doctor."

"I'll stay here with her, you go and get William."

"Terrence, please go quickly, and leave me here to try and help. Don't argue. There's no time to lose."

Terrence rushed out of the library and raced upstairs. He reached William's door and banged on it with his fists. "William, William, wake up."

William, still half asleep, wasn't sure if someone was actually banging on his door, or whether a dream was clouding his judgment. He groggily sat up and ran his hands through his hair.

"William, are you there?"

Fred appeared at his door across the passage and spoke to Terrence. "What's up old boy?"

Terrence turned round, his face looking pale in the half-light. "It's my wife, I don't know what's wrong. She's ... ill." His voice broke.

Fred bounded across the hall to him as William opened the door, his face a picture of shock. "What is all this Terrence?"

"We need a doctor, please be quick."

Hobbling on his twisted ankle, Terrence led the men back down to the library where Flora was looking green. "Call a doctor as quick as you can. There's a faint pulse but it is very sporadic."

Within half an hour the doctor had arrived and had Helen Porter carried up to her bed. "Leave me alone with the patient for a few minutes please."

The household had all woken up and were milling about downstairs in the hall, not quite knowing what to do.

A pale Flora was talking to Fred and William. "Her pulse was so weak. Do you think she needs a priest or something?"

"I don't know about those kinds of things, I'm afraid. I'll ask Terrence." William went over to the sideboard where his friend was drinking the brandy that Elsie had thrust upon him.

"Terry, is there anyone you want me to telephone, someone from the church perhaps? Tell me, and I'll put a call through for you."

Terry shrugged, his face stricken. "I'll have a think and let you know."

William retreated tactfully back to Fred and Flora.

Mary was sitting on an armchair whilst Peter Moore perched on the sofa next to her. She was feeling cross with herself, as she had fallen asleep on the chair behind the bedroom door where she had set up a lookout post to catch Jonty. On waking she had got up, shivering, and stretched. It looked like her knitting bag may have been in a slightly different position from where she thought she'd left it on the table under the window but that could just be her imagination. Switching the light on, she had made her way across to the window and examined the painted wood panelling, tapping around for a secret hiding place. It all appeared pretty solid, though. Next, she had got to her knees and examined the floorboards under the rug, but none of them were loose and nothing appeared to have been disturbed there for some time.

A commotion had then drifted up to her ears so she went down to see what was going on, and was met by the news of Helen's collapse.

"You're shivering," said Peter. "Are you alright?"

"I'm not cold, just shocked," replied Mary. "That poor woman. I wonder if she consumed too much alcohol and was poisoned by it."

Peter looked thoughtful. "I really don't know. Look, here comes the maid with a tray of tea. Can I get you a cup?" He rose, without waiting for a reply, and made his way over to the sideboard.

Jonty was shuffling from foot to foot near the stairs, looking uncomfortable, and avoiding Mary's suspicious gaze. Elsie was handing out cups of tea. She gave one to Terrence, who promptly tipped his brandy into it, and asked him if she could do anything to help.

"Well yes, perhaps you could phone the local vicar? William suggested it and I think it's a good idea, even though I'm sure Helen will be fine." His voice faltered.

"Of course she will be fine, but it won't harm to get some extra help. I'll get Jenkins to call the local one up right away, Terrence." She hurried away.

"I can't stand this any longer, I need to be with her." Terrence put his cup down and limped to the stairs. He painfully made his way up and went down the passage to his room.

Not much later a car was heard coming up the drive and the lights swept through the glass panel in the front door and slid across the back wall before being switched off abruptly. Within seconds a round face appeared at the door and William went to open it.

"I'm Reverend Bird," said a loud voice and in came the large form last seen on the 10.32 train the previous day.

Despite herself, Mary shuddered with irritation. Why him of all people?

William was shaking the clergyman's hand. "Come in, our patient is upstairs."

Reverend Bird followed William across the hall and tripped lightly up the stairs behind him despite his bulk. He was carrying a large bible in one hand and a prayer book in the other. "Last rites are usually carried out by the Catholic church," he said apologetically. "However, I can pray for the poor patient."

In the Porter's bedroom the doctor was holding Helen's wrist whilst looking at his pocket watch, and Terrence was sitting on the bed next to her looking worried. The curls on his head kept bobbing backwards and forwards, and his shoulders shook with emotion.

"Show me the patient please," said Reverend Bird in an important voice. "Make some space thank you doc." He muscled his way in and looked down at Helen's motionless face.

"Can I talk to you a minute please Mr Percival?" said the doctor in a quiet voice to William, who was hovering at the door. They went outside into the passage and the doctor shut the door behind him.

William looked expectantly at the medic. "What is it?"

"I'm sorry to tell you that Mrs Porter is barely holding onto life. Her breathing is very weak and I don't think she will last until the sun rises. Have you noticed the colour of her skin? It's changed colour since I've been here. I've only seen that once before, it's almost as if…"

"As if what?"

The doctor shook his head. "Her skin was quite red on my arrival but has now darkened. To me this looks like the result of increased venous haemoglobin oxygen saturation."

"I'm sorry, I don't understand. What does that mean, doctor?"

"In simple terms it looks like cyanide poisoning. The pigmentation on her fingernails has changed and she has been having convulsions. The police will need to be alerted. Please can you go and telephone them sir? Her husband is in shock and I need to give him something to calm him down."

"Are you… are you sure?"

"I'm afraid so. I was hesitant at first, but now I'm more or less certain."

William turned and raced down the passage, then seemed to change his mind and went back to his bedroom instead. He had an extension telephone in his room and preferred to call from there rather than in the hall downstairs where everyone would be able to hear his conversation.

The sun began to peep up over the horizon and filter its warm beams of light through the trees in the driveway, sending dappled spots of brightness onto the lawn. Watching its patterns changing and growing as if it were a giant kaleidoscope, Mary got up and stood at the window. The topiary peacocks looked absurd all of a sudden, and she frowned. She had no heart to talk to anyone at that moment. Jenkins, the butler, had entered the hall five minutes earlier and announced the passing of Helen Porter, and the cry from her husband upstairs still rang in her ears.

At that moment a police car came into sight and drove up through the tree-fringed driveway and stopped. Two men jumped out of the car and made their way up to the front door where Jenkins let them in and herded them over to William who was sitting at the bottom of the stairs, head in hands.

He looked up and gave them a weak smile. "Hello, I'm William Percival. Thank you for coming so quickly."

"We never take cyanide poisoning lightly, Mr Percival," said one of the men. He was middle aged with greying dark hair and a small moustache. "I'm Inspector Marcus Thomas and this is Constable Turner. How is the patient doing?"

"She died a few minutes ago."

"I see, well you have our sympathies, sir. Can you lead the way to the deceased please, and prepare a room where I can conduct interviews?" He turned to his constable. "You stay here Turner, and make yourself available in case anyone wants to talk to you. Make sure nobody leaves the room."

"Yes, sir." Constable Turner gave a small salute, the kind that always irritated his superior, and clicked his heels together.

Sighing, Inspector Thomas followed William up the stairs and down the west wing to the bedroom of Terrence and Helen Porter.

Constable Turner began to pace slowly around the hall shooting important little glances at everyone. He always liked the feeling of superiority he got from the beginning of a case. People looked up to him and saw him as a solid and intelligent figure to trust, or so he believed.

He cleared his throat and everyone looked up at him. "Now ladies and gentlemen," he said unnecessarily. "Let's stay calm and let the inspector do his job. He'll come and talk to you all soon."

"There isn't any suggestion of anyone being anything other than calm," said Mary turning from the window to fix him with a beady stare.

"Er, well yes that is true," replied the constable without shame. "Some people would find a case of cyanide poisoning rather hard to swallow. Oh er, pardon my unintentional little joke there..."

Mary raised her eyebrows in annoyance. "Constable, I do think..."

"Come on Mary, let's go and sit over there," interposed Peter Moore, coming over and taking her arm. He led her to a little sofa at the far end of the hall and sat down with her. "I've met more than my fair share of bumbling self-important policemen in my time, I can spot them a mile off."

Mary gave him a small smile and sat back silently.

An eerie quiet hung in the room, broken up only by the constable's plodding footsteps as he paced the room, and the methodical tick of the grandfather clock by the stairs.

Eventually William came back down and looked around at everyone. "Inspector Thomas has called for the police doctor who will come and give a second opinion, but I'm afraid it looks as if Helen was poisoned. There is a small granular powdery residue in her water glass which will need testing but it seems conclusive."

There was a collective gasp from the room, and everyone began to talk at once.

"Let's keep the noise down, respect poor old Terrence upstairs."

"Yes of course, the poor man, but why would anyone want to poison Helen?" asked Flora in a bewildered voice.

Fred, who was standing by her side, looked at her and said, "She may have poisoned herself. There's nothing to suggest foul play, or is there?" He directed his gaze up to William.

"I have no idea I'm afraid. The inspector has asked that we all remain here and he will be down in a minute or two to talk to us. He's just waiting for the other doctor to come. Ah, this must be him now."

A face appeared at the glass and smiled grimly at William as he opened the door. "There's been a fatality here?" he asked.

"Yes. This way please." William led him upstairs.

Chapter 8

Inspector Thomas had a quick look around upstairs to familiarise himself with the house and the rooms in it, then went downstairs and found the library. Before going in he wandered about self consciously, peeping through the doors that led off from the large hallway. He paused at the door to the long gallery and looked back at the people sitting down staring up at him from their chairs, curiosity written all over their faces.

"I'll need to see you all so if you could stay where you are I'd appreciate it."

He disappeared inside and the door clicked shut behind him. With a deep breath, he leaned on it for a second before wandering slowly down the length of the room and taking in the view of the large oil paintings that hung on each side of it. Many of them were sea pictures, and he wondered if the sea at Oakmere figured in any of them. Tiny boats were tossed about by storms, and sat on top of vast waves, making Inspector Thomas feel a vague seasickness. He'd never liked the ocean much.

Noting that a lot of blank spaces showed, where pictures had obviously hung before, he wondered if the Percivals were having them cleaned, or if they were being sold off to raise money.

"Won't be long now," said Constable Turner to the room in general. "He'll get started soon, and mark my words, he'll get to the bottom of it pretty quickly, don't you worry."

Inspector Thomas, finally ensconced in the library, crouched down on the floor where Helen had been found, trying to visualise her final moments. The pile of books that had fallen on and around her were still scattered on the floor. He stared at them, lost in thought, and fought the feeling of uselessness that often assailed him.

Somehow he'd risen to the revered rank of Inspector, but more by luck than brainwork. His cases somehow solved themselves, despite his determined intervention. So far he'd been lucky, but he was aware his luck would run out at some point, and he pushed down the creeping inferiority that threatened to overwhelm him. He cleared his throat out loud and shook his head as if to clear his mind of the negative fog that was rising and clinging damply to him. Right, he must get on with a little detection.

The large rug that covered the parquet flooring stopped short of the bookcase by about a foot, and he noticed some markings in the thin layer of dust that coated it. With a squint, the inspector leaned closer and discerned what looked like the letters D and I drawn with what could have been a finger.

Making a mental note of what he had seen, he called William and Elsie in to talk to him. They looked around the room as if seeing it for the first time.

"We don't often come in here," said William, interpreting the inspector's glance. "I must admit, now it's the scene of a crime, I like it even less."

"So you believe a crime was committed then Mr Percival?"

"Well, I can only guess, the same as you," stammered William. "It hardly seems likely really."

"Some people take arsenic for their skin. Do you think that it could be the same with cyanide?" asked Elsie, taking a seat in front of the desk where the inspector had made himself at home. She patted her bun, pushing a few straggling strands of hair back into it. "It may be good as a beauty treatment for all we know."

"Highly unlikely," said the inspector.

"Oh, well in that case I don't know what to say, apart from how tragic this all is," said Elsie. "Helen happened to be a wonderful woman, I can hardly believe she's gone. How is Terrence coping?"

"He's shocked as you can imagine. The doctor has given him a sleeping draught and the Reverend is sitting with him."

"That's good, the poor man."

"Can you give me the names of everyone here, please, and tell me exactly what happened this evening?"

"Yes, well we were having a party. Our cousin Mary arrived first…"

"Her full name please," interrupted the inspector, his pencil poised over the open page of his notebook.

"Mary Percival. Well, she's known as Mary but her full name is Diane Mary Percival."

"I see," said Inspector Thomas, scribbling hard. "Who else was here?"

"Frederick Adams, who is the son of our parents' friends. This is the first time he's been here. Flora James, who is my friend, and a frequent visitor."

William took over. "We also had Jonty Carshalton who is a friend from the village, and Terrence and Helen Porter, also from the village. Poor Helen." He shook his head sadly. "Oh, and our solicitor, Peter Moore, arrived late in the evening. Then we have the usual servants that have been with us for years."

"And who found Mrs Porter?"

"Terrence, her husband. He woke up and noticed she wasn't in the room so went looking for her. Apparently she'd told him she was coming here to the library to get some magazines."

"Were the magazines lying on the floor beside her when she was found?"

"No. None of my magazines have been moved, they're kept over there." Elsie pointed. "However, a pile of books had apparently fallen on her when she fell. Look, they're still there." She gazed over to the books with morbid fascination.

The inspector nodded dismissively. "So what was the nature of your party?"

"Nature?" frowned Elsie, her green eyes looking perplexed. "There was no special reason for it, we have parties all the time. However, we hadn't seen our cousin Mary for many years so in a way it was organised for her."

"May I ask the reason for the long absence of contact?"

"Oh Inspector, you know what families can be like. Our parents fell out, and we lost touch."

"I see," replied Inspector Thomas, looking as if he didn't see at all. "What made you get back in touch then?"

"It was time Inspector, that's all." Elsie spoke in a firm voice.

"Then what were the events leading up to the death of Mrs Porter?"

"The guests arrived, we all had cocktails together in the hall out there, and then we went to the dining room for dinner," said William. "That doesn't include Peter Moore, as he didn't arrive until later, as I said before. After our meal the ladies went to the drawing room and, some time later, I remember Mr Moore arriving. He didn't want to join the men for drinks, so went straight up to his room. I think the maid took him some food up on a tray. At some point the rest of us men joined the ladies and had a dance."

"Mr Moore didn't join you," muttered the inspector, continuing to write his notes down. "Then what?"

"Well, Mary went up to bed early, and the rest of us partied for quite some time; great fun. Actually, that didn't include all of us now I recall. Jonty didn't want to dance as he has two left feet, and he'd also gone up to bed."

"We danced and drank and laughed, until poor old Terry hurt his ankle that is," interrupted Elsie. "Mary appeared too, and we thought we'd been making too much noise."

"What had she wanted?"

"She came out with a funny tale about Jonty Carshalton appearing in her bedroom, and the experience scaring the life out of her. Poor old Jonty usually has the bedroom Mary occupied when he stays, and I expect he'd gone in by mistake. However, it had certainly given Mary a shock. She had a burglary not so long ago, and I expect she was still feeling sensitive. After that we all went up to bed. Terrence and Helen had been planning to go home, but because his ankle hurt him, we told them to stay."

Inspector Thomas knew he was out of his depth, but was too proud to show it. He fiddled with his pen and looked at William. "You all went to bed? So nothing else happened until Mr Porter knocked on your door and said his wife was ill?"

"Actually no," considered William, casting his mind back.

"Something woke me up before that. I got up and looked out of my door, but heard nothing more. I wish I'd gone to investigate now."

"What was it that woke you?"

"I have no idea at all."

"Well, could it have been a noise, do you think?"

"I guess it must have been, although I don't remember hearing anything particularly."

"Was it dark when you opened your door, or did you notice a light on anywhere?"

"It was dark. No, hang on a minute. I remember a light under someone's door across the passage from my room."

"Whose door?" Inspector Thomas sat forward and looked expectant.

"I...I'm not sure enough to say with conviction. It would either have been Fred's or Flora's. Their rooms are next to each other."

William turned worried eyes to Elsie and she gave him a small encouraging nod.

"Tell me, did Mrs Porter have any enemies to your knowledge? I take it you both knew her quite well?"

"Yes, we knew her extremely well," said Elsie. "She lived just down the hill and was a frequent guest here. I don't know of anyone who had anything against her, do you William?"

"No, I can't think of anyone," answered her brother. "She appeared to be an outgoing, friendly woman with no worries to our knowledge. Still, nobody knows what happens behind closed doors do they?"

"Closed doors? Are you trying to draw my attention to her husband?"

"Absolutely not!"

Inspector Thomas began to fiddle with his pen. "Mrs Porter was a woman of means was she not?"

"Well, yes, she had money. She received a large inheritance when her parents passed away."

"And Mr Porter? What do you know about him?"

"Terrence? Well, we aren't really aware of anything in his background. He tells a story of him being down and out with no money, and then he met Helen and his life was turned around."

Inspector Thomas looked up. "Did they have any children?"

"No."

"No dependents then," said the inspector beginning to jot down some more notes. "Do you know if a life insurance policy was taken out at all?"

"I'm afraid we haven't been told of their intimate financial situation," said William sounding a bit put out. "It would be vulgar to ask. You should put that question to him yourself."

"Don't worry sir I shall do just that. So, what else can you tell me about the people that are here this weekend? Please give me a run down on who they are and where they have come from."

A short while later William and Elsie materialised from the library blinking in the bright sunshine, and told Mary that she was wanted.

Mary, who had gone to fetch her knitting bag and was fiddling about with her yarns, got up and made her way into the library at once, her straight back seeming even more so.

"How can I help Inspector?" she said.

"Do take a seat Miss Percival," smiled Inspector Thomas, hoping to put the austere looking lady at ease. "Can you tell me a bit about how you came to be here this weekend, please?"

"Yes, well I was invited by my cousins William and Elsie. I hadn't seen them for many years and had an invitation out of the blue to come and visit."

"That must have been a nice surprise?"

"Yes, I suppose it was. At first I wondered whether to come or not, but then my house was burgled and I felt I had to get away for a bit, so I made the decision to come."

"I see. Was anything valuable taken from your house?"

"A box of my late father's effects."

"Sentimental value only?"

"I'm not sure, as I hadn't looked in the box because I couldn't face it. However, it was probably only some old letters and pictures. The burglar would have been most disappointed."

"Did you know anyone here?"

"Not a soul, apart from Elsie and William of course, and I hardly know them to be honest. I met Helen when I was a child staying here, but I wouldn't say I know her. It seems that I coincidentally found myself in a train carriage with most of the people who are here. Flora James, Fred Adams, Peter Moore and even Reverend Bird entered my carriage one after the other. Most disconcerting."

"That is rather strange, is it not? Did any of them know each other?"

"I don't believe so, as they all made great pains to introduce themselves. I tried to keep myself to myself, as did Peter Moore the solicitor."

Inspector Thomas looked Mary in the eye. "Why do you think you were invited here after all these years?"

Mary looked steadily back. "I'm hoping I will find that out for myself before the weekend is over."

"Can you tell me of the events of last night?"

"Well, we all arrived separately and had drinks in the hall, followed by dinner in the dining room."

"Did conversation flow, or did you notice any tensions anywhere?"

"I don't think there were any tensions, although I must admit to feeling a little tense myself. You see, I hadn't seen my cousins in many a long year and hardly expected there to be a crowd of people here. Plus, I was seated next to Jonty Carshalton who I found to be rather uncouth."

"Uncouth?"

"Yes. He didn't enter into any conversation, and had rather unorthodox table manners. In fact, the man rather gave me the creeps."

"Did anyone else share that opinion?"

"I really have no idea as it would be impolite to talk about the other guests in a derogatory fashion, particularly as I don't know them, but I can't fathom how he got an invitation here. Apparently he is a local and often comes to use the library. The library! I'd be surprised if that man could even read. If you ask me, he had an ulterior motive for being here."

The inspector leaned forward a bit. "What kind of ulterior motive are we talking here, Miss Percival?"

Mary sniffed. "Again, I really have no idea, however my opinion is that he is not to be trusted. Do you know, I found him in my room after I'd gone to bed?"

"Is that so? What was he doing there?"

"He says he went to the wrong room by mistake, but how can that be true? Anyone going into their bedroom would surely switch the light on, and not skulk about by the window in the dark."

"He was skulking by the window?"

"Yes."

"What did you do about it?"

"I sent him packing, and then went down to talk to Elsie and William as it had made me most uncomfortable. They said that Jonty was not a bad person, and probably told the truth. I went back to bed, but later on noticed my door handle turning as if someone were trying to gain access to my room again. It must have been him returning for whatever it was he had tried to get in the first place, but I cleared my throat loudly and frightened him off. I made sure to lock my door today." Mary produced a key from her pocket and brandished it at the inspector.

"You say he stood by the window? What side of the house does your window look out onto?"

"The driveway at the front."

"Is Mr Carshalton's own bedroom furnished with a front aspect?"

"I believe so. To my knowledge, his room is two doors down from mine, on the same side."

"I see, and was there anything in the alcove of your window that could have proved interesting to him, or anyone else for that matter?"

"No. My knitting bag sat there, a glass of water, and a vase of flowers. If he had been after my handbag he would have been out of luck as it was pushed under the bed."

"Which of the other guests were sleeping on your wing of the house?"

"Peter Moore the solicitor was the only other."

"Could Mr Moore have mistakenly your room for his when you saw the door handle turn?"

Mary looked at the inspector as if he had gone mad. "Well, of course not. That would not be likely would it? Both Mr Moore and Mr Carshalton mistakenly trying to get into my room instead of their own? Besides, Mr Moore's room was on the other side of the corridor, overlooking the back of the house. He was summoned here by my cousins, and had no motive for being here apart from work. I'm sure he has no need to try and steal from a fellow guest."

"Mr Percival told me that they had tried to put the solicitor off from coming until after the weekend. Why do you think he came so early?"

"I think there were some crossed wires. Peter Moore told me he had wanted to remain home and play golf, but that William and Elsie had asked him to specifically come this weekend."

The inspector seemed to remember his notepad and started to hurriedly scribble some notes down. He eventually looked up.

"So, what happened between dinner and you going up to your room?"

"Not very much. The men remained in the dining room and the women went to the drawing room where they continued to drink alcohol. I abstained myself. Then they put some music on and started to dance. I'm afraid it wasn't really my scene and so I decided to go to bed. Oh, before that, Mr Moore arrived and Elsie took him to see William. I met him in the east wing as I was going up to bed and we exchanged pleasantries."

"He was in the corridor?"

"Yes, why do you ask? Oh, don't tell me you're assuming he was having another go at gaining access to my room? What do you think these people were after in there?"

"I'm not suggesting anything Miss Percival, just trying to get the facts straight. Please continue with your version of events."

"Well, that is it really. Oh wait, I popped back downstairs to get a drink before I went to talk to my cousins about Mr Carshalton. I wanted to take a powder for my headache, but I don't like the taste of the stuff, so took my water glass down and Jenkins poured me a tomato juice instead."

"And you saw nothing suspicious then?"

"Well of course not," said Mary in a scornful voice. "Nothing had happened then, had it?"

Inspector Thomas was beginning to feel drained, and his interview not really getting him anywhere close to where he wanted to be. He limped feebly on. "What was your impression of Mrs Porter?"

"They all seem to be the same to me, these high society women. Dripping in jewellery and saturated with the latest in hair and clothes, drinking en vogue cocktails and laughing like maniacs at every little thing said by anyone else, particularly the male species."

The inspector seemed a little dazed after this verbal assault on the deceased and sighed to himself. "Thank you Miss Percvial, that will be all for now."

Chapter 9

A short while after Mary had left the library Constable Turner appeared in the doorway and plodded in to talk to his superior. "Anything of interest to report sir?"

"Well it seems as if there were some nocturnal wanderings around here," said the inspector.

"Ay, what's that?" said the constable looking confused. "Nocturnal wanderings? Sounds a bit poetic-like."

"Believe me, I see nothing poetic about it," said Inspector Thomas sitting back and looking thoughtful. "Have a look over in that corner, where Mrs Porter collapsed. See anything unusual?"

Constable Turner moved heavily over to the bookcase and knelt down on one knee, peering at the floor. "What am I looking for exactly?"

"Turner! And you say you want to be a detective." Inspector Thomas shook his head in despair.

"You don't mean these books, do you? Oh, do you mean these letters in the dust?" The constable squinted his eyes and stared hard at the floor.

"Ah, so you do reckon they're letters then, not just random marks? What do you think they stand for?"

"D and I. D and I. I don't rightly know, sir. It can't be the word DIE can it?"

"I shouldn't think so."

"Dim, dippy, diet? I'll ponder on it, sir."

The inspector inhaled through his nose and changed the subject in order to stop himself from speaking sharply. "Have you gleaned anything from anyone yet?"

"Well, my initial thoughts are that Flora James and Frederick Adams are more than a little friendly for people who have only just met each other."

"Very interesting, Turner. I'll have to keep an eye on their relationship. If that's all, perhaps you'd be so good as to send Mr Adams in to meet me now?"

Fred appeared at the door a few seconds later and gave the inspector his usual boyish grin; the dimples in his cheeks making him seem younger than his years. "Hi there, Frederick Adam's the name. You can call me Fred." He sat down and looked expectantly at Inspector Thomas.

Ignoring the invitation to be less formal the inspector said, "Mr Adams, I'm trying to get to the bottom of this little mystery. No one seems to think that Mrs Porter would be the kind of woman to commit suicide. Do you have an opinion on it at all?"

"I'm afraid I'd only met her a few hours earlier, Inspector. She arrived with her husband and did not look as if she had the weight of the world on her shoulders. Both of the Porters were friendly and outgoing, and I didn't sense anything negative at all from them. This is all rather a nasty shock."

"Yes, it is an unfortunate tragedy. Your opinion, I take it, is that Mrs Porter did not seem the type to spend the evening having fun and then, after everyone else had gone to bed, take her own life?"

"No, that seems a preposterous idea to me."

"So in that case the other alternative is murder?"

"Murder, but why? Surely there is another alternative, a mistake?"

"Ah, a mistake. Tell me how you think that could happen please."

Fred's face flushed. "I'm not an expert on these matters you know. I can't imagine either suicide or murder. There must have been a mistake. Perhaps someone suggested the benefits of drinking cyanide and she tried it, not realising it was a fatal dose. Some people swear by arsenic don't they? Maybe it has the same properties."

The inspector stared at the young man in front of him. "You're not the first person to suggest that today. What an interesting concept. Tell me about yourself, Mr Adams," he said with a small smile, and sat back as if he were an interested friend.

"Me? Well, there's not much to tell if truth be told," said Fred momentarily nonplussed. The inspector's change of tone was disconcerting and he felt on his guard.

"I'm sure that's not the case," said Inspector Thomas warmly. "What do you do, and where do you come from?"

"Oh, I'm sure you're not interested in boring old me," laughed Fred hesitantly. "Finding Helen's killer is far more important. Aren't we wasting valuable detection time talking about me?"

"Not at all, not at all. There's always time to get the background on the suspects in a murder case you know."

"Suspect? Murder? Gosh, yes I suppose I am, aren't I? Well, in that case, I'd better come clean!" Fred flashed a nervous grin at the man sitting opposite him.

"Yes if you would, sir."

"Well, I'm Frederick Penrose Adams and I come from a small town south of London called Haslemere. My folks have all passed on but I have the family home there, not that I am there very often. I travel around all over the country in my line of work."

"What is your line of work exactly?"

"I, er, well I sell things."

"A travelling salesman?"

"Of sorts, yes."

"You are being most cryptic, Mr Adams. May I have the name of your employers?"

"I work for myself, Inspector."

"I'm afraid I am getting somewhat weary of this conversation, we seem to be going round in circles. What is it that you sell?"

"Information."

"Ah, Miss James." Inspector Thomas stood up until Flora had sat down. He noted the beautiful blonde vision with striking red lipstick, expertly applied, sitting before him.

"Yes, please call me Flora. This is all rather upsetting, Inspector. I have met Helen a number of times here at Oakmere, and she came across as a pleasant enough woman. She didn't seem nervy or depressed, not that you can always tell I know, but she was just a fun person to be around." She began to fiddle with her earrings.

"And what did you make of her husband?'

Flora looked up. "Terrence? Well, he was fun too."

"Were they a happy couple?"

"Yes, I would say so," said Flora looking thoughtful. "Terrence was a terrible flirt, of course, but she never seemed to bat an eyelid."

"Did he flirt with you?" Inspector Thomas discreetly lowered his eyes and became interested in the pen that was lying on the desk.

"Yes, but I never gave it a thought, really. Innocent and harmless come to mind."

"So there was no suggestion of either Helen being upset with you, or Terrence hinting at a small affair of the heart?"

"You are way off the mark I'm afraid," said Flora with a frown, her cheeks flushing pink. "Terrence was respectful, just a bit playful, and Helen and I never had a cross word."

"Tell me, how did you come to be out of bed when Terence discovered his wife?"

"I thought I heard a noise, and I went out of my room to investigate."

"And what did you find?"

"Well, I'm not sure. Something disturbed me, that's all I know, and I got up," said Flora.

"I would have thought that most people waking up at a noise would sit up in bed and listen, and if they heard nothing more, would go back to sleep."

"I'm not most people, Inspector."

"Could the noise you heard have been Helen Porter falling into that bookcase, and the books tumbling out?"

Flora shuddered. "Yes, that's probably what it was."

"And yet your room isn't really anywhere near the library is it?"

"No, no, it isn't. William's bedroom is over the library, but mine is just across the way. It must have been something else that disturbed me." Flora looked steadily at the policeman opposite her. The inspector was the first to drop his eyes.

"So what happened when you went downstairs and saw Helen lying on the floor?"

Flora half shut her eyes, remembering the scene. "I felt for a pulse, and it was weak, so I sent Terrence to wake William up to summon a doctor."

"Wouldn't it have been quicker to have gone yourself, seeing as Mr Porter had twisted his ankle?"

"I didn't focus on his ankle, I'd quite forgotten about it in fact. My first instinct was to help Helen."

Inspector Thomas looked up. "I can't quite grasp why you wouldn't leave the husband with his wife and get help yourself."

"I can do first aid, Inspector, and I thought I might be able to help."

"And did you manage to do anything to, er, help?"

Flora frowned. "To be honest, it seems as if you're cross-examining me, and it's making me feel nervous. I did all I could to help, if you must know. I rubbed her cold hands to try and warm them up, and I put a blanket over her back."

"How did you come to know the Percival family, Miss James?"

"I met Elsie at a party and we became firm friends. She often invites me down here. I live just south of London with my mother."

"Your father?"

"He died some time ago, I'm afraid. He left Mother and I quite well off, though, so we're not destitute."

Inspector Thomas glanced at his notes. "Do you live near Haslemere by any chance?"

"Haslemere? No. Well, not too far really, maybe six miles or so. Why do you ask?"

"No matter. Now, can you think of anything worthy of note at all? A word, a look, a comment?"

"Well, nothing solid. The guest list for the weekend was a bit suspect if you ask me. We were all different from each other. Well, not all, but some seemed a bit out of place. Mary Percival for one. I realise she is a relative, but she seems so much older than her years. Not one for letting her hair down, that one. Then there's Jonty Carshalton. He's here often, making use of this room in actual fact, but he doesn't seem to have any conversation in him, just looks furtive and suspicious. I have met him here before and he was the same then too. Heaven only knows why he's so thick with the Percivals."

"Thank you for that insight. So, tell me, did Frederick Adams fit in?"

"Fred? Oh yes, he's a lot of fun."

Inspector Thomas averted his eyes from looking at the woman in front of him and instead fixed his gaze on a paperweight that was resting on an envelope at the far corner of the desk. "Is this the first time you've met him?"

"It is. Did you know we were in the same train carriage?"

"I did hear that, yes. So you're sure you've never come across him before?"

Flora frowned. "Of course I'm sure, I would have remembered."

"In that case, you may go for the time being. Thank you for your help."

Chapter 10

Inspector Thomas walked slowly out of the library, hands in pockets, and looked around at the people seated in the hall. They were expecting him to remove the veil so that they could view the truth beneath, but he was feeling increasingly insecure about his abilities. Putting on an air of confidence he breathed out slowly and spoke.

"I'll talk to you in a minute please Mr Carshalton, and Mr Moore afterwards. First of all, I must just check up on how things are going upstairs. You others may feel free to leave the hall if you would like, but please do not leave the house."

Upstairs, Reverend Bird was pacing the bedroom, his large feet squeaking over the floorboards, while Terrence Porter slept. Helen's body had been removed and the two doctors were talking in quiet voices in the corner.

"Ah there you are sir," said the police doctor. " We agree that cyanide was most definitely ingested from this glass, but it will need a test to confirm it. See the white residue around the sides?"

Inspector Thomas nodded and then looked around the room. "Where is the tray and water jug?" he asked. "Has somebody removed them?"

"Nothing has been removed since I've been here," said Reverend Bird, butting in. "I would have noticed. My wife, she says I notice everything. 'There's nothing hidden from your eyes Bobby Bird!' she says."

"I'm sure that is so," said the inspector frostily. He turned to Constable Turner who had appeared in the doorway. "Turner, go and ask the staff who removed the tray and jug from in here."

"Yes sir." Constable Turner clicked his heels and disappeared. They listened to his footsteps fading away. He was back in a few short minutes. "The butler says there wasn't a water jug in here as he didn't know the Porters were staying the night until the last minute, and he didn't think to bring one. The maid didn't bring one either."

"It looks like she got the drink from somewhere else, what?" boomed Reverend Bird in his cacophonous voice.

Terrence Porter stirred in his sleep.

"Oops, dear me, I must learn to speak in less of a loud voice," continued the Reverend in a loud whisper. "My wife says my voice is both a blessing and a curse."

Inspector Thomas raised his eyes to the ceiling. "You probably don't need to be here anymore, Reverend," he said. "Our patient has sadly gone, and Mr Porter is asleep, so there's no need for us to take anymore of your valuable time up."

"Oh no Inspector," brayed Reverend Bird waggling his finger. "Mr Porter sent for me. I'd be happier to stay until he dismisses me. He'll need some prayer and comfort when he awakens." He plonked himself down in a chair as if to imply that he would have to be physically removed if push came to shove.

Shaking his head, Inspector Thomas turned to the doctor. "Have you had a look at Mr Porter's ankle? He twisted it when dancing apparently."

"I had a brief look a minute ago, but both ankles seem fine. I couldn't tell which one he had hurt, and couldn't ask him as he had fallen asleep."

"Now that's interesting. Turner, can you fetch the finger printing kit from the car and take everyone's prints after you've dusted this glass? Then give the glass back to the doctor, here, who needs to take it away with him. Leave Jonty Carshalton and Peter Moore's prints until last as I need to see them."

Back in the library, the inspector called for Jonty who appeared at the door looking his usual shifty self. "Come in Mr Carshalton, take a seat."

"I can't tell you anything I'm afraid." He perched himself down on the edge of the chair and pursed his lips together.

"But I haven't asked you anything yet. You only need to answer my questions truthfully please. Firstly, I hear you often come here to use the library. What is it in here that you are so interested in?"

Jonty gave a start. "Well, I'm interested in the books. There ain't nothin' else in 'ere."

"You don't look like a reading kind of a man if I may say so."

"Looks can be deceivin' Inspector."

"Yes that is so. Tell me what books you like to read when you come here."

Jonty motioned towards the bookcase housing the classics but his eyes flickered briefly towards a different shelf, which wasn't missed by the inspector's sharp eyes.

"The classics?" Inspector Thomas stood up and walked slowly over to the books and picked one up. "Is this one of your favoured reads?"

Jonty cleared his throat. "Erm, yes. William Shakespeare was a genius. I could never get bored reading his plays."

Inspector Thomas was itching to test Jonty on his knowledge, but felt he was lacking in the literature world himself.

"Why don't you borrow the books and take them home to read in the comfort of your own home, Mr Carshalton?"

"I like to read 'ere, surrounded by all these old books. My house isn't nearly as comfortable I'm afraid." He gave a weak smile showing crooked teeth.

"The Percivals don't come in here do they? You have perfect privacy in this room to do whatever you choose to do."

"That is so, and I'm grateful for their generosity."

"From what I hear, you often make up the numbers when an extra man is needed at their parties."

Jonty stroked his moustache. "Yes. I don't feel very comfortable at those parties, but they let me use the library so I return the favour when needed."

"Did you know any of the guests here this weekend?" Inspector Thomas watched Jonty carefully.

"I knew the Porters as we all live fairly near each other, and I'd been at a party here with Flora James before. Miss Percival was a stranger to me, as was Mr Adams."

"What about the solicitor, Peter Moore?"

"He hadn't arrived 'ere when we 'ad dinner, so we 'aven't been properly introduced as of yet."

"What was your opinion of Terrence and Helen Porter?"

"I 'ad no opinion."

"Come now Mr Carshalton, we all have opinions, even if they're unspoken ones." Inspector Thomas leaned closer to Jonty, looking him directly in the eyes.

Jonty blinked once or twice. "Right, well if you're askin' for my private thoughts, I'll tell you 'em. I didn't trust Terry Porter one bit, now there I've said it." He pursed his lips up again, making him look more weasel-like than ever.

"Did he do something to prevent you trusting in him?"

"He was a bad lot, used to hang with a bad lot too. He may have said he had reformed when he met his wife, but mark my words, a leopard never changes its spots."

Inspector Thomas wondered if Jonty Carshalton had ever changed his own spots, but decided not to antagonise him more than was necessary. "So nothing concrete then, more of a feeling, yes? Tell me, why were you in Mary Percival's room in the night?"

Jonty looked as if he had been shot. He turned a sickly pale colour and opened and shut his mouth like a fish out of water. "I, er, I…"

A seagull wheeled past the window, squawking loudly as it called to its friends, and Jonty jerked his head round to look outside.

"Yes?" prompted Inspector Thomas.

"I entered 'er room by mistake. Mine is on the same side of the corridor, an' I didn't like to switch any lights on in case I disturbed anyone. Whenever I stay 'ere I usually sleep in the room she was stayin' in, so it were an easy mistake to make."

"How would switching your own bedroom light on cause any problem to anyone else who was sleeping along the east wing? Forgive my confusion, Mr Carshalton, but I can't seem to comprehend what you mean."

"I'm afraid I can't explain it, maybe I'd 'ad one too many drinks an' wasn't thinkin' straight."

"You can leave for now Mr Carshalton but please don't leave this house. Constable Turner will need to take your finger prints."

Jonty stumbled out of the room on spindly legs, hurrying a little as he heard the seagulls' raucous voices outside the window again.

"Hmm, very interesting," said Inspector Thomas to himself in a low voice.

He got up and moved over to the bookcase that Jonty's eyes had flickered towards earlier. He looked at the spine of one of the books and took it out, skimming the back cover. Replacing it, he removed another and flicked through the pages before putting it back and perusing the others on the same shelf. After he'd satisfied his curiosity he made his way to the door, almost bumping into Peter Moore who was standing outside with a raised arm as if about to knock.

"Pardon me Inspector, I've just had my finger prints taken and thought you wanted to see me straight after."

"That's fine, Mr Moore. Please go in and take a seat, I shan't be long."

Inspector Thomas strode, with more confidence than he felt, across the hall to the dining room where Constable Turner was tidying up his printing kit. Jonty Carshalton was wiping his fingers on a cloth and turned round and looked at him with a guilt-ridden expression before averting his eyes and hurrying out.

"Turner, Mr Carshalton has been spending time in the library reading up on poisons, murders and amateur sleuthing. He didn't want me to know that though. We need to keep a close eye on him."

Constable Turner raised his eyebrows and shook his head. "Doesn't surprise me at all, that man is a most suspicious character if you ask me. Perhaps he wanted to find out the tricks so he could try and pull the wool over our eyes. I'll make sure I know where he is at all times, don't you worry."

Just then Jenkins appeared and knocked timidly at the open door. "Excuse me sir," he said. "The lad who helps the gardener, name of Orson Cornick, would like a word with you. He's outside the back door if you'd like to follow me."

Inspector Thomas marched across the room and followed the butler to the back of the house, closely followed by Constable Turner who just about managed to prevent himself falling over as his large feet got caught under the corner of the rug in his haste.

Orson, the young under-gardener, was hopping about from foot to foot and twirling his cap around with nerves while a flock of seagulls swooped, plunged and squawked in the air above him.

"Now don't be scared sonny," said Constable Turner giving him what he perceived to be a gentle pat on the shoulder. "Tell the inspector here what it is you want to say."

"Well sir, I went to the tool shed this morning to get what I needed sir, and I realised something had gone missing."

"What was it?" asked Inspector Thomas impatiently.

"The cyanide sir."

"How do you know it was missing? Were you looking for it?"

"No sir, I never use the stuff meself sir. The head gardener is the only one allowed to touch the strong poisons. I just noticed a clean round space where a jar had stood. The rest of the surface and bottles were covered with dust sir," he finished proudly.

"What makes you think it was cyanide that was missing?"

"I found it by the potting shed, it was shoved underneath the seedling tray there, by the trowels. Here it is." He brandished a jar that he had been hiding under his cap and held it out.

"Careful there," said the inspector. "Turner, go and fingerprint it please."

Constable Turner gingerly took the jar and, his arm outstretched in front of himself as if he were holding an unexploded bomb, disappeared back inside to the dining room.

"Now sonny, Orson isn't it?" Inspector Thomas smiled tenderly at the lad.

"Yes sir, that's me name."

"Well, Orson, was your shed ever kept locked at all?"

"Yes sir, it was always locked up at the end of the day and unlocked first thing in the morning."

"So during the daytime the shed was left open, should anyone choose to take anything from it?"

"Well, yes sir, I suppose that's true," stammered the boy, his face falling.

"There's no suppose about it. Well, thank you for that. Perhaps you should keep that shed locked up for the time being. Tell the head gardener those are my orders."

Just at that moment the old gardener tottered around the corner of the house, and came into sight. He waddled up on his doddery legs.

"We were just telling your young helper here that the shed containing any poisons should be kept locked up until we've found the person who took the cyanide," said Inspector Thomas in a loud voice, over enunciating the words.

"I'm not deaf sir," said the gardener with dignity. "I may be old, but my hearing's as good as it ever has been."

The inspector stared. He took in the ancient face where nature had scored it with long deep lines, and noted the halo of grey hair perched uncertainly on top of his wobbly head. Instead of answering, he looked back at the boy.

"Off you go, sonny. I'm sure you have work to do."

"Yes sir, right away sir." Orson rushed away at top speed and disappeared around the corner of the house, his heart hammering wildly. He wasn't used to talking to the police, and hoped he wouldn't have to do it again in a hurry.

Chapter 11

Back in the library, Inspector Thomas found Peter Moore standing at the bookcase that Jonty's eyes had flickered towards earlier, hands in his pockets.

"Anything of interest there?" asked the inspector in a loud voice, making Peter jump.

"Not really Inspector," said Peter taking his hands out of his pocket and walking towards him with an outstretched arm. "I prefer real cases as opposed to fictional ones if truth be known."

The two men shook hands.

"Well this one is certainly a real case. Do take a seat, and please tell me how you came to be here this weekend Mr Moore?"

Peter sat down and seemed to consider his answer for a second.

"Well, my father used to be the Percival family solicitor but that job has now been passed down to me. The Percivals wanted to talk through something with me and asked me to come at once."

"Do you often visit clients at the weekend?"

"Sometimes, if it is important."

"And what was important about this visit?"

"I have no idea as of yet, as we haven't had a chance to talk."

"Did the Percivals express the importance of you coming over the weekend?"

"Yes. I was hoping to play golf this weekend as it happens, but you could say I was summoned." Peter steadily held the gaze of the inspector seated opposite him.

"How odd. The siblings say they were happy to see you after the weekend but that you had insisted on coming straight away."

"Well, that certainly is odd, Inspector. I can assure you that is not the case."

Inspector Thomas scribbled something down in his notebook. "So there is no clue as to why you have been asked here as of yet? No hint of anything at all?"

"Correct."

"I was looking in the long gallery earlier. Have you been in there yet?"

"No, I'm afraid not. Should I have?" Peter's face had a confused expression painted across it.

"Not especially. I noticed that a lot of the paintings were missing, and thought that maybe the siblings were in financial difficulties."

"They could be getting the pictures cleaned."

"True, and it did occur to me." Inspector Thomas inclined his head towards the solicitor, his eyebrows raised, silently telling himself he was just as intelligent.

"Anyway, I don't know anything about their state of affairs yet. There's nothing about financial woes in the family file that I brought with me. I had a flick through it yesterday."

"Anything interesting to be found?"

"Depends what you mean by interesting."

The inspector looked down at his notes. "It came to my ears that your clients were trying to renew interest in the missing Percival diamond, if you've heard of it?"

Peter Moore sat forward a little. "Indeed I have, and I read the article in the paper. It disappeared decades ago and hasn't come up for auction or been found in anyone's private collection. It was last seen in this house if I recall the details correctly. I did wonder if it were still here, and didn't get stolen after all. Wouldn't that be interesting?"

"Do you think you're here because of the diamond?"

"Well, that remains to be seen doesn't it?" replied Peter. "Anyway, I suppose whatever the reason they've asked me here, it will be eclipsed by the death of that poor woman. Is there anything I can do to help?"

"Just keep your eyes and ears open sir and let me know of anything you deem relevant. I hear you were in the same railway compartment as some of the guests here?"

"Yes," replied Peter with a small laugh. "Reverend Bird seemed to hit it off with the young people, but I tried to remain hidden behind my paper, apart from a brief interlude with Miss Percival in the dining car. I didn't imagine I'd run into any of them again, especially not in the same place."

"Did you get the impression that Frederick Adams and Flora James had been previously acquainted?"

"No," said Peter looking surprised. "They introduced themselves in the carriage so I don't think they'd met before."

"What impression did you get from them?"

"To be honest, I tried not to listen most of the time. Fred seemed like a fun-loving young man, Flora…well, I'm not sure I really formed an impression. She's a pretty young thing, takes care of herself and wears nice clothes. Mary Percival seemed reluctant to be there, I felt quite sorry for her at one point, as the reverend was keen to get everyone involved. She and I got on rather well when we went for tea. My impression was of a no-nonsense spinster who'd had a hard time, but with a hidden soft heart underneath her spikiness."

"And you sir? Are you married? Do you have a family?"

"No, marriage seems to have eluded me. I live on my own with my housekeeper."

"Thank you. Perhaps you'd like to join the others. I'm sure I heard the breakfast gong sound."

No one really wanted to eat breakfast, but they went through the motions anyway. William and Elsie tried, and failed to bring about a cheerful atmosphere but persevered on through the silence. Terrence was absent as he was still asleep, but Reverend Bird tripped down the stairs when he smelled bacon drifting up to his nostrils.

"Well, what have we here? Breakfast, what?"

"Come in Reverend," said Elsie in a bright voice. "Do help yourself to the food on the sideboard. There's coffee here too if you'd like some."

"Thank you my dear, thank you," beamed Reverend Bird. "Don't mind if I do. That poor man is still out for the count, and I don't want to leave until I've talked to him properly." He picked up a plate and began piling food on to it liberally.

"I'm sure he'll appreciate it," said Elsie lamely.

"Nice to see you again Miss Percival, and you Miss James. Mr Adams, I didn't imagine I'd run into you again, but I feel as if I am in the company of friends." Plastering a bright smile across his face, the reverend noisily pulled a chair out from under the table, scraping it across the parquet. He threw himself down on it, banging his plate in front of him.

Mary frowned.

"What a terrible thing to happen to your friend," went on the reverend, unperturbed. "Cyanide is a dreadful way to go from what I hear."

Flora's eyes widened, and Fred moved closer to her, putting a protective hand on her arm. "Let's not talk of it now please Rev. We're all very upset. Let's eat our breakfast in peace."

"I understand, I understand totally," tweeted Reverend Bird. "Death is not easy, particularly unnatural death. We'll all need to be brave for that poor widower upstairs."

"I couldn't agree more," said William brightly. "By the way, this bacon is delicious. Have you tried any yet, Mr Moore?"

"Indeed I have, it is delicious," replied Peter, taking the hint to change the subject. "I think I will help myself to some more, and please do call me Peter."

Inspector Thomas had drunk a hurried cup of tea, which was scalding hot and exactly what he needed, and eaten a light breakfast in the kitchen with Constable Turner and was now talking with him about the case.

"Thoughts so far, Turner?"

"Thoughts? Well for starters, that fingerprinting kit is a marvel, sir. How the police got good results before that was invented I really don't know." He picked up the delicate handle of his cup with his large hand and drained the dregs of it, looking round for the teapot to get a refill. Cook waddled across and obliged.

"So Turner, are you sure that the other fingerprints on that glass of water belonged to Mary Percival? You've obviously confirmed Helen Porter's prints."

"Absolutely certain sir, and there was a smudged mark too that looked like a different print. I can't quite make it out as of yet, but will take my findings down to the police lab in a minute for them to have a look. As I say, the kit I have is fantastic, but the equipment's better down there."

"Yes, good idea. I think I'd better go and have words with Mary Percival, something's occurred to me." He got up, stretched and made his way out into the hall where the others were filtering out of the dining room. Their faces showed strain.

"Miss Percival, might I speak to you in the library please?" He opened the library door and stood back to allow her to go in before him.

"What is it Inspector?" Mary sat down and put her hands in her lap, her back straight.

"I'd like to ask you if you gave Helen Porter a drink before she went up to bed last night."

"Gave her a drink? No, certainly not. I don't really drink alcohol myself, and was not involved in serving or pouring drinks for the others."

"I don't necessarily mean alcohol. It could have been a glass of water for instance," prompted Inspector Thomas.

Mary shook her head. "No, I didn't give anyone a drink, and besides I went up to bed before the others."

"Yes, but didn't you go back down before they went up? You wanted to talk to your cousins about Jonty Carshalton having been in your bedroom."

"That is correct, but I would have remembered giving someone a drink. What is all this about?"

"Your fingerprints were found on the glass of cyanide that killed Helen Porter."

Mary gasped. "But how? That can't be possible."

"I can assure you it is, so if you'd like to cast your mind back and recall how that could have happened, I'd like to hear it. In fact, I'm all ears."

Fred and Flora were talking together in low voices, sitting on the floral window seat in the drawing room. Flora looked out of the window and saw the gardener weeding one of the borders and occasionally flapping his hands at an inquisitive gull. The under-gardener was prancing about looking as if he might take off himself.

"Why do you think the inspector has summoned Miss Percival again," asked Fred. "She can't have poisoned Helen, surely? I know she must have thought we were all a bit uncouth and noisy last night but I don't think she's unhinged enough to murder because of it. I'd stake my reputation on it."

"What reputation's that then?" smiled Flora. "I don't know, they say you can never really know a person, don't they? She certainly seems the uptight sort. That policeman is probably just picking her brains as she's an older woman."

"Hmm, maybe. Who do you think did it then?" Fred lowered his voice and moved closer to prevent being overheard, despite no one else being in the room with them.

"That's a tough question to ask, let alone answer."

"I know, but I always think a woman's instinct is spot on."

"Flatterer! Well, I suppose Terrence is the most likely person, I'd say. I heard the constable talking on the telephone earlier and it turns out that there had been rather a large life insurance policy taken out last year." Flora patted her blonde hair and smoothed it into place. She then took her lipstick out of her bag and removed the cap, half lost in thought.

"Gosh, great detection work, Flora! Well things certainly don't look too good for him, do they? Come on, let's go and do some detective work of our own and see if we can solve this mystery before the police."

Inspector Thomas looked directly into Mary's eyes, wishing he didn't feel so intimidated. "So, have you come up with anything yet Miss Percival?"

"I'm thinking of the glasses that I touched yesterday." Mary held her head high. "When I went to my room I decided to take something for my headache, as I told you before. There was a glass of water in my room, but I don't like the taste of the headache powder so I took the glass downstairs and left in on the sideboard. The butler came and poured me a tomato juice into a fresh glass, and then I took that one back upstairs with me."

"So you left the glass of water downstairs. Had you drunk anything from it?"

"No, I hadn't. Are you saying that someone came along and put cyanide into my water glass and gave it to Mrs Porter?"

"I'm not saying anything yet Miss Percival. However, it looks quite likely."

"Well, I hope you are not suggesting that I put the cyanide in it. First of all, I'd like to think I would be intelligent enough to wipe my prints off the glass. Second of all, how would I know who would drink from it, if anyone?" She glared, her cold expression making the inspector quite glad that looks couldn't kill. "I suppose that is why you're asking if I gave anyone a drink. As if I would poison anyone!"

Just then, to Inspector Thomas's immense relief, Jenkins tapped on the door and poked his head around it. "Excuse me sir, the doctors have gone and Mr Porter has woken up."

"Thank you Jenkins, stay here a second will you? Right, Miss Percival you may go for now."

The butler stood still, his face showing no emotion, and he stood back politely to allow Mary to pass.

"Jenkins, do you recall giving Miss Percival a drink last night?" The inspector peeked guiltily out of the door, hoping he hadn't been overheard by the cross spinster.

"Yes, sir, I remember."

"What did you give her?"

"Tomato juice, sir."

"Can you talk me through what happened?"

"Yes," said the butler, looking surprised. "I met Miss Percival in the hall and she had a glass in her hand. She put it down on the sideboard, so I went to her and asked if she needed anything. She said she'd like a tomato juice, and so I poured one for her."

"You didn't empty her water out and use the same glass?"

"Oh no sir, that wouldn't be the right thing to do at all. Not good etiquette. Besides, there isn't a sink in the hall, so I would have had to have taken the glass to the kitchen. I gave her a fresh glass and off she went, back up the stairs."

"What did you do with the unwanted glass of water?"

"Nothing. I usually clear all the glasses away at the same time, once the guests have gone to bed."

"And did you clear it away once the guests had gone to bed?"

Jenkins frowned. "No sir. It wasn't there, now I come to think about it."

"Now think carefully, was anyone else in the hall, or did you notice anyone shortly afterwards in the area?"

Jenkins answered immediately. "No, there wasn't anyone about, I'd have remembered. It is my job to pay attention to the details and make sure everyone is taken care of properly."

"I'm sure you do an excellent job. Were any of the other servants still up at that hour?"

"Oh no, sir. I was the only one about."

"Thank you, you may go now." Inspector Thomas went out of the door, crossed the hallway and leapt up the stairs two at a time, followed at a slower pace by Reverend Bird, who was off to check up on Terrence.

Chapter 12

Terrence was sitting up in bed with a hot red face, his curly hair sticking up at different angles where he'd laid on it, and looking absurd. He picked his gold cufflinks up from the bedside table as Inspector Thomas entered the room.

"Have I really got to answer a load of nonsensical questions?" he asked. "My wife is dead, and you need to find out why. What more is there to say?"

"My sincere commiserations Mr Porter. It is a terrible tragedy, but I'm sure you would like to get some answers too. Can I fetch you anything? A drink perhaps?"

"Coffee, strong coffee."

"I'll get it young man," boomed Reverend Bird from the doorway, making the inspector jump. "You just take your time, and talk to the inspector here. A hot coffee will be with you shortly." He disappeared off down the passage and Inspector Thomas got up and pushed the door shut behind him with a bang before seating himself on the chair next to the dressing table.

"Tell me, Mr Porter, about the glass of water your wife drank last night. Where did she get it from?"

"What kind of a damn fool question is that?" snarled Terrence. He placed his cufflinks into his pocket. "How would I know where she got her water?"

"Calm down please sir and try to recall. Did she have it in her hand when you went up to bed?"

Terrence lay his head back on the plump pillow and shut his eyes for a second. "Well, now that I think about it, yes she did. I'd twisted my ankle, and she was trying to help me up. She had a glass in her other hand."

"Can you think where she got it from sir? Did she have it when she left the drawing room where you were dancing?"

Terrence screwed his eyes up. "I can't remember. I don't think she had it then, though, as we were all drinking from the long stemmed glasses."

"So it is probable that she picked it up from the sideboard in the hall where the drinks were kept?"

"She must have I suppose. I don't remember anyone handing a glass to her."

"Thank you sir. Now, this question will seem more than a little impertinent but I do have to put it to you. Last year, you took out a life insurance policy for a rather large amount of money."

"Well, what of it? Plenty of people have life insurance policies. Are you accusing me of bumping my own wife off for a bit of money?" Terrence's face turned a puce colour, and he sat upright again.

"Now, now sir, there are no accusations as of yet. Please try to calm yourself."

Just then the door opened and Reverend Bird came into the room with a steaming cup and saucer. "Here you go Mr Porter, a nice strong coffee will do you the world of good. Cook's put a nice slice of fruitcake on the side there too, got to keep your strength up. Now, would you like me to stay with you while you talk to the inspector here?" He perched himself on the edge of the bed.

"Yes, in actual fact I would," said Terrence folding his arms and glaring at Inspector Thomas.

"Now hold on a minute," began the inspector. "This is a murder investigation…"

"Exactly, and I shan't say another word unless I can have the reverend here to be a witness," said Terrence in anger. "Ridiculous questions about drinks and insurance policies."

Reverend Bird beamed.

"Fine, have your clergyman present if you so wish," said Inspector Thomas, exasperated. "I'd like to ask you how well you know Flora James?"

"Flora James? Is she your number one suspect?" Terrence's eyebrows rose up his forehead and disappeared under his curls, his eyes widening in surprise.

"There isn't a number one suspect at the moment, more's the pity."

"Then why...? I hope you're not insinuating there's anything untoward with my relationship with that young woman. I know her from parties here and have never met her anywhere else. Check with her yourself."

Another knock came to the door and Inspector Thomas sighed in despair.

"Sir," called Jenkins. "Constable Turner is on the telephone for you."

Turning on his heel, the inspector stalked out of the room to go and take the call.

"Yes, what is it?" barked Inspector Thomas down the receiver.

"It's me sir," said Constable Turner sounding wounded. "I'm at the lab. I wanted you to know that the other prints on the glass look like they might be Jonty Carshalton's. The cyanide found by the gardener has no prints on it, however. It looks like someone wore gloves."

Inspector Thomas said a few more words, gave some instructions, flung the receiver down and then marched into the drawing room where most of the guests had congregated. They all looked round when he entered.

"Mr Carshalton?" he enquired between gritted teeth.

"He hasn't joined us," said William. "I believe he's in his room. Shall I get Jenkins to fetch him for you?"

"No, that's quite alright." Inspector Thomas marched back up the stairs and made his way down the east wing until he came to a door. He knocked and tried the handle but it was locked and no sound came from inside. Presuming correctly that it was Mary Percival's room he carried on down the passage and knocked at another door.

"Who is it?" came Jonty's voice from inside the room.

"Police Inspector Thomas. I'd like a few words with you please."

Jonty opened the door looking surprised. "Yes, what is it?" he asked.

"I'd like to come in for a minute please," said the inspector pushing past Jonty into his bedroom. He took the room in at a glance, noting the expensive furnishings and modern design, and then sat down in the plush chair next to the window, looking briefly out at the garden in the front. "Now, Mr Carshalton, tell me how your finger prints came to be on the glass of water that was in Mary Percival's room."

Jonty looked at the inspector in fear, his mouth opening and shutting like a door in a gale. He sat down on the edge of the bed and his legs started to shake.

"I'm waiting for an answer please Mr Carshalton," snapped Inspector Thomas.

"I have no idea what you expect me to say, Inspector. Anyway, I thought that it was Mrs Porter's glass that had got the poison in it."

"At the moment, I'm leaning towards thinking that Mrs Porter's death was an accident. The poison was meant for Mary Percival, as I'm sure you already know."

"I don't understand what you are on about," said Jonty mutinously.

"Enough of this pussyfooting around, please. You are well known to the law for your past dubious activities Mr Carshalton. I know you seem to have turned over a new leaf of late, but what if I were to suggest you knew something of a burglary that took place at Miss Percival's house not so long ago? What if Miss Percival were to positively identify you as the man she saw in her road? What if your thoughts were to get rid of her before that happened? I take it you see the way my mind is working."

"'ere," muttered Jonty looking more panic-stricken by the second. "I don't know nothin' about it. Arrest me if you like, but I didn't poison no one, or rob no one for that matter."

"And yet your fingerprints were on that glass as clear as day. Why were you in Miss Percival's room? We both know that it wasn't a case of a mistaken bedroom, don't we?"

Jonty pursed his lips obstinately and said nothing.

"Have it your way sir. I'm afraid you will need to stay here in this room while I continue in my investigation. If nothing else comes to light you have been warned of the consequences. I will come back to you later, and I hope you will tell me all that you know." The inspector stood up and left the room abruptly, slamming the door shut behind him.

Peter Moore was making his way up the stairs to go to his room and he passed the inspector walking towards him.

"Were you looking for me, Inspector?"

"No sir, but actually I would like to have a quick word now that you mention it."

"Come this way." Peter gestured towards his bedroom and led the way to it. "You get a fantastic view of the gardens and can just about see the sea in the distance from up here."

Once inside Peter shut the door but the inspector opened it up again an inch or two and stood peering out through the gap.

"Is something wrong?" faltered the solicitor.

"I'm keeping an eye on Mr Carshalton's door. I told him to remain in his room but I'm not sure how obedient he is going to be."

"Ah, I see. Is there a reason he has to stay inside?"

"His finger prints were on the glass of cyanide."

"What? You mean he poisoned Mrs Porter?"

"I'm not sure as of yet, but he certainly handled the glass."

"When and how?"

The inspector turned away from the door for a second and looked at Peter. "He won't say. However, the glass was in Miss Percival's room until she took it down to the hall."

"Mary's? What on earth was it doing in her room? You're not suggesting that she put the poison in the water are you?"

"Now why would she want to poison a woman she'd only met once before as a child?"

"Exactly, that's my point. She's not a murderer, I'm certain of it."

"That's a strong opinion towards a woman you've known less than twenty four hours if I might say so, Mr Moore?"

"I'm a solicitor, Inspector. I come across crime and criminals a lot in my line of business, as you do too. You tend to get wise to certain types, and I don't think Mary is one of them. Besides, she's an intelligent lady, and she would know to wear gloves or wipe her prints off a weapon of murder afterwards."

"People can be very good at pulling the wool over our eyes when they want to. However, I suspect you're right, I can't imagine Miss Percival as a murderess either, but I wouldn't go so far as to swear to it." He took another peep through the gap in the door but Jonty's door remained resolutely shut.

"If the poison was in Miss Percival's room, could it be that it was meant for her instead of Mrs Porter? And if so, how did the stuff get to be in Mrs Porter's room?" Peter looked thoughtfully at the policeman.

"I'm sure all will be revealed in due course sir. It is possible that the poison was administered into the drink when it was on the sideboard downstairs, after Miss Percival had taken it down, but I don't know.

"When the time seems decent I'd like you to find out what you were summoned here for. Perhaps the Percivals will be willing to carry on with business as usual."

"Certainly. I'm as intrigued as you are Inspector."

"By the way, you said you found it easy to be wise to certain types just now. Have you identified anyone here that fits in to that mould?"

"Now that's a tricky question. I would have to talk to them all for a bit longer before accusing anyone of being a criminal type, Inspector. However, on saying those words, I don't trust Jonty Carshalton one little bit."

Chapter 13

Constable Turner had arrived back at Oakmere Hall and was passing the time of day with the gardener in the driveway. "This is a fantastic place to work," he said chattily. "Been here long?"

"Years and years, far too many to mention," twinkled the gardener. "I expect I was here before you were even born. Worked for the Percivals before the present Percivals took over. Can't really see myself anywhere else now. I should've retired long ago, but I doubt I ever will."

"Well, as long as you've got the energy, why not?"

"I'd only get under my wife's feet if I shuffled about at home all day long."

Constable Turner imagined himself being under his own wife's feet all day long, and gave an involuntary shudder. "What do you make of the happenings this weekend?"

The gardener leaned on his spade and looked off into the distance with his faded delphinium blue eyes. "There are some that might think this old house were cursed. My missus, now, she's one of 'em. It certainly ain't the first tragedy to hit this old place. You heard what happened to the owners before, I take it? Went clean off the edge of the cliff they did. Terrible it was too, their kids were too young to be orphaned like that." He clicked his tongue and shook his head sadly.

"Very sobering indeed," said Turner, putting on a suitable expression.

The gardener nodded slowly.

"What do you use the cyanide for, anyway?"

"We haven't had to use it for a long time now, but it was a pest control for the rats."

"Ah, I see. I take it you don't have rats now then?"

"Not one."

The under-gardener, hovering about and trying to listen, flung some weeds into the wheelbarrow to show willing.

"Boy, take the barrow round to the bonfire and pile them there weeds up on it, then you can rake that bed over there. Now, where were we Constable? Ah yes, this murder! Let me show you where the cyanide was taken from." The gardener, strutting in an important fashion with his flat cap perched at an unusual angle on top of his tufty thatch of hair, led the policeman round the side of the house.

In the distance Fred and Flora were walking at a slow pace together, arm in arm. When they spotted the constable they moved slightly apart and unlinked their arms. Constable Turner pretended not to notice and continued on his way to the shed.

Inside the house Mary was talking to Elsie who was looking upset. "It is a terrible thing to happen Elsie, but you need to try and be strong."

"I know, Mary, but I feel so terribly responsible. There are so many emotions going around my head at the moment. If Helen did take her own life, how selfish that she would do it in my house. If she was murdered, who did it and why did they do it? I just don't have any idea what to think."

Mary put her knitting down and looked at Elsie. "Listen Elsie, the police will get to the bottom of it. I know it is easy to say, but try not to fret."

"You're right, I shouldn't fret. I'm a natural optimist, I need to show the world." She reached up behind her head and pulled the hair tie out of her wayward hair.

As she was retying it neatly, the inspector descended the stairs and made a beeline for the two women. He nodded at them.

"Any news Inspector?" asked Elsie looking up at him, the worried expression still on her face.

"We're just carrying on with our enquiries, so nothing to report at the moment. What I need the answer to is if anyone went outside at any point yesterday evening before the gardener's shed was locked. Did anyone have a chance to pop outside and get that cyanide? Also, who knew it was in the shed?"

"Everyone went up to their rooms to freshen up before dinner, so no one can be accounted for fully. It would have been easy for anyone to slip outside unnoticed," replied Elsie looking thoughtful. "I'm not sure that anyone was aware of us having cyanide, though. I didn't know about it, to be honest. All that kind of thing was in the gardener's hands, but I suppose the shed *would* be the obvious place to keep the poisons. Anyone looking for some would surely look there before anywhere else."

"Hmm. Who was in the drawing room when Miss Percival here came down and left her glass on the side?"

"I wasn't aware of her bringing her glass down, but I would guess all of us, apart from Peter Moore and Jonty Carshalton."

"Mr Carshalton's fingerprints were found on the glass."

"What?" exploded Elsie. "But I don't understand. Jonty wouldn't poison anyone! He may be a bit uncouth but he has no reason to kill anyone. Perhaps he came down for a drink himself and moved Mary's glass out of the way or something."

"That's highly unlikely, I'm afraid. He would have said if that were the case."

"Unless he forgot," interposed Elsie.

"The thing is, the man is refusing to say anything at all. I also have an inkling that he liked reading up on amateur sleuthing and the effects of poisons, right here in your library."

Elsie grasped the arms of her chair. "Where's William?" she said quietly.

"I'll go and find him," said Mary in a firm voice. "You just wait here a minute Elsie." She left the hall with a swish of her skirts.

William had gone upstairs and was talking to Terrence, despite Reverend Bird's constant interruptions. When he heard Mary's voice calling out to him he got up and left the room at once.

"Is everything alright Mary?"

"Elsie needs to see you. I'm afraid Mr Carshalton's fingerprints were found on the glass of cyanide, and she's a bit upset."

William raced down the west wing to the stairs and went to find his sister.

Constable Turner had come inside and was standing outside Jonty Carshalton's room, trying to look official, occasionally rising up on his toes and clasping his hands behind his back.

"Constable, is there something wrong?" complained Jonty opening the door. "Are you preventin' me comin' out? I've done nothin' wrong. I must have touched that glass by an accident when I was in Miss Percival's room."

"Hold your tongue my man," replied Constable Turner sternly. "You're not a prisoner, I'm just keeping an eye on you. The inspector will be along when he has something to say to you."

Jonty subsided into silence and slammed his door shut.

Peter Moore had been stretching his legs outside, and walked around a bush nearly bumping into Fred and Flora who appeared to be loitering near the drawing room window.

"Pardon me," he smiled at them.

"We were trying to figure out who could have planted poison in Helen's glass," said Fred in a conspiratorial whisper. His freckles seemed more defined out in the open, and his eyes shone bright with an ill-concealed excitement.

"Yes, it's an absolute shock," said Flora watching a seagull land nearby and begin to peck at something on the ground. "Fred and I just can't even begin to pin anything on anyone."

"We heard that Jonty Carshalton's prints were on the glass, but no one in their right mind would leave their prints on a murder weapon would they?"

"Not on purpose," agreed Peter. "Well, unless they happened to have been disturbed in the act, or if they happened to be a bit simple and thought they could bluff the police. Would you say that Mr Carshalton was simple? I haven't seen enough of him to form a firm opinion as of yet."

"Well," began Flora doubtfully. "I don't really know. Looks can be deceiving, and he is quite well read by all accounts."

"What do you make of the letters D and I being found in the dust by her dead body?' asked Fred eagerly. "Do you think they're the start of the word diamond? I can't think of another word that could be relevant, can you?"

"No," agreed the solicitor. "However, the marks could have just been marks made by falling books, or by a shoe when someone was standing by the bookcase. It isn't conclusive that they were deliberate letters."

"If this were a fictional story, the letters would have been the start of someone's name, the murderer's name! However, this isn't fiction, and no one here has a name beginning with D and I. In my mind, this murder and the diamond story are mixed up together, though, and that Helen was trying to tell us something," said Flora.

"I think you'll find that…" Peter hesitated and lapsed into silence.

Fred and Flora exchanged looks.

Just then there was a knock from the inside of the window, and William beckoned to Peter, his sister at his side.

"Excuse me, I'll leave you to your sleuthing," said Peter and made his way back round to the front door.

"So what do you take to be the right course of action?" asked William after a rather long talk with the solicitor. "It doesn't seem like great timing what with Helen, but Elsie and I do need to try and trace that diamond."

"I don't quite know how to advise you. You've had a newspaper interview, so the public are aware of it. All you can do is sit back and wait for any possible witnesses to come forward, or people that have heard rumours of what might have happened."

"But what about cousin Mary's father and his receipt?"

"If you insist on trying to get to the bottom of that you'll have to ask her straight out. The direct approach is the only way to go. Frankly, I don't see why you contacted me for help. Couldn't we have corresponded about this by post or over the telephone?"

"Yes, I suppose you're right, we could have. We were just so caught up in the moment and wanted to talk it over with you."

"Are you in any financial difficulties? The inspector was wondering why the gallery was lacking in pictures."

"Was he now?" said Elsie, her eyes narrowing. "Why didn't he ask us that himself then?"

"I have no idea, perhaps he will later."

"Well, if you must know, we do need a bit of extra income, but we are not destitute." Elsie avoided eye contact with the solicitor and looked at William in a determined way. "We always have the other paintings to sell if need be. Anyway, regarding Mary, let's strike while the iron's hot. I'd rather think about that than about Jonty's fingerprints being on her glass."

Before William could reply the luncheon gong rang out.

"Ah, I wondered why I was feeling hungry," said Elsie. "Let's all go and eat, though it seems rather callous in the face of the events here so far."

"We have to keep our strength up." William gestured towards the door as the sound of footsteps padded across the hall outside. "After you."

"Thank you." Peter walked to the door and opened it. As he left the room he heard William telling Elsie that they should talk to Mary as soon as they had eaten.

Chapter 14

Jonty Carshalton opened his door. "Constable, was that the lunch gong? I'm rather 'ungry you know. Will I be allowed to go and eat or am I on starvation rationin'?"

Constable Turner cleared his throat. "The maid will bring your food up here. Until the inspector gives further instructions I'd rather you kept away from the rest of the household. I'm off to the kitchen myself to eat so I'm trusting you to do as I ask."

Terrence, white and shaken, was sitting at the dining table, close to the large and ponderous figure of Reverend Bird, who seemed to dwarf him with his large frame. Mary looked towards them in distaste as the reverend sycophantically tucked Terrence's napkin into his collar.

Peter Moore came in the room and took a seat next to Mary, giving her a small sideways smile. She returned it at once.

William and Elsie sat together trying to be cheerful, aware that they were the hosts and had to try and keep the morale of their guests up.

Fred and Flora also sat together, looking bright eyed, having spent the morning discussing motives and murderers. They surreptitiously looked at each person in the room in turn, occasionally nudging one another and giving each other knowing looks.

"I wouldn't mind going in the maze later," said Fred to the room in general.

"I love that maze," laughed Flora. "I always seem to get lost though. We should go and explore it after lunch."

"We seem to have paired off," murmured Peter to Mary under his breath. "Do you think that's the natural order of things when there's been a murder?"

"I expect you would understand more about the human condition than me," said Mary. "Do you suppose we all veer towards the one we least suspect of being a tyrant?"

"Well if that's true, then I'm flattered to hear you trust me!" Peter raised his glass to her. "However, are you aware of the saying that we should keep our friends close and our enemies closer?"

"Yes indeed. So are you suggesting that the pairings are strategic because we all suspect each other?"

Peter laughed as Mary raised an eyebrow at him.

Jenkins served the food and there was a silence for a few minutes until he had left the room.

"Where's old Jonty?" asked William as Inspector Thomas entered the room and began walking around it. "He's not still in his room is he? Perhaps he didn't hear the gong."

"He's eating upstairs sir," said the inspector as he took a seat by the sideboard. "Please don't let it worry you for now."

"Don't let it worry us?" burst out Terrence in a loud voice. "Has that cad killed my wife or not? If he has, you'd better make sure he remains in his room or I won't be responsible for my actions." Reverend Bird shushed him as if he was soothing a baby, and Terrence subsided at once.

"Inspector, you must be hungry," said William brightly. "Your constable is eating in the kitchen. Why don't you join him and come and talk to us afterwards?"

"I think I'd prefer to stay here and talk to you all while things are fresh in my mind and I've got you all together Mr Percival," replied Inspector Thomas tartly. He began to circle the table.

Mary put her knife and fork down in irritation.

"Let's start with the confusion caused by your visit Mr Moore." Inspector Thomas looked at the startled face of Peter. "You claim that you were summoned this weekend, but Mr Percival says you were told that Monday would be suitable. Would you both like to explain this to me?"

"My secretary received a telephone call asking me to come this weekend as a matter of some urgency," began Peter.

"I didn't send an urgent message," said William turning to his sister. "Did you?"

"Of course not. Why does it matter anyway, Inspector?" asked Elsie.

"It might not matter Miss Percival, but I like to get these things clear in my mind. So you, Mr Percival, telephoned the secretary of Mr Moore did you?"

"As it happens, no I didn't. I left Jenkins a list of things to do that day, and that was one of the points. Would you like him to show you? He has a notebook and I leave him instructions in there."

"Yes, humour me if you would sir. I'd like to view that notebook."

Just as William was getting up, Jenkins appeared at the door with a tray of glasses that he took over to the sideboard.

"Ah Jenkins, please can you show the inspector here your notebook? He would like to see the message asking you to invite Mr Moore over?"

"Yes sir, certainly." Jenkins left the room and came back a few minutes later with a leather-bound book. He handed it to Inspector Thomas.

Flicking through the pages, the inspector quickly found the page and looked up at the butler. "It tells you to ask the solicitor over as soon as possible after this weekend."

"That's correct sir, it does," said Jenkins reading over the inspector's shoulder.

Inspector Thomas turned to look at the solicitor. "What do you have to say about this information Mr Moore?"

"Well I'm not sure where the crossed wires happened, but what I said stands. Ask my secretary if you don't believe me. She told me it was urgent that I came this weekend."

"Excuse me sir," interposed Jenkins. "I had another note, not written down in this particular book. It was on the kitchen table and said to ignore my previous instructions, and I was to ask Mr Moore to come urgently."

Peter looked triumphantly at the inspector, his eyebrows raised.

All eyes turned to look at William who was looking confused. "You had another note?" he said to his butler. "But I didn't write another note. Besides, I always leave you instructions in your book."

"That is so sir," replied Jenkins. "I was a bit surprised to see it on the table, but who am I to question how you instruct me?"

"Do you still have the note?" asked the inspector at once.

"No, I believe the cook put it on the fire in the kitchen."

"Was it written in Mr Percival's writing?"

"I presumed it was," said the butler casting his mind back. "I'm afraid I didn't really think about it, I was busy during the morning. All I did was read it and then go to make the telephone call."

"Do you know anything about this at all?" asked the inspector looking at Elsie with his piercing eyes.

"Nothing, it's all most confusing," said Elsie looking at him. "Who would have written that?"

"Who happened to be in the house that day?"

"Well, only us and the servants," said Elsie. "We don't usually have any guests during the week."

"Did you receive any visitors that weren't staying with you, just popping over to say hello perhaps?"

"No." Elsie shook her head.

"Actually, I believe old Jonty was here in the library," said William looking thoughtful. "He came here quite a few days in a row didn't he?"

"Yes, of course, Jonty. He's such a regular to our library that I hardly notice him most of the time. I remember him being here when we were arranging the weekend as you asked him if he'd like to come, didn't you?"

William nodded.

"Jenkins please can you ask Constable Turner to go and get Mr Carshalton and bring him down here?" asked Inspector Thomas.

The impassive butler left the room and went to the kitchen, where the constable was sitting at the scrubbed table chatting away to the cook between large mouthfuls of food. His wife had never been much of a good cook, although she tried her best, so it was a treat having food in a house like this, a perk of his job. He was just raising his loaded fork towards his mouth when Jenkins appeared and passed on the inspector's instructions.

The fork was lowered again and Constable Turner got heavily to his feet. He was exhausted from being up most of the night and had hoped his lunch break would revive him, but even that was being interrupted. He went and tramped up the stairs with as much noise as he could and went to fetch Jonty.

They appeared at the dining room door together and entered, both a little huffily.

"Ah Mr Carshalton," said the inspector. "Please take a seat at the table over here please." He steered him to the chair furthest away from Terrence, who was glowering at him.

Jonty lowered himself slowly down onto the chair, darting nervous glances across the table towards Terrence, and cleared his throat. "What can I do for you?"

"Mr Carshalton, I believe you were here the day that this house party was arranged? Is that so?"

"Well, what of it?"

"Were you here? I'm asking you a question."

"Yes I was as it 'appens. William asked me himself when I was coming out of the library. Ain't that so William?"

William nodded but said nothing.

"If you live so near, why do you stay the night? The Porters don't usually stay." Inspector Thomas's eyes bore into Jonty like gimlets.

"He takes pity on me, like. I live on my own you know." Jonty's voice became a whine.

The inspector slipped a piece of paper and a pen down onto the table in front of Jonty. "Please can you write down your address details for me?"

"I already have his details sir," interrupted Constable Turner and then turned a deep shade of red at the inspector's frown.

"He said he has 'em," said Jonty looking defiant.

"Please do as I ask Mr Carshalton."

Jonty picked up the pen and painstakingly began to write on the paper.

"How you can sit there so calmly when you've just poisoned my wife, I don't know," burst out Terrence.

"But I didn't murder no one," muttered Jonty, his eyelids flickering.

"Then how do you account for your fingerprints being on the glass that contained the cyanide?" finished Terrence in triumph.

Reverend Bird cooed at him, which was a tactic he employed during church services when trying to quieten down wayward children, while Mary tutted under her breath and looked down at her lap.

Fred and Flora were taking in the scene before them with something amounting to glee. They looked from Terrence to Jonty and back again.

"I'd really like the answer to that question too, old boy," said William in a quiet voice, but Jonty remained silent.

Inspector Thomas picked up the paper offered up to him from Jonty and thrust it at the butler. "What can you tell me about this writing, Jenkins?"

"I'm afraid I couldn't say," said the flustered looking butler. "It seems just like normal writing to me sir."

The inspector put the butler's open notebook on the table and placed Jonty's written piece of paper next to it. "These seem similar to me. I, for one, wouldn't be able to differentiate one from the other if in a hurry. What do you think Mr Percival?"

"Me? Well, I suppose it is quite similar to my writing if you squint your eyes a bit." William screwed his eyes up as he was talking.

There was an uncomfortable silence as the inspector walked over to the window, his shoes squeaking on the parquet flooring. He peered out, and then slowly walked back with his hands behind his back. He looked at Terrence and a puzzled expression crossed his face.

"Mr Porter..."

"Call me Terrence, everyone else does." He flicked his hair off his collar and smiled a smile that didn't quite reach his eyes.

"Mr Porter," persisted the inspector. "Was your wife in the habit of drinking water in the night?"

"What a very odd question." Terrence shook his head again to move his curls out of his face and stared at the policeman squarely. "Our maid always puts fresh water in our room, but 'No', in answer to your question. Call me sarcastic, but neither of us ever woke up on purpose to drink anything in the night."

"Then why did she take water up with her here?"

"Why? Well, for me to take my painkillers with, of course. Honestly, what kind of foolish questioning is this?" He looked at Reverend Bird with an expression that clearly stated his feelings about the inspector.

Inspector Thomas smacked his hand down on the table loudly, making Flora practically leap out of her chair. "Then why haven't you queried who the cyanide was for then? Surely that would have been your first thought? I think the water was meant for you, sir. Why haven't you presumed the cyanide was meant for you too?"

Terrence stared at the inspector with wide eyes and his mouth gaped open. He floundered, not knowing quite how to answer.

"Well, Mr Porter? What do you have to say about that?"

Terrence found his voice at last. "It didn't cross my mind for a second. I was just upset about my wife. It never entered my head that it could have been meant for me. Do you think it was?"

"I don't know," admitted Inspector Thomas. "However, it is perfectly feasible, and I imagine your vanity would have cottoned onto that before anything else."

"Frankly, I find that offensive," muttered Terrence.

"Someone was trying to kill you?" gasped Reverend Bird, surreptitiously moving his chair a little bit back. "But that's ridiculous. A good fellow like you! No, someone so callous, so evil, can not be amongst us."

"Do you have an explanation for all this then?" Inspector Thomas looked wearily at the reverend.

"I'm all for this being a terrible mistake. Is it possible that the gardener was handling the poisons and forgot to wash his hands or something? Perhaps a grain was left on his gloves and somehow ended up in a glass..." his voice tailed off and he pulled his obstinate hair over his smooth head, trying to flatten it down. "That young lad, the gardener's mate, he's not the brightest spark is he? I saw him flapping his arms up and down like a bird earlier and looking as if he was trying to take off."

"Much as I like your rosy way of looking at the world, and seeing good in everything, life just isn't like that in reality. I'm afraid this is a murder investigation. I don't believe Mrs Porter took her own life." The Inspector Thomas turned to Jenkins. "Please could you fetch Mr Carshalton's tray and bring it down here if he hasn't finished? I think it best if we all eat here together."

Chapter 15

Constable Turner had been despatched off to the police station again to find out more on the backgrounds of each person in the house. He went off in a hurry hoping that the cook would keep his food for him. The inspector, thoroughly exhausted by now, was sitting in the kitchen thumbing through his notes. He'd talked to the servants but had gleaned nothing of interest from them. Apart from Jenkins, they'd all been in bed when the household had called it a night. Cook, who was stirring mulled cider in a great vat ready for the evening's wassail, put a cup of tea down in front of him, and a plate of food.

Mary had taken herself off to her room to lie down, as had Terrence with the irrepressible and ever-present reverend at his side. William and Elsie were lounging in the hall, having decided that now was not the time to talk to Mary after all, and instead they sipped at hot drinks, and talked through their options. Jonty had gone to the library, and Peter up to his room to look through his paperwork again.

Fred and Flora, the only people who seemed genuinely cheerful, donned coats and rushed off together to see if it were possible to conquer the maze. Inspector Thomas watched them from the kitchen window, cup of tea in hand, and wondered how they could be so upbeat in the face of unnatural death. He remembered Constable Turner's supposition that they may have known each other before and, on a whim, decided to follow them. Creeping out of the kitchen door, he went after them much to Cook's chagrin. She shook her head at the untouched plate of food, picked it up and banged it loudly down on the side next to Constable Turner's plate, startling a robin that had flown on to the window ledge.

Fred and Flora were walking down the garden. They bypassed the orchard and skirted the bushes on their way towards the maze.

Inspector Thomas, feeling much like a spy, tiptoed from one bush to another, willing himself to be invisible. At each hiding place he would hold his breath, wait a few seconds, and then peep out quickly.

"Nearly there," said Fred, his voice filtering back to the inspector's ears. "Do you suppose we can get to the middle and back?" The couple rounded the row of hedges at the entrance to the maze and made their way inside, chattering loudly. Inspector Thomas rushed the last few feet to the hedge border but remained on the outside, listening intently.

"So, that turned out to be a tense meal didn't it?" came Fred's cheerful voice. "Jonty really is a suspicious character, if you ask me. I wonder why his fingerprints were on that glass? There doesn't seem to be a rational explanation, whichever way I look at it."

"I can't figure it out either. His prints were smudged apparently, whereas Mary's were clear ones. Does that mean he was in a hurry and put the glass down all of a sudden or something? Was he seen? He could have been disturbed, I keep trying to remember something, anything, but nothing comes to mind."

"Do you think he wrote that note summoning the solicitor?"

"Who else could have done it," replied Flora, her voice sounding excited. "He is a strange man, that one. Why would he want the solicitor here this weekend though? That's what I can't understand."

"Beats me," said Fred, his voice sounding a bit further away. "There's something going on that hasn't come to light yet. I don't know who would want to murder poor old Helen either. I didn't know her, but she seemed like a very nice lady. Then there's the fact that Terrence had taken out an insurance policy not so long ago. Could Terrence and Jonty be in it together do you think, or is that a bit far-fetched?"

"I don't see why they'd be in it together, and having a solicitor here doesn't help a murderer though, or am I missing something?"

"Maybe they are all involved in it together. Jonty and Terrence appear to hate each other, but that may be all part of their plan."

Flora spoke again. "Hang on a minute, what about this? The inspector seemed to think the poison could have been meant for Terrence, seeing as Helen was taking the water up for him to take his painkillers with. If that's true, maybe Helen had been trying to kill her husband? Don't forget that they had updated their insurance policy."

"I'm not sure if it does or not, but didn't Helen have a lot of money herself? Why would she want to claim on the insurance? It doesn't make sense."

"We don't know what her financial situation was like. Perhaps she'd run out of money. Maybe Terrence was working his way through it, and there wasn't much left."

"Seems a bit mad to murder your husband because he was spending your money, though. Why not just divorce him, or restrict him from getting his hands on it some other way?" Fred's voice sounded confused.

"I told the inspector that Terrence was a bit of a flirt. What if he happened to be more than that? What if he was having affairs, and Helen found out? Some women would find that grounds for murder, wouldn't they?"

Their voices faded off and Inspector Thomas clicked his tongue in irritation. Now he'd have to follow them in. He had been following the line of hedges at the perimeter but would now have to double back on himself and go into the maze entrance. Quietly tiptoeing back, and freezing for a second when his foot snapped a twig, he crept into the maze and trailed after the couple. Their voices came to him from behind an ornately sculpted hedge and he stood still, hardly daring to breathe.

"I know we've discussed it before, but do you honestly think any of this has anything to do with the missing diamond?" asked Fred.

"It certainly seems like a possibility, though I can't quite work out how it could be. Who knew about the diamond?"

"Well, you hadn't heard of it before, had you?"

"No." Flora paused for a second before shaking her head.

"Oh look, we've reached a dead end."

"So we have, let's retrace our steps to that bush down there. Hold on a minute, haven't we been this way before? I recognise that bit of branch that's bent over at the tip." The couple began to walk back the way they'd come, and the inspector had to squeeze himself behind a convenient swathe of green foliage. He waited a minute until sure they had passed, mentally trying to fashion himself into an abundance of ornamental grass, and then followed. He meandered along quietly, mulling things over in his mind.

Fred and Flora had left the maze and were talking nineteen to the dozen as they made their way down the long stretch of lawn towards the dilapidated fence at the edge of the cliff.

"Did you know that William and Elsie's parents fell to their deaths from this cliff?" Fred looked squarely at Flora's horrified face.

"I had no idea, how did that happen?"

"My parents told me that it was a horrible accident, during one of their house parties. It was windy, I presume much more than today, and they were playing hide and seek in the grounds by all accounts. No one knows quite how it happened, and William hasn't talked about it to me so I'm not going to bring it up."

Flora shivered. "How dreadful, the poor things. Imagine hurtling down there with the knowledge that death is on its way to claim you. They say that your life flashes before your eyes, don't they? How horrid."

"I'm sorry if I upset you, I imagined you would have known, being Elsie's friend."

"I didn't." Flora paused, thinking deeply. "Wait a minute, how do you know about it, if William hasn't brought it up?"

Fred looked out to sea. "My parents were here when it happened."

"Oh goodness, how awful. I don't really want to hear any more about it, can we change the subject?"

"Yes of course."

"Well, we've given motives to most of the household and yet not one of them seems to stand out clearly," said Flora. "You've put Helen on my mind. The thing is, only someone very stupid would have put poison in some water to kill their husband, and then end up drinking it themselves."

"She didn't appear to be a stupid woman. What if she'd intended to give it to Terrence but decided to drink it herself at the last minute, if she was depressed?"

Flora looked thoughtful. "Or what if she was going to poison him, and he switched the glasses when she wasn't looking?"

"No, there was only one glass, wasn't there?"

The two paused, thinking hard.

Fred spoke first. "Who else would have been trying to kill Terrence? Jonty seems the most likely. There's certainly no love lost between them."

"What about the solicitor? He was summoned here and there's some confusion whether or not that is even true. Could he have had a motive?"

"Anyone could have a motive? We haven't given motives for either one of us yet, have we?" smiled Fred. "It could just as easily be you or me."

They had reached the old brittle fence that stood on top of the cliff and were peering over it at the desolate scenery beneath them. The sea was foamy and white with anger as it raced in towards the rocky base below, and repeatedly rose up as if reaching for them. Spray rose up into the air and the droplets clung together in little wispy clouds. A flock of noisy seagulls buffeted about in the wind as they circled and fought over some food.

"Us?" laughed Flora. The wind began to whip itself up where they were standing open to the elements, and her hair kept blowing into her face. She hooked the front part behind her ears. "You're right, I most certainly haven't given that a thought. Are you considering me then?"

"Not seriously," smiled Fred with an impish glint in his eye. "However, it is feasible. Now, what if I were the guilty party? Perhaps the reason you woke up was because you heard me sneaking back off to my room having killed Helen."

"Yes," joked Flora, joining in. "Funny you should mention it, but I did see you now I cast my mind back, and my mother always told me to beware of men with freckles!"

"Ah yes, the freckles, a dead giveaway! Anyway, did you have a reason for getting up? You said you heard a noise, but what was it?"

"I don't actually know."

"Don't know, or don't want to say?"

"Why wouldn't I want to say? I've nothing to hide, and I'm not protecting anyone."

"I don't know, it seems strange to get up and leave your room in the night just because you heard a noise. There are plenty of people here this weekend, surely a noise isn't really unexpected?"

"Inspector Thomas was suspicious of that too. I can't answer as I got up on instinct."

"I expect you are high up on his list of suspects," grinned Fred.

Flora climbed up onto the first rung of the fence, peered downwards and felt giddy at the sight of the rushing water circling the rocks that were breaking the surface far below. She could just about make out a small portion of the old steps that had been cut into the cliff long ago, and thought how dangerous they looked. A long way out to sea a little boat bobbed about like a cork floating on the water.

"I believe you're suspecting me of something too, Fred," she said slowly, unable to tear her eyes away from the hypnotic movement of the sea. "Now why would that be, I wonder?"

Fred's face was full of mischief. "I'm merely pointing out what the police are most likely to be saying. After all, you allegedly heard a noise that no one else noted, and took yourself off downstairs. Next, you told Terrence to go and get William, leaving you alone to alter any evidence against yourself, or indeed create new evidence. Helen could have just been knocked out, and you had the perfect chance to get her to drink the cyanide-infused water. Perhaps it was you that wrote the letters D and I in the dust to fool everyone too."

Flora looked serious. "Then how did I get the glass back up to the Porter's room, and why?"

"You could be in it with Terrence, in all fairness. He would have taken the glass back to his room. Maybe you two wanted to run off together with his wife's money."

Flora pouted. "I know you're only pulling my leg, but it is feasible that I murdered Helen, isn't it?"

"No more than anyone else here. Isn't it suspicious that we all congregated in the same train compartment before ending up in this house? The whole weekend is full of mystery and intrigue if you ask me."

Suddenly, without any warning, the portion of fence Flora was standing on collapsed and she plunged forward. Letting out a shrill scream, she grabbed blindly at the struts but felt her body plummeting towards the edge of the cliff as if in slow motion. Her heartbeat was loud in her ears, all other sounds blotted out by the roaring of the blood that was racing around her body. It was then that she fainted.

A while later, having been lost in thought, it dawned on Inspector Thomas that he hadn't heard the voices of Fred and Flora for some time. Where on earth were they, and how was he supposed to find his way out of the maze? Groaning, he realised he had got himself completely lost. What now?

"Flora, Flora, can you hear my voice? I've got you but I need you to help me." Fred's panicked voice filtered through to Flora and she weakly opened her eyes. She was face down and halfway over the edge of the rocky ridge, and she could see the swirling, writhing sea way down below, its jaws open and waiting to devour her. She felt light-headed. Fred's voice came again.

"Flora, please. I've got your legs, but you need to help me. I'm holding on to the fence post with one hand but I'm frightened you'll slip out of my grasp. Can you try to leverage yourself up at all? Please try."

Using all the strength she could muster, Flora's arms flailed around over her head, trying to find something solid to hold onto. Her hair was over her face and whipping backwards and forwards painfully in her eyes. She sobbed loudly. At last, her hands grabbed at solid rock and she pushed hard as Fred tried to hoist her back up.

"Nearly there, keep going Flora." Fred's voice was tinged with fear, although he tried hard to cover it up. "Come on, you can do it."

With the last vestiges of remaining strength, Flora gave a final push and Fred heaved her up onto the ground. The two collapsed on the grassy edge, Flora too shocked to even speak. Fred's face was white, and he was shaking all over.

"Let's get away from the edge. I can't believe the Percivals allowed this rotting old fence to remain here, especially after what happened to their parents. What if you had been killed? I can barely take it in. Look at your hands and knees, you poor thing. They're all scratched and bleeding. You need a strong cup of tea with some brandy in it, let's get back to the house."

The two stumbled off towards the house and away from the hungry sea.

Chapter 16

The afternoon took a slow stroll into early evening before Constable Turner arrived back at Oakmere Hall. He had found out all the information he wanted, but had unfortunately nodded off in his chair at the station for longer than was appropriate for one on duty. On waking, he'd rushed off back to the big house but no one seemed to be about, apart from a sleepy looking William and Elsie who were talking in low voices on sofas in the hall.

He went into the library looking for the inspector, and a surprised Jonty looked up from a chair by one of the bookshelves where he was avidly reading something. Constable Turner beat a hasty retreat and popped his head around the kitchen door but the only person in there was the cook who was putting the finishing touches to her cider. It smelled wonderful, but he didn't wait around to savour it. He could see his plate of lunch on the side and was tempted to go and eat, but thought the better of it, and hurried up the stairs, down the east wing and knocked on Peter Moore's door.

"Come in." Peter Moore was sitting down in front of a desk, papers spread across the top of it.

"Mr Moore, I don't suppose you've seen the inspector at all?"

"Not since lunchtime I'm afraid. Is something wrong?"

Constable Turner edged closer to the desk and his eyes alighted on the newspaper that was open to reveal a photograph of William and Elsie. "Is this the interview about the Percival diamond? I haven't seen it before."

"Yes. Feel free to take a look."

"I should really be looking for Inspector Thomas, but I'll just have a quick glance. All in the name of research." He picked up the article and began to read, sitting his bulk down on the edge of the green leather-topped desk.

Peter Moore felt a bit irritated and moved his chair a few inches back, looking at the back of the newspaper that was very close to his face. Didn't the constable understand about personal space? He gave a start, blinked, and then double took.

"Look at this Constable!" He snatched the newspaper out of the startled policeman's hands and folded it over, jabbing his finger at an article on the back page.

"A flight of geese flew over the..." began Constable Turner in a bewildered voice.

"No, not that bit, this bit here. Can you see who wrote the article at the bottom of the page?"

"Miss Flora James," began the policeman uncertainly. "What of it? Oh! Oh, I see. Miss Flora James! That's a coincidence, or is it?"

"Hmm, well I can tell the penny has dropped."

"But what of it?"

"Constable, Miss James has claimed she had never heard of the Percival diamond before this weekend, remember? Apparently everyone put her in the picture about it during dinner last night, or so the inspector said, anyway. She can't have missed it, if she had written an article for the very newspaper that the story was published in, don't you see?"

"Ah, yes, I get what you mean, unless she just turned to the back page where her article had been printed. That doesn't seem too likely though does it? Did you know she was a reporter?"

"I had no idea, but then again I haven't asked anyone about their chosen professions. Isn't that your job?"

"Yes sir, but she didn't disclose this information to me, and I'm sure the inspector would have mentioned it if he'd known. I've been looking into everyone's backgrounds down at the station and there was nothing there about a reporting career. Perhaps it's a different Flora James, or maybe it is just a little hobby of hers. I'd better go and find him." With that the constable disappeared out of the door on his flat feet and made his way down to the kitchen.

"Cup of mulled cider, Constable?" asked cook. "I could do with a second opinion. Your lunch is here too."

"Now that's a temptation and a half I must say. I think I'd better go and find the inspector first though. Have you seen him? Looks like he's disappeared into thin air."

"I saw him in the garden earlier. Hopping about from hedge to hedge he was. It reminded me of a headless chicken dashing about the yard."

Constable Turner stared at her blankly. "Well, I'll look for him outside then." He majestically took his leave, disappearing out of the kitchen door and into the garden.

Inspector Thomas was fed up; he'd walked past the same bit of sticking out branch three times now. Where on earth had the exit gone? He'd learned nothing of interest from eavesdropping the conversation between Fred and Flora, and was now well and truly lost. It would be dark soon. What a day! Why hadn't Constable Turner come looking for him? He must have returned from the station by now. The tired inspector sat down on a bench in an alcove of the maze and sighed heavily, watching his breath disappear into the air like smoke. Thankfully he happened to be shielded from the wind where he was sitting, for it looked to be picking up strength. He shut his eyes, and tried his best not to feel too upset with himself, but he sometimes despaired of his own intelligence. Yes, he'd managed to arrive at a good place in his career, but all his cases seemed to be solved with only minimal input from himself. He could never seem to shake these negative thoughts. With a tired head full of doubts, he nodded off, his head lolling forwards and then resting on the hedge next to him, startling a mouse that was in there.

Fred and Flora returned to the house and sat down shakily in the hall with William and Elsie.

"Did you manage to get to the centre of the maze and back again? That was quick!" said Elsie. She peered closely at her friend, noting her tear-stained cheeks. "Oh goodness Flora, what happened to you? Did you fall over or something?"

"We went to the cliff's edge, and the fence collapsed, nearly sending Flora off to her death," said Fred through gritted teeth. "She's in a state of shock. We both are."

Flora said nothing but looked at her dirty knees and the palms of her hands that were flecked with blood from where she'd cut them on the rocky cliff. She was very pale and her face was smeared with dirt and tears.

Elsie turned white. "William, the gardener told you the fence needed replacing a long time ago. How come you didn't get him to make a new one?"

William looked sheepish and horrified in equal measures. "I always thought there were so many more important jobs that needed doing in the garden, and hardly anyone ever goes that far, not after what happened. Besides, money was tight. Flora, I'm so sorry. How can we make it up to you?"

"I'm just shaken up, but you need to get the fence mended before it happens to someone else."

"William will talk to the gardener at once, won't you Wills?" said Elsie. "I don't know what to say Flora. Thank goodness you are alright. What on earth is going on here this weekend? It has turned into a nightmare."

"I feel absolutely awful this has happened. Let me get you both some brandy, it's good for shock. I'll have a word with the gardener too." William got up and left the hall.

"I'm so glad you didn't fall right over, I would never have forgiven myself if something had happened to you," said Elsie. "Oh how awful, it takes me back to my parents' accident." Tears welled up in her eyes.

"I heard about that, and I'm so sorry for you, but please can we talk about something else now please?" said poor Flora.

"Of course, as soon as I've had your cuts and scratches bathed. I've no idea where the police have gone," said Elsie. "One minute they're here locking people up in their rooms, and the next they've completely disappeared."

William came back with two glasses of brandy and handed them over. "You do like to exaggerate don't you, sister of mine? They only asked old Jonty to stay in his room for a while, he wasn't locked up!"

"As if Jonty would murder anyone. We've known him years and he's never been psychopathic before. I don't believe he's done anything wrong."

"No, but it seems strange that his fingerprints were on the cyanide glass."

"You can never really know anyone," said Fred, draining his brandy and putting the glass down. "People only show you what they want you to see."

"Are you trying to tell us something Fred?" said Flora with an attempt at a smile. "Do you have a hidden side?"

"Nothing I care to reveal," grinned Fred. "And what about you? What is your secret?"

"That would be telling wouldn't it?" said Flora. She was still very white. "Listen, I need to thank you Fred, you saved my life today. I'm so grateful to you."

"Think nothing of it. Actually, I feel responsible for the accident."

"Why?" asked Flora. "It was absolutely nothing to do with you, how can you take the blame?"

"I walked us down that way, didn't I? If we hadn't gone there, well, the accident wouldn't have happened."

"The thing is, it could have happened to someone else, and with worse consequences," interrupted Elsie, noticing Flora's face. "Fred, you're not to blame. William and I are to blame because we should have had the fence mended a long time ago. The thing is, because of what happened to our parents, we don't ever go down there. Out of sight, out of mind. Now, let's do as Flora said, and change the subject. Do you think we should ask Terrence if he'd like to join us down here for some tea? I feel so dreadfully sorry for the man."

"He seems to have found solace in the reverend." William put his teacup down on the table and poured another one. "Cake anyone? A strange man for someone of the cloth, a bit clingy, don't you think?"

"Absolutely," agreed his sister picking up a slice of cake and placing it on her plate. "You'd imagine he'd want to get back home to his wife and flock by now. It isn't as if he knew Terrence beforehand or anything. Do you think we should gently shoo him off?"

"Perhaps we should, but if Terrence needs him..." William's voice trailed off.

"I'll go up and find out if they want to join us, shall I?" said Fred. "I need to get changed out of these dirty clothes anyway. Are you going up Flora?" He got up at William's nod and held his hand out to help Flora to her feet. The two made their way upstairs together and Flora disappeared off to wash her face and put on clean clothes before going back down in haste. She wasn't in the mood for being alone.

Briefly pausing outside Terrence's door, Fred heard the sound of muted voices coming from inside. He knocked smartly on the door and opened it. Reverend Bird and Terrence wheeled round in surprise from where they were sitting by the window.

Composing himself at once, Reverend Bird plastered his big smile across his face. "Fred, well what a nice surprise. Look Terrence, Fred has come to enquire after you."

"Actually, I've come to see if you'd both like to join us downstairs for a drink," faltered Fred, looking from one to the other.

"I think we can manage that, can't we?" twittered the reverend at Terrence, who nodded sagely. "Come on, let's go."

Fred didn't wait, but made his way to his room to change, feeling a little nauseated by the reverend's fawning behaviour.

Chapter 17

Mary had had a nap and was now ready for a cup of tea. Unlocking her door she went down the corridor, stopping outside Peter's door, which was ajar. She gave it a little tap and called out.

Peter appeared at the door at once. "Are you going down? Right, I'll come with you."

The two of them wandered slowly down the east wing together in a companionable silence, only broken when Peter told Mary about Flora's newspaper article.

"How extraordinary! Why ever didn't she say? Sounds more than a little suspicious don't you think?"

They stopped before they got to the top of the stairs.

"Let's discuss this in layman's terms," said Peter in an undertone. "The Percival siblings do a newspaper interview raising interest in the diamond. Your house is burgled. You get invited here after decades of silence. Who else should be here but an alleged reporter, Flora James, who denies having heard about the diamond before this weekend, and yet must have seen the article. I am summoned urgently although the Percivals deny the urgency. A strange note, presumably not written in William's hand, is given to the butler asking him to make sure I am here this weekend. It mysteriously gets burned in the kitchen fire. How am I doing so far?"

"You're doing fine, keep going," prompted Mary.

"Each of us in the same train carriage turn up here; that in itself is strange. Jonty Carshalton is found looking for something in your room…"

"We don't know he was looking for anything," interjected Mary.

"That's true, but it seems he was up to no good anyway. Jonty's fingerprints are found on the glass of poison along with your own ones. It seems as if he must have planted the cyanide in your room, but why? Later that night he, we presume, tries to get in to your room again. Local neighbours come to the party and cannot get home again as one has hurt his ankle. Incidentally, when I was talking to Flora and Fred outside this morning, she told me that Terrence had all but run upstairs to get William when she sent him, but what about his bad ankle? It is as if he only hobbles when he remembers he is meant to be hurt. Then Helen dies. What do you make of all that?"

"I can't begin to piece anything together in my mind. It's awful but all I can focus on is Jonty Carshalton being in my room."

"You don't suppose he was your thief do you?"

"My thief? I'd hardly call him *my* thief. However, I know what you mean, but why would he burgle my house then coincidentally appear here this weekend, trying to burgle me again. What on earth would he be after?"

"Your diamond perhaps?"

"Does he imagine I carry the thing around with me wherever I go? And why have you been brought here this weekend? People don't usually do business at the weekend, and in the middle of a house party. Could your life be in danger too, do you think?" Mary's face looked quite alarmed as she turned to the solicitor.

"I doubt it very much," replied Peter cheerily. "Maybe, as a man who works in law, I'd be a good witness to something or other. Trouble is, I haven't witnessed anything at all!"

Constable Turner was loitering around by the garden sheds, half looking at the under-gardener weeding a flowerbed. He stood back a bit and began to watch intently. This was the boy that had discovered that the cyanide was missing. Orson, wasn't that his name? Didn't the inspector always tell him that criminals could never help interfering in an investigation, and often went back to the scene of the crime? Why was the lad digging? Feeling clever, he cautiously made his way over to the boy and knelt down heavily next to him, staring at the dirt and frowning.

"Is something wrong sir?" asked the boy looking rather scared.

He turned his face from the constable and back to the flowerbed again. What was the policeman looking at?

"Let me help you, sonny. We don't get far in life without helping each other." Constable Turner grabbed the trowel out of the startled boy's hands and began to scrabble about in the earth.

"It's fine sir, it's me job. No need to 'elp me at all." The boy scrambled to his feet as clods of dirt started flying about as the policeman stabbed wildly at the border.

"What's goin' on 'ere?" shouted a voice, and the head gardener loomed into sight and walked over with his bowlegged gait. "Orson, I need you to help me fix that fence down at the cliff's edge. It'll just be a patch up job as we've finally been given permission to renew the whole lot, so will need to get hold of some good timber. Constable, can I 'elp you with anything?"

Not even knowing what he had been looking for, Constable Turner took one last jab at the earth and then flung the trowel down. There was nothing buried there at least. Rather embarrassed, he got up and brushed the dirt off his hands and knees before nodding curtly at the gardeners and theatrically taking his leave. They watched him go in bewilderment.

Before he realised it, the constable had arrived at the maze. He loved mazes, and carried a fond memory around of courting his wife in one. She often joked that she'd only agreed to marry him because she was afraid of not getting out of the maze again. He began to recreate the scene in his mind: humming the tune he'd serenaded her to all those years ago.

"Pom pom pompety pom, tumty tumty tum."

Inspector Thomas awoke with a jerk. What on earth was that sound? He stretched, sat up and the sound soon wafted up to his ears again.

"Pom pom, tumpety tum."

"Is that you, Turner? Where are you? I'm lost in this blasted maze."

"Sir? Is that you?"

"Well of course it's me, you nitwit."

"Where are you?" Constable Turner's surprised voice sounded from behind one of the hedges.

"If I were aware of that, Turner, I wouldn't be lost would I?" The inspector's voice rose scathingly up to the constable's burning ears.

"Keep talking sir and I'll come and find you."

"We need some more tea in the pot," said Elsie peering into it. "I'll give the maid a shout."

"Oh, don't do that Elsie," said Mary who had ascended the stairs with Peter but had not yet sat down. "I'll pop along to the kitchen myself, I could do with the distraction. I think we need some more cups and saucers too."

Fred got up at once and picked up the teapot. "Here, let me help you."

The two disappeared up the length of the hall and disappeared through a door at the end.

"Shouldn't we call Jonty through? I'm guessing he's still in the library." William wandered off to find him.

"So, Miss James," began Peter. "I don't really know much about you. Do you have any hobbies or interests?"

Flora looked up at him in surprise. "Me? Well, no not especially. I love fashion, but what woman doesn't?"

"None that I know of!" laughed Elsie. She was kneeling on the floor and dabbing at her friend's grazes with some iodine, making her wince.

"You're not interested in writing then?" probed Peter.

"Writing? Now what makes you ask that?" Flora's bright smile began to fade.

"I thought I might have seen your name somewhere before, that's all."

Flora looked down at her lap but said nothing.

"Flora?" Elsie put the iodine down on the table and looked at her friend. "What's he talking about?"

Flora sighed. "I take it your hint refers to an article I wrote for the newspaper?"

Peter nodded.

"It isn't a hobby as such, I imagine you're talking about an article I sent in some time previously, not really expecting it to be printed."

"Oh, what article? Darling, how exciting!" Elsie clapped her hands together.

"Nothing, really it was nothing."

"The article was in the same edition that your interview was printed in," said Peter looking at Elsie.

"Really? I'd love to read it. Perhaps I did read it, and didn't notice your name. What was it about? Wait, it was in the same paper? Then…?"

"Then she knew about the Percival diamond," finished Peter.

"I can't believe you didn't mark the way you came in," said Inspector Thomas accusingly.

"Well you didn't either sir," said Constable Turner in an injured voice. "I'm sure it was this way, though. Come on, let's try."

The two men walked single file down the pathway that Constable Turner was gesturing towards. Suddenly the constable gave a little cry.

"Look sir, we've made it to the middle. Aren't we clever?" He did a little jig, much to Inspector Thomas's disgust.

"Constable, pull yourself together at once. Our goal isn't to get to the middle; it's to get out. I've been stuck in here long enough today as it is. How are we supposed to conduct a murder investigation when we're marooned in here? It's practically dark. Why, who knows what the murderer is getting up to now without us being there to thwart him."

"Or her," pointed our Constable Turner. "It could be a woman."

"Just get us out of here Turner," said the inspector in a withering voice.

Jonty Carshalton joined the others for a cup of tea but sat slightly away from them, and as far away from Terrence as he could manage.

"I can't think where the police have gone," Elsie said to the room. "Their car is still here, so they must be about somewhere."

"Perhaps they've discovered a clue in the grounds," replied William. "That's where the cyanide was found so they must be on the track of something or someone."

"Well I wish they'd hurry up and get to the bottom of it," said Terrence throwing a nasty look across at Jonty. "I'd like them to take the tyrant to task."

"Tell me what you found out at the station earlier," said Inspector Thomas, trying not to feel irritated as the two men came up against yet another dead end.

"Right, good idea and a good use of time if I might say so sir."

Inspector Thomas clenched his fists against his sides and clamped his teeth shut so he wouldn't say something he might regret.

The action wasn't lost on the constable, who hurriedly continued.

"Peter Moore sir. He is exactly who he says he is, the Percival family solicitor. His father before him took care of the family's legal matters."

"So his father would have been solicitor when the diamond went missing all those years ago."

"Yes, he was. There's nothing untoward with the way they conducted their business, it's all above board so to speak. Then we have Mary Percival, second cousin to William and Elsie Percival. She lives a frugal existence miles from Oakmere, on her own. It seems her father cut off all contact with the family here decades ago."

"Do we know why?"

"Not yet sir, but this is the first time the cousins have met up again since childhood."

"We will have to find out about that. What about Flora James?"

"She's a firm friend of Elsie, and a regular visitor here. She lives with her mother in a large house and seems to be a young woman of means. However, it seems she has designs on being a writer and had an article published in the paper that printed the story about the Percival diamond. I only just found that out earlier as Peter Moore has the newspaper article in his room, and Flora's article is on the back page. Her father, now dead, was a writer and had quite a few books published."

"What kind of books?" asked the inspector with pricked up ears.

"Oh, mainly ones about crimes that were solved by anyone other than the police, some amateur sleuths and even a solicitor. Not our kind of read I'm afraid sir," chuckled the policeman.

"Sleuthing? Do any of his books happen to be in the Percival library? Jonty has a penchant for reading those types of books."

"I don't know but I'll look when we get out of here. Have we tried this way?"

The two men tramped valiantly along in silence for a few minutes, trying to dodge the muddy edges, and concentrate on getting out.

"There's only one thing for it," said the inspector at last. "You kneel down here Turner, and I'll climb onto your shoulders and see if I can look over the hedge to see where we are. We'll have to be quick, before we're stuck in total darkness."

"But it's dirty here sir," protested Constable Turner.

"All in the line of duty."

"But you're taller sir, you should be the one on the ground. I'll climb onto your shoulders instead, shall I?"

"Was that a serious question, Turner?"

Seeing the expression on his superior's face, Constable Turner at once dropped to the ground, planting his large hands into a dirty puddle.

"Ooh, let's move over there a bit where it isn't quite so swampy."

The two men walked over to a patch of greenery.

"Right then, down you get Turner."

Constable Turner got gingerly down on his knees, steadying himself with a branch.

"Ouch!" He leapt up again making Inspector Thomas jump.

"What is it?"

"Nothing sir, just a thorn." Sucking his thumb, Constable Turner knelt back down again.

"Right, ready?" Inspector Thomas clambered onto the policeman's knees, grasping at the hedge as he placed one foot firmly on his shoulders and hauled himself up. "No, I can't see over this hedge. You'll need to stand up."

"Stand up? I'm not so sure I can."

"Give it a try Turner."

The constable, muttering under his breath, raised himself up a bit and planted one foot firmly on the ground.

"Woah, steady yourself there." The inspector swayed about and grabbed at a branch.

"I'm trying my best sir," replied the constable in a wounded voice. He clamped his muddy hands around his superior's ankles, stopping the trousers flapping in his face, and staggered to his feet.

Anyone spotting the two men would have thought they were witnessing two clowns practicing their acrobatic act. The constable tottered about from side to side while his inspector half squatted on his shoulders, calling out well-intentioned instructions, his arms flailing about.

Chapter 18

"So did you really not know anything about our missing diamond, Flora?" asked Elsie to her friend. "How could you have missed the interview? The paper made a big thing of it."

Flora looked embarrassed. "Look, alright, so I was aware of it. What does it matter?"

"I'm sure it wouldn't matter but for the fact you told us you'd never heard of it before."

"Yes, that was a mistake. I'm sorry I said I didn't know about it, when I did. Everyone knows about it. I was just interested to hear about it, so I claimed I knew nothing."

Mary gave Flora a hard stare. "Miss James, you cannot give your friend that statement as an excuse. Surely she deserves more than that? You must have more to tell."

"Well, well, I..." stammered Flora. She covered her face with her hands.

Fred stepped in. "Look here, what does it matter if Flora had heard about the missing diamond or not? It isn't as if she stole the thing, is it? What's the big deal?"

"Thanks Fred, but she's right, I should tell the whole truth." Flora turned to Elsie and gave her a small smile. "Else, I've wanted to be a journalist since I was a girl. I started off writing short articles and sending them in to various publications in the hope that one of them would print my humble thoughts. A few did over the years, but I didn't get any regular work, which was what I really wanted. It's a man's world out there."

"Surely you didn't need to work Flora, didn't your father leave you pretty well off?" Elsie stared at her friend, a frown furrowing her brow.

"Oh yes, he did. It wasn't about the money; it was simply my passion to write. Not many men allow women to do this kind of work so whenever I had an article published I felt as if I'd scaled a mountain. One day I heard about your diamond and I thought that if I were to find out what had happened to it, I would get more recognition and perhaps be taken more seriously." She took a deep breath. "I went out of my way to introduce myself to you, to befriend you. My goal was to get to the bottom of the mystery, to find the diamond for you. I didn't realise one of my articles would appear in the same paper as your interview."

Elsie gave a shocked gasp. "You duped me?"

William shook his head sadly and moved closer to his sister, putting a protective arm across her shoulders.

"Elsie, I'll admit that was my motivation at first, but please believe me that when I got to know you I thought you were amazing. You truly were, and are, my friend. The story became insignificant in the face of our friendship."

"What exactly did you find out about the diamond?" interrupted Peter. "My clients would appreciate any information that you have found out."

"I, well, I saw the letters in the trunk you hauled down from the attic," stammered Flora, going rather red in the face. "Please forgive me for snooping. I was hiding in the room and considered climbing into the trunk. I opened it and had a quick peek."

"I'm not sure I can take this in," said Elsie looking upset. "I thought you were my friend. You say you *are* my friend, but how can I believe you after this? What friend goes through someone's personal items?"

"Listen Elsie, just hear me out." Flora ran her hands through her blonde hair, inadvertently drawing attention to her chipped red nails. "I wasn't snooping as such. Each time I came here I would systematically search rooms, just in case the diamond had been lost or hidden away somewhere. Really, I wanted to help! I traced the diamond as far as Mary's father."

"We did that ourselves from the letters," said William.

"Yes, well I went to try and find out a bit more about Miss Percival here," said Flora gesturing towards Mary. "I even saw her in the village shop near her house…"

"I thought I had seen you somewhere before," said Mary sternly. "Are you responsible for my burglary young lady?"

"No, I swear that was nothing to do with me. Nothing. I noticed you seemed to live a modest life and guessed you did not have the jewel. I made some enquiries and came to the conclusion that there was no way you were hiding a diamond away. What would be the point? Surely anyone with something worth so much money would sell it and live a handsome life?"

"Maybe you would Miss James, but not everyone thinks in terms of luxury," retorted Mary witheringly.

"Are you saying you did have the diamond then Mary?" asked William. "You led us to believe that you didn't remember ever having seen it before."

"I told you the truth, I don't remember seeing it."

"Then what happened to the diamond after your father took it?"

"Took it? You make it sound like he stole the thing. Father wouldn't talk about what happened when we were here and left so suddenly, but over time he hinted that he might have it."

"Hinted?" said Reverend Bird before he could stop himself. He was leaning forward listening to the conversation with interest.

"Yes, hinted Reverend, not that it is any of your business," bristled Mary.

William gave his cousin a hard stare. "Well he did have it, and left a receipt with our parents. Did he not leave information as to what happened to it when he died then?"

Everyone's eyes were on Mary, making her feel rather like a specimen under a microscope. She busied herself pouring another cup of tea from the teapot, and her cup rattled in the saucer as she picked it up.

"Father died a poor man, and left me a small box of his effects: letters and such like. I never felt able to look through it as his death hit me hard and I found it too painful. The box was put in my attic and was left until I thought I would feel strong enough to go through it, but I never got to that point. It was almost as if, in looking, I would have to acknowledge that he had gone, and that was something I didn't want. Then the blow came a short while ago when it was stolen."

Flora gasped. "Someone was after the diamond. I mean, do you think the diamond was in that box?"

"I think it may have been, yes. The thing is, who else knew about the possibility of me having it?"

"Us," said William looking at his sister. "Only us. Does that make us suspects in your burglary?"

"I'm afraid it does," stepped in Peter. "You had seen the correspondence between your fathers in your trunk. You were the only ones that could have guessed where it was."

"No, we're not," said Elsie quickly. "What about Flora here?"

"I didn't steal it! If I had why would I still be hanging around here? Besides, my motivation was returning the diamond to you and getting an article in the papers. I didn't want it for myself, I don't need the money."

"How can I trust that you are telling the truth?" Elsie wiped a couple of stray tears away from her green eyes and leaned closer to her brother.

"Elsie, please. I am aware I have a lot of making up to do, but I didn't take your diamond."

"My diamond," interrupted Mary tartly.

"Yes, I'm sorry, your diamond. Anyway, what about the interview in the newspaper? Many people would have known about the missing jewel."

"Known about it, yes. However, I was not mentioned in that article so they would have to be good detectives to trace it to my door." Mary crossed her arms tightly as a defensive mechanism to keep everyone out.

"How would you know that you weren't mentioned if you claim you didn't read that newspaper?" replied Flora stubbornly. "It seems as if I wasn't the only person hiding the truth."

"Well, if we're all about telling the truth, why don't you tell me exactly why you asked me here?" retorted Mary, looking hard at her cousins. "I suppose your purpose was motivated out of a desire to get information out of me about that blasted jewel."

"I see the entrance Turner!" said Inspector Thomas. "Right, let me just make a mental map and then we can get out of here."

"Right-o sir." Constable Turner's legs shook with the strain of having his superior balanced precariously on his shoulders. His foot, inadvertently finding itself in a muddy patch, slid to one side.

Elsie stole a quick look at William who was looking decidedly uncomfortable. "It looks like we're all coming clean so yes, Mary, I'm afraid we did invite you to find out what had happened to the Percival diamond. I'm so sorry."

"And what if I did have it? What then?"

"We had hoped that you were fantastically rich and living the high life."

"Again, what of it?"

"Mary, perhaps this conversation should be had in private," muttered William, aware of the others listening with their mouths open.

"Oh come now William, just when we're all being so honest and open with each other," said Mary in a sarcastic tone. She sniffed and sat back in her chair, looking cross and mutinous in equal measures.

"Let's calm this down and try to think in a clear manner," said Peter. "The police seem to have disappeared into thin air. Right, well you say that only William, Elsie and Flora knew about the letters in the trunk. Was anybody else here present during that party?"

William looked thoughtful. "Well, let's see. Yes, Terence and Helen were here, and probably Jonty too. Were you here Jonty? All our parties seem to merge into one, and I'm blessed if I can remember."

"He was here," interposed Terence before Jonty could say anything. "I remember."

Jonty coughed. "I'm not even sure which party you are referrin' to? I'm afraid I don't remember seein' no trunk."

William and Elsie looked at Terence.

"Don't get suspicious of me! I've just lost my wife, for goodness' sake. I distinctly remember a large trunk in the corner of the room after we'd been playing hide 'n' seek, and it hadn't been there at the start of the evening. I didn't look in it, though."

"Now, now young man. No one is accusing you of anything," said Reverend Bird. "I like to think I'm here to pour oil on troubled waters, so if anyone is distressed please do speak out."

"To be perfectly honest Reverend, and with the greatest respect, I believe it is time you got on your way now," said William. "There's no need for you to remain here, and I'm sure your family are wondering where you have got to."

Reverend Bird's face fell. "Oh, but I want to stay, really I do. I am the neutral party, and so can soothe over any problems and help you all."

"We don't need soothing," said Elsie. "We need to get to the bottom of a problem, and I don't see how you can help us."

Reverend Bird turned big eyes towards Terence. "It is up to you Mr Porter? Would you like me to go and leave you in peace?"

"Not at all," said Terence. "I'd like you to stay, please. This lot are at each other's throats, and no one seems to understand how I'm feeling, apart from you. Besides, that infernal policeman suggested the cyanide could have been for me, and I need protection."

"I think that says it all," said the reverend firmly. He turned stubborn eyes to the rest of them. "You heard him, that cyanide could have killed him. What if the killer strikes again and I'm not here? I would find it extremely hard to forgive myself."

"Fine, you stay," said William exasperated. "And you're right, Terence, we don't know how you're feeling, but we are trying our best. I'm going to go and look for the police."

"I tell you I'm sorry sir," said Constable Turner in a small voice as he ineffectually tried to wipe the dirt off his uniform with his handkerchief. He was sitting in a patch of wet mud, and his thick regulation trousers were soaked through to the skin where he'd slipped into rather a deep puddle.

Inspector Thomas hauled himself up into a seated position, winded. His face was covered in brown putrid mud from the puddle he had slid head first into on his rapid descent from Constable Turner's shoulders.

"The worst thing about this, Turner, is that it has hardly rained in days. The puddles must be a permanent fixture in this maze. Here, help me up."

The two men struggled to their feet, slipping about and trying to steady themselves.

"Come on sir, let's get out of here. Cook will make us a nice cup of tea and we can dry off." Constable Turner waved his handkerchief in the general direction of his inspector's lapels but was swatted away brusquely. Feeling fed up, the two men hesitantly picked their way over the mud towards the direction of the exit.

William was on his way out of the kitchen door when he saw two woebegone figures in the distance, covered from head to foot in mud, and tried to hide a smile behind his hand. He slipped back inside, pretending he hadn't noticed them.

"Anyway Turner, you never did finish telling me about the background of our suspects. What did you find out about the Porters?"

"Ah, the Porters." Constable Turner wriggled his toes luxuriously, enjoying the heat of the kitchen stove. His socks hung drying on the clotheshorse, and he was sitting back with his feet up on a chair, sipping at a hot cup of tea. "Helen Porter came from a well to do family and was the only person in line to inherit a rather nice fortune. She had lived in this area for many years, and was well-liked amongst her peers, although rather fond of a drop or two of the strong stuff. Not that I'm one to judge," he added quickly, noting the blank look on the inspector's face. "Terrence was trickier to find out about, but it turns out he wasn't always called Terrence Porter. He claims he was falsely imprisoned on charges of theft some years back and had to change his name on leaving prison to stop being hounded by the press. My belief is that he changed it to prevent his brothers-in-arms coming after him and giving him what for."

Inspector Thomas raised his eyebrows in interest. "I knew he had been a thief, but what did he steal?"

"Allegedly, a string of pearls and a couple of diamond rings which were taken from the home of Lady Stirling, as well as other petty burglaries. He has always denied it but, as the saying goes, mud sticks."

The inspector shut his eyes in irritation at the mention of mud again.

"By all accounts he met Helen at the races and they got along almost immediately," continued Constable Turner. "They got married, and the rest is history. Nothing else happened to get him into trouble."

"I don't suppose he needed to find trouble, having married into money," replied the inspector with a cynical tone to his voice. "Did Lady Stirling get her jewellery back?"

"No, I don't believe so."

"Is there a possibility that someone here was duped at some point or other by him? Perhaps the cyanide was pay-back."

"I haven't found anything out to that effect, sir, but it isn't out of the question."

"What if he'd stolen Mary Percival's diamond, and she found out about it? She could have been getting her revenge on him. Mind you, there wouldn't be any point in poisoning the man without first getting her diamond back, or at least information as to what had happened to it."

"True, but maybe she did find out the information and we just don't know about it yet.

"Anyway, who else is there to report on?" He ran his hands through his now dry hair, and some flakes of dried mud drifted onto the floor. "Jonty Carshalton for starters. He seems most shady but has escaped trouble with the law for some years now so we don't have anything on him. Once or twice in the past he was accused of things, but always had a valid alibi. In fact, more than once his alibis were that he was here spending time at the Percival's house."

The inspector sat up straighter. "His alibi was from the Percivals?"

"Yes sir, they backed him up. He lives a modest life, has no wife or family, and no friends to speak of, unless you count the Percivals. By all accounts he used to hang about with a bad lot, but hasn't been known to do so for a long time."

"Bad lot?"

"Yes, a bunch of chancers, in and out of prison for petty crimes. Maybe he saw the error of his ways and distanced himself from them. All we know about him is that he is an avid reader and keeps his nose clean."

"I'd like to find out a bit more about the men he used to hang around with when you get the chance. It seems like his kind of gang would be the type that Terrence Porter once knew. Is there a history there?"

"Possibly so, but I'll find out for sure, sir."

"The Percivals are funny friends for a man like Jonty Carshalton. He would fit in more with their servants than them, and I think there's more to their friendship than meets the eye. What do you know about the Percivals?"

Constable Turner began to drum his fingers on the table. "Only that they have always lived in this house, neither having married before. They enjoy their money and are always hosting wild parties that are notorious for their high alcohol content if you get what I mean sir. They have been trying to get that diamond back, prompting local gossip that they're in financial trouble."

"And are they?"

"Yes sir, I believe they are. There's no proof of that, mind, but just the idle gossip from the servants."

"What happened to their parents?"

"An unfortunate accident, they fell to their deaths from the cliff at the bottom of the property when the Percivals were children."

Chapter 19

As soon as Inspector Thomas had begun to feel warm, dry and not so silly, he decided to do a little exploring. "Come on Turner, let's have a proper look around the house. No one here wants to talk frankly with us, or if they do, I can't for the life of me work out which ones they are."

"Ah, some proper detecting. Sounds good to me." Constable Turner's face presented the inspector with a smile.

"Yes Turner, the authority is ours. Let's have a poke around."

The two men went up the back stairs together, appearing in the servants' quarters at the top. Striding across the passage past the rooms, they descended the small staircase at the end that led to the door that opened up at the back of the west wing. They went out and loitered on the landing for a few seconds, wondering what to do next.

"Do you want to search the rooms sir?" asked the constable.

"I don't really know. Actually, I do. Here's an idea for you. I'm going to go to Flora James's room. If you make your way to the library and throw some books down or something, I'll listen out for the sound. Remember, she said there was a noise that disturbed her in the night? Let's see if she could have heard Helen falling onto that bookcase."

"But sir, if she did hear it, does it prove anything?"

"No. However, if she didn't hear anything, what was she doing up, and why did she say she heard something that no one else seems to have heard?"

"Ah, I see," murmured the constable, looking more confused than ever. "Right then, I'll just be off downstairs then. Listen out for some noise."

Inspector Thomas tapped on Flora's door to make sure it was empty and then disappeared quietly inside.

Constable Turner walked down the stairs and alighted in the hall where some of the household were still sitting around. They all looked up at him, half expecting him to ask them a question, but he strolled nonchalantly past, avoiding all eye contact and whistling to himself. He disappeared into the library, looking important, and shut the door behind himself.

"I wonder what he's up to," grinned William, still with the delicious image of the two muddy and bedraggled policemen in his head.

Nobody had to wait long to find out. A few seconds later a resounding and prolonged crash came to their ears as the constable swept a large volume of heavy encyclopaedias on to the floor. William leapt to his feet and rushed to the library door, throwing it open.

"What on earth...?"

Constable Turner looked up guiltily. "Just an experiment Mr Percival, nothing for you to worry about." He bent down, picked up one of the heavier books and threw it back down again on the wooden part of the floor where the rug didn't reach. It sounded like a clap of thunder and William stared, quite lost for words. The policeman squeezed past him and hurried back up to the inspector, leaving William gazing after him open-mouthed.

"Did you notice any noise, sir?"

Inspector Thomas shook his head. "No, not a thing. How very interesting, Turner. So, unless Miss James heard something else that nobody else on this wing was aware of, I suggest she was probably lying to us."

"Unless she just happened to wake up, and thought she heard something, but it was really something in her dream."

Inspector Thomas looked at his constable in a mordacious way but said nothing. He left the room and began to walk down the corridor towards the stairs, and along to the east wing. He could hear the murmur of conversation drifting up from the hall, but didn't want to talk to anyone yet. Constable Turner followed slowly, not really knowing what he was meant to be doing.

At the end of the passage the two men stopped. A small door that looked like it must open into a cupboard stared at them. The inspector turned the handle and the door swung open. "Ah, the attics lead up from here. I suppose they must just take up this half of the house, as the servants reside in their own quarters above the other wing."

He poked his head in and switched on the light, noticing a carpet of dust on the ground. However, something large and heavy must have been dragged through it recently as clear marks showed up on the floor. "Come on Turner, let's take a look in here."

The two of them bent their heads to get in the doorway and followed the path of the object that had been dragged about. It didn't take long to find the trunk that had been returned to the attic not too long before. It sat at the bottom of a wooden ladder that went up to the higher attic space above.

"Now what have we here? This looks like it has been of interest to someone of late." Inspector Thomas perched on one of the ladder rungs and pushed back the lid of the trunk. Inside there were piles of newspapers, letters, photographs and pieces of aged paper.

"Mostly private letters I think sir," said Constable Turner hurriedly. "Perhaps we shouldn't be looking through these. They can't have any link to the poisoning."

"Turner, not for the first time, you have me wondering why you entered the police force in the first place." Frowning, the inspector picked up one of the envelopes from the top of the pile, slipped it out of the envelope and began to read.

William and Elsie were in the library, picking up the encyclopaedias that had been thrown to the floor. Elsie was laughing. "Honestly Wills, if we ever decide to commit a crime, let's do it in this area. The police don't have a clue what is going on around them. I guess I shouldn't laugh really, Helen lost her life, but they really are too comical for words."

"You should have seen them dragging themselves across the garden earlier, looking as if they'd been having a mud bath. It reminded me of the pigs at the farm down the hill!"

The siblings collapsed against each other, laughing silently, with tears of mirth running down their cheeks.

"There's a lot of anger in these letters Turner," said Inspector Thomas, passing them over to the policeman for him to peruse. "A lot of accusations too. It looks as if Mary Percival's father was furious with his family. It is a pity we can't read the letters that went back to him in reply, if indeed any were sent."

"That's right, they might not have replied, sir. Anyway, this here receipt shows that he had the diamond at one point. No one seems to know what happened to it after that though."

"Yes, well I don't think we're going to get much else done here today. Let's tell them all we're going. It'll give them a chance to talk to us, if they've decided to stop shielding each other. I'm certain someone knows something."

Inspector Thomas summoned everyone to the hall, and stood waiting for them to sit down and pay attention to him. "Right," he said, once they were all seated. "Constable Turner and myself are going, but will be back first thing in the morning."

"Have you found anything out?" asked William.

"We're piecing together the information we have, and will inform you as soon as we know anything solid."

"So you haven't then," muttered William under his breath.

"As I said before, please do not leave Oakmere Hall until I give you permission to do so."

"Are we quite safe?" asked Elsie, more to put her guests minds at ease than her own.

"Of course we're safe," said her brother in earnest. His handsome face turned to look at everyone. "If anyone is concerned, please do come to us and say. We shall all keep an eye out for each other and nothing horrible shall happen. Terrible as it is, I'm sure Helen's poisoning was accidental."

Terrence, who was sitting next to the ever-present reverend, snorted but remained quiet.

"If that's all, we shall go, or does anyone want to talk to me first?" The inspector paused. "Right, come on then Turner." The policemen went to the front door and disappeared outside, leaving Jenkins to shut it behind them.

As the car wound its way back down the drive, the inspector turned to his constable. "Turner, give me your opinion. Do you honestly think the death of Mrs Porter and the Percival diamond are linked?"

"I don't know sir, but it wouldn't surprise me one little bit."

"Let me say what's in my head, and you can chip in with anything you think relevant. Mary Percival seems to imagine that the diamond could have been in her father's box that was hidden in her house. The box is taken and her cousins, who are incidentally trying to trace the diamond, invite her to visit after years of silence. Perhaps the Percival siblings arranged the burglary and when the diamond couldn't be found, they asked her here. Strangely, the same guests were on the train with her, and even in the same carriage. Were they all after the diamond too? Somehow Mrs Porter could have got herself mixed up in it and got herself killed in the process."

"It sounds plausible but I can't see where anything fits to be honest."

"Me neither, Turner, me neither." Inspector Thomas drummed his fingers impatiently on the car dashboard and scowled.

"I can't help wondering whether they are all in it together, a large gang of them."

"All in it together? All in what together? What are you talking about Turner?"

"Just thinking aloud too sir, but it seems funny how they were all in the train together, highly suspicious if you ask me. Could they be a gang of jewel thieves?"

"They'd hardly be travelling together would they?" said the inspector in an acerbic voice. "I wonder how long it would take me to get a warrant to search the Porter's house? Maybe you should scout around there after you've dropped me home, see if you can find anything out."

"Ah yes, I understand, you can trust me sir," said Constable Turner, tapping his finger on the side of his nose in a knowing way. "In actual fact, I know the gardener down there. I'm sure I can engage him in conversation and get myself invited in for a cup of tea."

"Right, that's settled then. You do whatever it takes to gain access and have a look around for goodness' knows what. Maybe you'll even find Lady Stirling's lost jewels, though I doubt it after all this time. Let's go over everything again before I'm home."

Dinner was awkward for everyone; each one lost in their own thoughts. As soon as it was over they heard a distant wailing coming from outside.

"What's that?" asked Fred at once, looking towards the window with wide eyes.

"It sounds like chanting," replied Flora. She put her napkin down on the table and cocked her head to one side, listening hard.

"Oh goodness, it's the crowd from the village," said Elsie getting up. "I'd forgotten it's the wassail tonight, we should have sent word that they shouldn't come here after what's happened."

"Bother, it's too late for that now," said William. "I'm really sorry Terrence."

Terrence shrugged in a manner that suggested he couldn't care one way or the other.

"Well, let's hope the gardener has lit the bonfire, and that the servants haven't forgotten what they're meant to have done in preparation." Elsie got up and hurried off to the kitchen to see the cook.

William stood up and smiled around the room. "This isn't ideal, but it will take our minds off things for a little while. Come on, let's go and grab warm coats and make our way out to the orchard."

Only Fred and Flora managed to look in any way enthusiastic, and followed William eagerly. The others filed after them in a listless fashion.

Once outside they heard the singing again, this time nearer than before, and the roll of drums started up, loud and deep. Mary trembled as the bass sound of the drumming vibrated in her chest, and went to stand near the bonfire that was crackling merrily away in the orchard. Its orange hands unfurled and pointed up towards the sky, shooting little sparks out of its fingertips.

All at once a large crowd of people appeared around the side of the house, banging ancient looking instruments and bearing medieval torches. Children were flitting about in delight and getting in everyone's way. At the forefront of the procession was the queen of the wassail, looking startling in a starched white pinafore and wearing a crown made from twisted chestnut sticks and holly leaves. Everyone was dressed up in costume. It was all rather sudden and surreal.

"Golly, how exciting," said Flora clapping her sore hands together. She took her lipstick out of her pocket and applied it to her lips without a mirror. "How sweet the children are, and how beautiful the queen looks!"

The cook and maid appeared at the kitchen door with a large steaming vat and a ladle. The butler followed with a tray of glasses and then disappeared back inside to get some more. Slices of cake were piled up high on a trestle table.

The drummers banged out the last of their rhythms and a hush descended across the garden. Everyone's eyes turned to seek out the owner of the property, waiting for his speech.

"Welcome everyone," said William in a loud voice, and everyone cheered. He was standing on a chair by the kitchen door in order to be seen. "This annual tradition is an important one for us here at Oakmere, and we're happy you made the effort to come. To the queen we bow down to you, and to the common folk we pay you the greatest respect as has been done at this place for many years. As you know, tonight's wassail will hopefully awaken the apple trees and scare off any evil spirits in order to give us a good harvest at the end of summer."

Someone pushed the queen forward, and she skipped up to William's chair, smiling. William jumped off his chair and bowed to her, then turned to face the crowd and raised his arms up to prompt them to bow too.

"We honour our queen."

"We bow down, we honour our queen," echoed the crowd, bowing down as one.

"Come, drink and eat, and we will dance and sing our songs of blessing."

The crowd cheered again. Somewhere at the back, a baby howled and was shushed.

"What a load of nonsense," said Mary in a low voice that only Reverend Bird heard. She crossed her arms across her chest, half from annoyance and half from cold. "And those children shouldn't be out on a cold night like this."

"I agree my dear," he said. His sparsely combed-over hair was waving about in the breeze like a flag of surrender. "A pagan tradition that holds no truth, but a bit of fun nonetheless. Oh look, there's my wife, I must go and see her." He pushed his way through the crowd, sending small children skittering across the path out of his way.

Those that had been brandishing lit torches lined up behind one another and moved forward to throw them onto the fire, sending it blazing higher into the sky, crackling and spitting in delight.

The drumming started up again, rhythmical but menacing, and seemed to get louder with every second. A sense of danger hung in the air, primeval and earthy.

The gardener stood near the bonfire, poking and prodding with a stick to keep it in check. It roared away hungrily in the orchard as it was fed more wood, and many of the guests gathered around it to stay warm, clasping their hot apple cider with both hands. The butler was hastily ladling more drinks into glasses as the crowd queued up for seconds.

The gardener's lad had tied a pale blue ribbon to the largest apple tree and the queen of the wassail was busy pouring cider around the roots of it and whooping loudly, one hand holding her skirts above her ankles. Flora watched in fascination.

"Hold her up," shouted a voice from the crowd, and the queen was suddenly lifted up by two burly men and hoisted into the boughs of the tree. Laughing in delight, she took some of the cake that was held up to her and dipped it into her glass before carefully placing it in the branches. Everyone began to sing. Their symphonious voices were lifted up high by the wind and whipped about hauntingly.

"The bread be white, and the wassail be brown, so here my fellow I drink to thee and also the health of each other tree. Well may ye blow and well may ye bear, blossom and fruit for apple and pear."

There was a pause as the crowd began to bang sticks on the ground, picking up on the rhythm of the drumming before the singing recommenced.

"Stand fast root, bear well top. Pray the God send us a howling good crop. Every twig, apples big, every bough, apples now."

A violin began to play and people began to dance, lifting up their skirts and stamping on the ground in a way that was wholly mesmerising. Women held the hands of their children and friends, and twirled them around trying not to lose their bonnets, while men clapped in time and roared with laughter.

Fred glanced across at Flora who was joining in with the celebrations, her newly applied red lipstick showing up in the light of the bonfire. It was smeared from drinking the wassail, and reminded him of blood. He shivered suddenly.

Elsie weaved in and out of a group of dancers, waving the ribbon on a stick that had been thrust into her hand by one of the villagers. William went to find her, taking her free hand and they danced off into the midst of the crowd.

Peter was standing near the servants, enjoying the spectacle, but not wanting to join in with the celebrations. He half-heartedly wondered where Terrence was, hoping he wasn't finding everything too overwhelming, but Terrence was nowhere to be seen.

"And now," roared a voice from somewhere in the centre of the group of dancers. "We rid ourselves of the evil amidst us."

The drumming got faster as the dancers whirled around trying to keep up with the beat, and the sound filled everyone's ears so much so that they couldn't concentrate on anything apart from its hypnotic pulse. Flora's dress was a blur of colour and Fred couldn't make out her outline very well. He blinked and turned away.

"Evil must flee, evil must go," roared a large man as he waved his stick in the air. The crowd chanted the words after him, repeating it over and over again.

"Go, go, go."

Mary imagined the witch hunts of days gone by and shivered, thinking of the poor women that had been accused of putting spells on people.

"EVIL MUST GO."

All of a sudden guns were produced from cleverly concealed pockets, loaded and pointed up to the sky as Flora's dizzy eyes widened in fright.

"Now don't you worry," said a voice in her ear. It was Jonty. "This is all part of the ritual." He slid away into the crowd.

"Everyone ready? Three, two, one, FIRE."

A deafening sound exploded into the night as the guns were fired up into the tops of the trees. The thunderous roar split the night sky for several seconds and just as suddenly stopped. There was a pause before Flora began to scream.

"I've been shot, oh someone help me." She swayed and fell backwards onto the hard ground as the crowd parted around her.

Fred, who had taken his eyes off her, pushed his way round the bonfire, shouting out as people scattered out of his way in shock. People began to wail in fright, and children rushed about wildly trying to find their mothers.

"Flora, FLORA." Fred scooped her up in his arms and ran blindly towards the house.

Chapter 20

"Give her some air, move back a bit."

"Move, move I tell you."

"Are you sure she's not badly hurt?"

"Yes, it's only a flesh wound. See for yourself."

"Look, she's coming round at last."

Swirling in and out of consciousness, Flora could hear everyone talking around her. She tried to open her eyes but just as quickly drifted back into darkness as the voices echoed and faded away.

"Here are my smelling salts." Elsie rushed into the hall and thrust a small bottle towards Fred. "You do it."

Fred uncorked the small bottle and wafted it under Flora's nose. She gave a start and opened her eyes wide.

"Flora, thank goodness, how are you feeling? See if you can sit up."

"I think I'm okay." She pushed herself up into a sitting position with one arm and pushed the hair out of her pale face. Her arm was throbbing and she looked down at it, noticing the bloody trickling down. "What happened?"

"A stray bullet grazed the skin of your arm. All we needed to do was clean it up. It's still bleeding a bit but I'm going to put a bandage on it now. Are you in a lot of pain?"

"A little sore, but it isn't too bad. I thought all the guns were pointed upwards."

"Yes, well they were meant to have been, obviously," said William with a grim expression on his face. "One of the farmers said that when he reached for his gun, it had been removed from his pocket. He must have been jostled about a lot in that crowd, and didn't notice when it fell out."

"I don't understand. If it fell out, how was I shot?"

"Perhaps it went off as it hit the ground," suggested Reverend Bird doubtfully.

"That isn't really possible, surely?" said Fred. "It must have been taken from his pocket, let's be serious here. Some of the men had a scout round, and the reverend found it on the ground near the back of the orchard."

"You mean I was shot on purpose?" Flora's white face seemed to pale even more. "Why? What for? I didn't do anything wrong." Tears began to well up in her eyes and she hastily rubbed them away.

"No, of course you didn't, no one's suggesting otherwise. It must have been an accident, one of the children trying to be grown up and join in with the men." William shuffled about looking uncomfortable.

"A child?"

"We think so." Fred dropped his eyes. He couldn't bear to think of any other option.

"Was I unconscious for long?"

"A few minutes, that's all." Fred squeezed her hand.

"You're in shock, my dear," said Reverend Bird. "Thank the Lord the wound wasn't a serious one, for it could have been fatal."

"Reverend!" said Elsie crossly. "There's no need to speculate on what might have been." She began to wind the bandage around her friend's arm.

"Oh yes, quite. You're right of course, I'm sorry my dear. Rest assured, you'll be on the prayer list next Sunday, and the congregation will petition for your speediest recovery."

Elsie sighed and looked at her brother. "Do we need to call the police? Get some fingerprints taken?"

"It isn't worth it tonight," replied William. "I handled the gun, the owner handled it, and so did Reverend Bird. We would all have smeared any prints. Besides, whichever child fired that bullet will be mortified enough as it is. A policeman chastising them will not help now, tomorrow will be soon enough."

"I have to agree," said Fred in a decisive manner. "The inspector will be back here in the morning anyway, so we can fill him in with the details then can't we?"

"Exactly. The farmer has allowed me to keep hold of the gun so that Inspector Thomas can see it when he arrives. He's gone home now and so have all of the revellers. They were quite upset, poor things."

"Where have you put the gun Wills?" asked Elsie.

"In the library. I've wrapped it up in a cloth, no one will disturb it so don't worry."

"I've had two near misses this weekend," said Flora. "Should I be worried?"

"Of course not. Here, drink this brandy." Elsie handed a glass over to her friend who drank it up obediently.

"Do you think we should perhaps all head off to bed now?" asked William. "It's been a very long day. I'm glad Flora isn't badly hurt, as you can all see. Flora, can we get you anything, or would you like to talk some more?"

Flora shook her head. "No, I feel quite alright now, thank you. Just a little shocked, but a sleep will sort me out. I don't want to make a fuss." She got shakily to her feet and smiled at everyone to show she was fine.

"Well in that case, goodnight." Mary took her leave and began to make her way to the staircase, followed by Peter and Jonty. Terrence and his shadow, the reverend, went up together.

"Are you sure you want me to stay with you for another night?" Reverend Bird asked.

"Yes, I shall be alright tomorrow, but I can't stand to be alone in this house without my wife. Someone is after my blood." Terrence hobbled on his sprained ankle, and turned left at the top of the stairs and down the west wing to his room.

Fred took Flora's good arm and escorted her up to her room, while William disappeared back outside to make sure the servants were putting the fire out properly. It had got really windy, and the embers were glowing in anger as they were being raked out. Elsie watched them for a while from the kitchen door, deep in thought, and then took herself off to bed.

Mary thought the weekend had aged her by at least ten years, and longed to go home to peace, quiet and sanity. She wondered if she should be brave and wait behind her door to catch Jonty sneaking into her room again, but as it was so cold, she felt less inclined to do so. Instead, she remained in her clothes but got under the bed covers to keep warm, leaving the curtains open for some natural light. Before long her head began to nod and her eyes shut. She tried to fight it but was soon fast asleep, still sitting upright in bed.

Time passed. Jonty was sitting on his bed with his door ajar, he wanted to hear any noise that might occur in the house. Although certain that everyone had gone to their rooms, he decided to wait a bit longer. It was imperative that everyone was sleeping before going to get what he wanted.

Terrence seated himself on a chair at the dressing table in his room, the place he'd last seen his wife sitting. He could almost see her there now, brushing her dark bob in the mirror. Reverend Bird snored in the other chair where he'd abruptly dropped off to sleep mid-sentence.

Terrence got up and began to pace the room, thinking deeply. He opened his door quietly and looked out onto the corridor. All was quiet apart from the distant ticking of the clock in the hall below. Looking back into his room he noticed the fruit knife in the bowl of apples, the blade glinting in the shaft of moonlight that was coming through the gap in the curtains. He walked over to it, picked it up by the ivory handle, and pocketed it.

One person hadn't gone to bed along with the others. That person had gone upstairs and then doubled back down once the lights had gone out, and was now sitting in the shadow of the clock in the hall. Nothing could be seen of him apart from the soft light from his eyes when the moon sailed out from behind the clouds and cast an occasional lambency into the room.

All was quiet, and the house appeared to slumber. There was a movement in one of the upstairs bedrooms and, should there have been an onlooker, they would have seen a door handle turn slowly and a door opening. The occupant peered out and looked from left to right before seeming to make a decision and slipping out into the east wing, moving swiftly towards the stairs. Warily walking down, the figure made their way across the back of the hall to the kitchen and disappeared inside, clutching a bag under their arm.

The person who was hiding in the shadow of the hall clock exhaled softly, aware that they'd been holding their breath. They made as if to get up, but discerned another noise coming from upstairs, and subsided back into the darkness.

A second person crept downstairs and followed the first into the kitchen and out of the open back door.

Terrence once again peered out of his bedroom door and was surprised to see two people creeping about in the dark. He waited a few moments to make sure that no one else was around, and then followed suit down the stairs, his hand reaching into his pocket to hold onto the handle of the knife.

Reverend Bird snored gently.

Chapter 21

Mary was in the middle of a feverish dream where an unknown assailant, determined to steal her knitting bag, was pursuing her. An artful look crossed her face and she decided to hide it where no one would be able to find it. No, those woollen booties had to be secreted away to protect the owner's identity. Mary's dream weaved in and out of reality as she tucked her knitting bag under her arm and made her way towards the maze. Was that thick mud or sinking sand that she was struggling through? Someone or something was trying to slow her down. A sound somewhere behind her alerted her to the presence of another person, and she hurried along occasionally darting worried looks over her shoulder. She passed the smouldering fire and bypassed the orchard, doubling back to fool her stalker.

Jonty Carshalton was aware that Mary was sleepwalking, and followed her stealthily, hopping behind convenient trees or bushes when the moon sailed in front of the scudding clouds. He could tell she was making for the maze and wondered if she knew it well. The diamond must be hidden in one of her knitting needles, the large ones with the screw top. Hadn't he heard, with his own ears, the Percivals talking about hiding toys in it last night at dinner? Well, hide it all she liked; he would be watching where she put it and would soon have it in his grasp.

Mary rushed along, her paranoia growing and growing. Someone was definitely following her; that was certain. The person she was protecting would be in trouble if she didn't get rid of the evidence at once. Unaware that she was sleepwalking, Mary hurried on, her cheeks flushed and her breathing uneven, with her heart hammering in her chest painfully. Reaching the entrance of the maze she plunged inside.

Seconds later Jonty also reached the maze and raced in, slipping on the mud and only just recovering his balance in time. He paused, waiting for his eyes to adjust to the darkness, and cocked his head on one side to see if he could hear Mary's footsteps. There was a muttering coming from further ahead, and Jonty noticed her shadowy figure disappearing around a hedge further on as the moon momentarily appeared. Furtively, he moved forwards, unaware of Terrence behind him, his knife blade glinting in the moonlight.

Inspector Thomas lay in bed trying his hardest to drop off, but sleep eluded him. His mind began to swim round and round in circles, trying to make connections between each of the guests at Oakmere Hall. Something was troubling him, but he couldn't put his finger on it. It seemed to him that, although Terrence Porter was possibly the intended victim, someone had been trying to kill Mary Percival, and Helen Porter had been murdered in error. She must have taken that glass of cyanide quite by accident when Mary took her unwanted glass of water downstairs. So who would want to murder Mary? Well, it must be someone who wanted her diamond, but why kill her if they weren't aware of the diamond's hiding place? Perhaps the Percival siblings wanted her dead so that they could inherit it, but again, why do it until they knew where the diamond was? It didn't make sense. His thoughts darted from one possibility to the next, none of them ringing true in his head. There was always the possibility they had stolen it from her. It may have been in Mary's father's box, and they needed to get rid of her so that they could announce to the world that the jewel was once more in their possession. That seemed the likeliest thing he could thing of, but could he prove it?

Jonty was peering round a tall bush and watching Mary digging in the dirt with her bare hands, the mud wedging itself in her nails. They had trailed around and were now at the centre of the maze. The moon had been kind and decided to stay out to shine its cold light on the proceedings.

Mary reached into her knitting bag and dragged out the booties, still attached to the needles. She stuffed them into the hole she'd made and began to pile the earth back on top, panting from her exertions, and muttering incoherently.

Jonty moved forward into the pale light and Mary gave a start, sprang back, and cowered by the hedge in fright.

"What are you doing? You mustn't," she croaked. "Are you one of us, or are you on the enemy's side?"

Ignoring her, Jonty knelt down and began to scrape at the freshly filled-in hole with his hands. Terence stood in the shadows, the knife held loosely at his side.

"'ere, what's this?" Jonty suddenly held up a muddy woollen booty. "What've you gone buryin' this for?" He looked back into the hole, scrabbling about frantically, trying to find something else. "Where are they? Them large knittin' needles, where've you hidden them?"

Before Mary could speak, Terence emerged from his hiding place and launched himself at Jonty, wildly grabbing at the knitting which began to unravel itself, getting tangled around the men's hands. A scrum ensued while Mary gave little screeches and hit out with her knitting bag in the general direction of the two men.

"Where is it? Where is it? Give it to me now." Terence shouted loudly, holding the knife up to Jonty's throat.

"It isn't 'ere, I tell you. Ask 'er where she's put it, this must be some kind of set up."

Mary was sitting on the ground rocking backwards and forwards and moaning softly.

"Stop right there and put your hands above your heads where I can see them." Fred Adams stepped out from the darkness provided by one of the sculptured hedges and pointed a gun at Jonty and Terence who were wrestling on the ground. The two men continued to struggle with one another prompting Fred to point his gun up into the air and fire a shot. Both men leapt apart, covered in dirt and breathing heavily.

Peter Moore was sleeping fitfully when a distant shot sounded out. Something inside of him knew it wasn't part of a dream, and he sat bolt upright in bed. He had felt hot and stuffy earlier, despite the wintery weather, and had opened his window to let the air circulate in the room. Getting out of bed, he went to the window and looked out, but all was silent. As his eyes swept over the shadowy garden a lone seagull screeched suddenly and flew past, making him jump back in fright.

Flora, who had been awake the whole time, was sitting in bed scribbling something down in a notebook. She thought she might as well make the most of her sleepless night and write down her version of events, as someone might want to print it in the newspaper at some point. Her arm was painful, but it didn't prevent her putting her account onto paper.

She also heard the shot and raced to the window to look out, but despite the moonlight lighting up the garden, she couldn't see a thing. The waves crashing over the distant rocks could be faintly discerned, making her shiver, as she remembered how she had almost fell victim to them. She strained her ears to try and hear something else, but to no avail.

Fred moved closer to Mary who had fully woken up at the sound of the shot and was looking confused. "It's alright Miss Percival, I've got them covered. You were sleepwalking. Give me your hand." He helped her to her feet and gave her an encouraging smile, before turning to Terrence and holding his hand out for the knife. He slipped it into his pocket.

"Mr Adams, you came just in time." Mary offered him her hand gratefully.

"You two, let's go," said Fred, his usual jovial voice having disappeared and been replaced with a harder edged sound. "Walk in front where I can see you and follow your footsteps back to the exit. The path is very muddy where we've walked, so you won't get lost. Any funny business and I shoot. It's up to you whether or not you want to test whether I'm serious. Now, off you go, march."

Jonty and Terrence, looking mutinous and worried respectively, marched as instructed, muttering profanities under their breaths. Fred followed after with Mary trotting behind him.

Chapter 22

Flora opened her bedroom door. She knew a shot had been fired, and her heart was beating nineteen to the dozen. Was someone after her? Who should she go to for help? Should she trust anyone here?

"Is that you, Miss James?" Peter Moore loomed into the crepuscular light at the top of the stairs, looking as if he were about to descend. He peered at her as she emerged fully from her room, holding on to her bandaged arm. "Were you aware of a loud bang coming from outside?"

"Yes, whatever was it?" Flora tied her dressing gown belt up with one hand and looked at him suspiciously.

"It sounded like a gun shot to me. Would you like to come down with me to investigate?"

Flora hesitated. What if Peter were luring her downstairs to kill her? She wasn't sure if she could trust anyone at all. "I'm not sure, perhaps I should stay up here if there's a madman about."

"It would probably be safer. I say, you don't think someone took the gun that William put in the library, do you?" said Peter.

"Oh golly, yes I do think that. Let's have a look together." Flora decided to trust her instincts that Peter was a good person, and the two of them crept down the stairs together and across to the library, pushing the door open and snapping the light on. Flora was shaking, a little from cold but also from fear.

"Where would you hide a gun in here?" Peter turned around looking at the rows of floor to ceiling bookshelves. "William didn't say exactly where he'd put it did he? You look in the desk drawers while I see if it's been put on top of any of the books."

The two hunted in silence.

"Look, here's the cloth that William must have wrapped the gun in," said Flora a minute or two later. "I found it in the top drawer of the filing cabinet. What shall we do?"

"We need to find out who is absent from their beds. Quick, let's go." The two of them hurried to the door, through the hall and up the stairs, both instinctively turning right at the top.

Peter reached Mary's door first. "Miss Percival, are you awake?" Peter knocked on the door loudly. "Mary, it's Peter, I'm out here with Miss James. Please wake up."

No sound came from Mary's room and Peter turned to Flora looking worried. "You should go in. I wouldn't like her to wake up and find another man in her room. It might frighten the life out of her."

Flora turned the handle and entered, peering in the half-light towards the bed. She groped her way over and touched the covers.

"The bed is empty!" Flora turned back and saw Peter silhouetted in the doorway. His shadow was elongated and monstrous, making Flora's hair stand on end. She was wondering whether or not to scream when he put his hand around to the wall, felt for the light switch and turned it on.

Flora blinked at the sudden brightness and turned back to look at the bed, her heart beating fast. "I don't understand. She can't be outside firing a gun."

"No, but someone could be firing at her," said Peter looking grim. "Don't forget that the cyanide was in her water, someone must be desperate to bump her off. Let's see who else is out of their room."

Flora went over to Peter looking scared. "Do you think someone was trying to shoot her earlier in the orchard, when I got hurt?"

"Was Mary standing near to you at the time?"

"I, I don't know," frowned Flora trying to recall. "She may well have been. I remember hearing her voice at one point."

The two hurried down the corridor to Jonty's room, and Peter rapped on the door before turning the handle and boldly entering. He turned the light on and noticed the empty bed. "Look, the covers haven't been disturbed here at all. I think Jonty Carshalton is trying to murder Miss Percival. He was in her room the first night; his fingerprints were on her glass, and now this. We need to wake the others up and get outside to help, though I fear we're too late after hearing that gunshot earlier. Let's hope she's had the foresight to hide somewhere clever. Don't forget she knew this place like the back of her hand when she was a child, all children explore and find the hidden nooks and crannies that are to be found."

Racing down the corridor and down onto the west wing, Peter and Flora reached Fred's room. Forgetting all etiquette, Peter entered and turned the light on, before turning to face Flora with a confused expression on his face. "He's not here either. Whatever does this mean? Quick, whose room is next?"

"Mine's next door, but we don't need to go in there," said Flora quickly. "I think the Porters' room is on the other side of mine though, let's see."

Reverend Bird's snoring could be heard before the two reached the room. Peter opened the door and turned the light on noting straight away that Terrence was not in his bed. The reverend spluttered in his sleep, tried to roll over, and promptly woke up. "Yes, my dear, I'm just coming on up to bed," he said with a yawn. "Oh, oh, it's you two!"

"Where's Mr Porter, have you seen him?" asked Peter in an urgent voice.

"Terrence, why he's sleeping isn't he?" Reverend Bird opened and shut his eyes a couple of times and looked at the unoccupied bed. "Oh dear, the poor man obviously can't sleep for grief. He must have gone downstairs so as not to disturb me."

"He isn't downstairs," said Peter through gritted teeth. "And how come you're sitting here fully dressed. Have you been outside?"

"Outside? Are you mad? No, young man, I've not been outside since the wassail. I'm dressed because my night things are not here." The reverend smiled, showing his horsey teeth.

Flora thought quickly. "Were you with Mary Percival outside during the festivities?"

"Why yes, I was my dear, for a while at least. Then I spotted my wife and went off to find her. Why do you ask?"

"I remember hearing your voice. Were you both standing near to me?"

"Right behind you, I seem to remember. You were dancing."

"Oh no!" Flora looked at Peter whose face had been drained of all colour. "It looks like Mary could be the intended victim."

The two, followed at a slower pace by the sleepy reverend, rushed out of the room and across the corridor to William's room where they knocked loudly, hardly daring to find anyone there.

"Yes, who is it?" William's voice, alert and surprised, drifted through the door.

"It's me, Peter Moore, and I've got Flora James and Reverend Bird here too. Can you please come?"

Footsteps sounded, and William's face appeared at the door. "What on earth's the matter?"

Another door, further down, opened up and Elsie appeared. "Is anything wrong?"

"Yes, I'm convinced something is very wrong. There was a shot outside, and Miss James here heard it too. We investigated and found that the gun you hid, William, was missing from the library. Also missing are Mary, Jonty, Fred and Terrence."

"I'm worried. Something is most certainly wrong. Mary's water glass contained cyanide and now she's missing from her room in the middle of the night, along with the gun," said Flora in a panic. "I thought at first that someone was after me, but I now think they're after Mary. Whatever is going on in this house?"

"Hang on, I can't quite get my head round this. Are you saying that you believe someone is trying to kill our cousin?" William looked at Elsie, who had joined them in a huddle at his door. She shuddered as the wind danced about under the doors and lifted the edges of the rug.

"We need to get outside and find out what's happening," she said.

"Myself and Peter will, if that's okay with you?" William turned to look at the solicitor who nodded in affirmation. "Reverend, can you take Flora and my sister down to the hall and take care of them please? Keep them occupied, perhaps put the kettle on? If everyone is outside in this weather, they'll need a hot drink when they return."

"But of course. Come on, ladies." The reverend, looking relieved at not having been asked to go outside, ushered Flora and Elsie down the stairs, followed a few seconds later by William and Peter after they'd quickly gone to don shoes and coats. Elsie was looking disgruntled at being told to stay inside, but one look at Flora's terrified face, and she knew she was doing the right thing.

William grabbed two flashlights and disappeared out of the kitchen door with Peter close on his heels.

Fred had his gun pointed into Terrence's back and they were following Jonty towards the patched up fence on the cliff top, Mary walking at Fred's side and looking cold and shell-shocked. The old lighthouse was working, and swept its electric beam out to sea in the distance, the ocean mist illuminated in its rays.

"Stop here," demanded Fred and the party of four came to a halt next to the place where Flora had nearly fallen to her death earlier.

"Why do we need to be here?" asked Terrence, his back to the sea, reluctantly leaning against the fence. He looked over his shoulder, noting the black face of the cliff as it stretched itself along the coastline. Darkness was thrown over the sea like a discarded cloak while the clouds hurried past the moon busy at their nocturnal business.

Jonty stood next to him, not daring to look out at the undulating water, and tried to blot out the continual sound of the waves and spray dashing against the jagged rocks beneath.

The beam from the old lighthouse cast an occasional dull light upon the proceedings, its fingers stretching out to try and touch the cliff they were standing on, but never quite reaching it.

The wind began to pick up and moaned across the garden whipping up debris, while the moon kept disappearing as if it were playing hide and seek with the scampering clouds.

"We need to be here in the open where I can keep an eye on you, and besides, I don't want to wake the whole household up if we go inside," said Fred, looking as if he might be regretting his decision.

Mary shuddered at the sound of the furious sea rolling and heaving below, the waves slamming themselves down with determined force. "Perhaps we should move away from the edge. We'll get blown clean over if this wind gets any stronger. Miss James nearly became a victim to the sea earlier, and I can't help but think about William and Elsie's parents." She licked her lips nervously, tasting the salt in the air.

"Not until we've got to the bottom of this," replied Fred, raising his voice to be heard above the whining of the wind. "Jonty, you first, get talking."

Jonty had his hands held up in front of him as if in surrender. "What do you want me to tell you? I 'aven't done nothin' wrong."

"Then why were you following Miss Percival here?"

"Who says I was followin' 'er?"

"I was in the hall, and I noticed you. Let's not play games here."

"She were sleepwalkin', like. I've heard it's not safe to wake someone in that state, so I followed 'er instead. She went in the maze and buried some knittin'. Next thing I know, Terrence were jumpin' on me and threatenin' me with a knife."

"I don't believe a word of it," said Fred in disgust. He raised his voice again. "What makes you say she was sleepwalking, and why weren't you in your bed? If you don't start making sense soon, this gun may just start to do some talking of its own."

Jonty looked at the gun with a nervous expression on his face, and swallowed hard. He smoothed his greased back hair off his face where the wind was battering him from behind. "I couldn't sleep, like. I heard a noise and peeped out of my door to see Miss Percival here leavin' 'er room and lookin' glassy eyed. I guessed she were asleep."

Fred turned to Terrence. "What have you got to say about all this?"

"Well, for starters, I object to you pointing that gun in my direction. Who do you think you are?"

"That will be revealed in due course. However, I'm the one with the weapon, so I'd advise you to tell me the truth."

The wind suddenly dipped and soared, howling around the cliff top like an angry banshee. Mary's hair was plastered to her face and sea spray was whipping up off the surface of the water below and sending tiny droplets of briny water over them all.

"I can't stop imagining my poor relations tumbling over the edge all those years ago, and I really believe we should go back in now," she insisted, shivering all over. "We'll catch our deaths out here."

Fred nodded curtly. "Perhaps you're right. I can't stop thinking about poor Flora either; she was very lucky not to have fallen. You two, Terrence and Jonty, walk in front of me back to the house. We can talk more there. Miss Percival you can walk with me, quick let's go."

Wet through and shuddering from cold and exposure to the elements, they began to walk back towards the house, Fred still brandishing the gun.

As they were nearing the orchard a voice hailed them. "Hey, what are you doing out here? It's freezing cold. Come back to the house with us, we've been worried." It was William and Peter, their flashlights picking out the faces of the four, and making them blink.

Peter shrank back a bit and prodded William warningly, nodding towards the gun in Fred's hand. The two lapsed into a momentary silence as the group trouped up and continued walking towards the house. Peter and William fell into step behind them, looking confused.

Chapter 23

Reverend Bird had boiled the kettle and was spooning tea into the fat brown teapot. Elsie was busying herself filling the jug with milk and putting sugar into a bowl while Flora sat at the vast scrubbed table resting her injured arm on its surface.

"Here we are," said the reverend in a cheerful voice. "Tea and sympathy, isn't that what you ladies say? Right, shall we sit here or take the tray into the hall where the fire is still aglow in the grate?"

They all voted for the hallway and made their way through, stifling both their yawns and their worries about what could be happening outside. The windows rattled in their frames making the trio look towards them in concern. Flora went and peered out, recoiling at the monstrous shadow projected onto the lawn from the topiary peacocks.

Elsie dispiritedly stoked the fire and wondered whether or not she should wake the servants up, before deciding against it and sinking into one of the chairs, looking tired. The clock ticked as if with a heavy heart.

Reverend Bird began to talk about his church, but the other two didn't listen to him, their thoughts elsewhere.

Presently a sound came to their ears, and the three looked up to see the group of missing guests trouping through the doorway from the kitchen, followed by a bemused William and Peter.

Elsie leapt up. "Oh, you're all here, thank goodness. What on earth...?"

Fred was still holding the gun and had a grim expression on his face. "Sit down you two," he barked at Terrence and Jonty and the men slid onto the nearest couch. "Miss Percival, you need to warm up. Go and stand by the fire."

Mary moved over to the fireplace as Elsie picked up a blanket from the back of her chair and placed it over her cousin's shoulders.

"Are you alright Mary?"

"I'm perfectly fine thank you," said Mary in a clipped voice.

"I don't understand what is happening."

"I'm sure Mr Adams here will explain far better than I could."

Fred took command again. "I advise everyone to sit down before anyone else gets hurt. If we have to stay here until sunrise we will."

Everyone sat down obediently.

"The time has come for me to tell you who I am," said Fred, pacing the hallway and scratching his temple with the barrel of the gun.

"Please tell me you're not another so called friend with an ulterior motive?" said Elsie.

"Elsie please don't," begged Flora. "You *are* my friend, I only wanted to help. Yes, it is true I wanted to get a jolly good story out of your diamond, but please understand I never meant to upset you."

"I think that's enough for now Flora," said Fred. "I really do have to tell you all who I am."

"Well, who are you then?" demanded William. "Are you saying you're not the son of my parents' friends, some kind of imposter?"

"If you'll let me speak I'll tell you," said Fred in a frustrated voice.

The wind, like an angry bully at school, shoved the climbing wisteria with all its might and one of its neatly tied back sections snapped, sending it crashing down, its branches screeching across the window of the glass as it fell. Everyone jumped in fright.

Mary put her hand across her heart, feeling it's rapid beat. "My nerves won't take much more of this."

"Look everyone, settle down, please." Fred was finding the situation difficult and wished he didn't have the gun in his possession.

Everyone turned back to him and gave him their full attention.

"I am the son of your parents' friends, William and Elsie. However, I am more than just that. My job is as a private investigator, and I travel around finding out information for whoever pays me to do so. The reason I am here this weekend is because of my work, I was employed for a specific reason, and that is to protect someone here."

"Who?" expostulated William, his face half hidden in shadow looking wary. "Was it Helen?"

"No, not Helen…"

"Well who then, for goodness' sake?" Elsie leaned forward in her chair impatiently.

The clock whirred and chimed the hour.

"He is working for me," said Mary at last. "I employed him."

"You employed him? Whatever for?" Elsie looked at her cousin in surprise. Everyone's eyes roved from Mary to Fred and back again, wondering what on earth was going on.

"I had a burglary not long ago, as you know. Someone stole my father's box, and in that box was the Percival diamond."

There was an audible gasp around the room.

"You said you didn't even remember seeing it!" cried Elsie accusingly. "How are we expected to believe you had it all along? You lied to us!"

"And you lied to me!" Mary's voice rose up with emotion. "The only reason you invited me here after all these years was to get your hands on that diamond. Never once did you try to get in touch with me before, not even when Father died, and we only heard about your own parents' death by chance. It seemed a most curious coincidence that the diamond should be stolen and then for you to suddenly want me to visit you."

"But how should we have known the diamond was stolen?" asked William who was sitting very still and upright in his chair.

"Perhaps you paid someone to steal it, and they double crossed you, and told you it wasn't there," said Mary triumphantly. "You asked me here for information."

"That is preposterous Mary, we asked you here to see you."

"And now you still continue to lie," hissed Mary. "I shall have no more to say if we don't all speak the truth. However, to clear my name, I did not lie to you. My father told me the diamond was in the box, but I never felt able to go through his things, and the diamond did not interest me in terms of financial gain and so I kept putting off looking. I guess I should have had it put in a bank vault, but never got round to it. Fred, you can continue." She pursed her lips together tightly as if to stop any more words spilling forth.

"Thank you." Fred cleared his throat and carried on pacing up and down while the others sat as still as statues and looked at him. "As I was saying, Miss Percival here employed me. She had an idea that her cousins had got someone to plan a burglary at her home to see if the diamond was there, as she knew that they had put forward some publicity to try and find it. When she received her invitation to come to Oakmere Hall she suspected that either they wanted to bump her off to claim the diamond for themselves without opposition, or hadn't got the diamond but wanted information about it. She puzzled over it for a while before contacting me and requesting that I get myself invited too, and to be here to protect her."

"So it was no accident you ran into me in the bank that day then?" frowned William.

"No, it wasn't an accident William."

"Well I'm sorry to hear that, I thought we had got along rather well."

"We did, and I'm glad I met you anyway. I knew we'd get along well together."

"You didn't seem to take your duties in a serious manner," drawled Terrence. "The cyanide that was allegedly meant for Miss Percival ended up killing my wife, though I still think I was the intended victim. Your detection skills didn't manage to prevent anyone from getting harmed."

Fred's face fell for a second. "You're right, I hold my hands up to that. It is unfortunate we are fallible and can't always get it right."

Terrence looked at his hosts with a nasty expression on his face. "Are you saying that William and Elsie are responsible for the death of my wife? That they tried to poison their cousin but their plan went horribly wrong?"

Elsie leapt to her feet, followed closely by her brother. "We did nothing of the sort. We are not thieves or murderers. Oh tell them, William." Elsie sat back down quickly, covering her face with her hands.

"There's nothing else to say," said William quietly. He sat down, shooting defiant looks around the room. "We are not guilty of this, and you can choose to believe it if you want. If you don't, I can't do anything to alter your point of view."

"Fred, why were you on the train with Mary? Did you suspect someone would try and murder her in the carriage?" asked Flora. "It all seems a little dramatic. Perhaps you suspected me? After all, I did hide my identity as a hopeful journalist."

"I got on the same train partly to keep an eye on her, yes. Obviously I was on my way here too, so it made sense to travel at the same time. I didn't suspect anyone before coming here."

"Let's face it, we're all in a bad position," said Peter. "For me, there is a question mark around me coming this weekend, when it has been made quite clear that I shouldn't have been here until next week."

"And me and my wife never stay here: this was the first time we'd spent the night, just because of my blasted ankle turning over like that." Terrence leaned over and touched his bandaged leg.

"But did it really turn over?" asked Fred. "It's been noted that you only limp when you remember to."

"How dare you?" shouted Terrence going red in the face. His curls bounced around on his collar. "My wife dies, a guest gets shot at, and you accuse me of faking an injury?"

"You omit to mention your attacking Mr Carshalton with a knife out in the maze earlier, Mr Porter." Fred stopped pacing and leaned against the sideboard looking at Terrence. "Perhaps you'd like to explain that to us all?"

"I thought he might be attacking Miss Percival, so I pounced, if you must know. I couldn't sleep, I heard a noise, and peeped out of my door to see her walking downstairs followed by Jonty. I followed to see what was going on and grabbed the knife on my way outside. It was in my fruit bowl in my room. They went to the centre of the maze, and when I thought he was going to strike her, I jumped on him."

"Never mind that, I still can't get my head around your belief we would murder you," said Elsie in a small voice. She looked at her cousin. "Mary, William and myself are struggling in the financial sense, I admit it. We found a trunk in the house with a receipt written by your father, a receipt for the diamond. There were letters from him, angry ones saying what our parents did was preposterous and wicked. We wanted to find out what it all meant. It's true, we did only ask you here because we hoped you might want to help us out, but murder would never have crossed our minds. How could you possibly even imagine such a thing?"

Mary held her head up and eyed her cousin in contempt. "I remember you saying something to your parents the summer I visited, although you weren't aware that I overheard you. However, it rattled me so much that I began to sleepwalk again, and that only happens when I'm disturbed."

The room was so quiet by then that you could have heard a pin drop. Even the wind outside seemed to have held its breath in anticipation.

"Well, what did I say?"

"You, my dear, said that if they didn't give you what you wanted, you would throw them off the edge of the cliff."

There was a pause, and Elsie laughed. The sound echoed through the hall, sounding far more chilling than it was meant to. "But that's just something a child would say. I *was* a child, and obviously didn't mean it."

"Doesn't it seem uncanny that they ended up falling over the cliff to their deaths then? I'd very much like to hear your explanation."

"You believe I pushed them over?" Elsie began to cry and looked over at her brother helplessly.

"Leave her alone," he spat out. "Are you actually accusing my sister of murdering our parents? An accident happened, pure and simple. Neither myself nor Elsie were outside when it happened, we were fast asleep."

"Do you have witnesses?"

Fred interrupted. "My parents were here the night the Percivals died, apparently it came as the most awful shock. They were playing some party game or other, but no one quite understood why they decided to go down by the cliff edge. However, there was no suspicion it could be anything other than a horrible accident. They said the children were woken up by the police, and they'd never forget their screams."

William put his arm around Elsie, who had started to weep in earnest.

"My father told me about the tragedy too," said Peter. He smiled kindly towards Mary. "He served as their solicitor so was summoned to deal with everything. He said the police believed it to be an unfortunate accident."

"Did he say my father had the diamond?" asked Mary.

"I'm not sure if that was disclosed to him or not. He believed it had been stolen, but he never quite convinced me that he was certain of the fact. He was fascinated by the diamond, and passed that fascination on to me. It is meant to be spectacular."

"Well I guess we'll never know," said William, still with his arm comfortingly around his sister. "What are we supposed to do now?"

Reverend Bird, who had been sitting wide-eyed drinking everything in, gave a little cough to clear his throat. "I think perhaps we all need to calm down a bit. Fred here has centre stage, let him continue with his detective work."

"Er, thank you for that," said Fred. "Let's continue then. Terrence, you were a thief when you met your wife Helen, and your story, which you allegedly churn out at every house party you attend, is that she reformed you. You became a new man when you fell in love with her…"

"What of it? I tell the story because it is true." Terrence stood up, anger written all over his face.

"I suggest that, rather than becoming a reformed character, you simply had no further need to steal. You were the same crooked person inside but with wealth at your disposal, and no longer in need of taking other people's jewels. I suggest another thing too;

that you decided the Percival diamond was too big a deal to just ignore. You wanted to see if you still had the nerve to break into someone's house and take their property."

Terrence hobbled towards Fred and lunged at him. Fred sidestepped him and Terrence crashed into the sideboard sending some silver trays tumbling onto the floor with a loud clatter.

William and Reverend Bird got up at once, and went over to Terrence, each one taking one of his arms and leading him back to his chair firmly.

"There is also the fact that you took out a hefty life insurance policy not long ago, and your wife is now dead, leaving you even more wealthy than you were at the start of your marriage."

"You're disgusting!" fumed Terrence.

"Let's turn to you Mr Carshalton, sitting there so quietly," continued Fred, as Jonty shifted uncomfortably and smoothed his hair back, his moustache twitching with emotion. "Why are you here so often? You're not the usual acquaintance of people like William and Elsie are you?"

"I use their library, they're good to me."

"But why are they so good to you exactly? Do you hold something over them?"

"'ere, I resent that remark. I like readin' them books, and the Percivals don't mind me bein' 'ere."

Fred turned to William. "Why do you let him come here?"

"It's as he says," replied William. "He reads books, we don't. Why not let the library be of use to someone who's interested in dusting off those ancient covers? He helps us out when we need an extra man at a party."

"No, I don't buy that story, there's more to it than meets the eye."

William shrugged. "I don't really care if you buy the story or not, to be honest."

A ray of bright golden sun suddenly shone through the window with startling effect and made Flora, who was sitting in its path, blink.

"My goodness, morning already!" Elsie got up and drew the curtains further apart. "What should we do now?"

Chapter 24

Fred felt totally out of his comfort zone. He was pacing about in a room full of people, and was holding a gun. What should he do now? The women shouldn't have to sit through this scenario, but he couldn't exactly let them leave the room. What if one of them were the guilty party? Most of them were looking to him for direction, but he'd run out of ideas. Reverend Bird began to hum Onward Christian Soldiers under his breath.

"What is your plan?" said William at last. "Do you have any firm ideas Fred? We can't all just sit here for hours on end while you brandish a gun, or are you waiting for the inspector to turn up?"

"I think that's what we should do, it would be the safest thing by far," replied Fred, making up his mind.

At that moment the maid appeared down the stairs and gave a start when she saw them. She turned towards Elsie with a red face. "I'm sorry I'm sure, it was so early I didn't use the back stairs. I was coming to light the fire here and really didn't expect to see anyone up at this time." She bobbed down in a hurried curtsy.

"That's quite alright. It is early, but perhaps you and cook could serve breakfast in here this morning. I've kept the fire stoked up so no need to do anything here."

The maid nodded her head, glanced nervously at the gun in Fred's hand, and disappeared into the kitchen at top speed. Soon, the sounds and smells of breakfast cooking drifted in to the hallway, and before they knew it the food was placed on the sideboard for them to help themselves to. As well as dishes of eggs, bacon, tomatoes and mushrooms there was also a plate of slices of the cake left over from the wassail.

Reverend Bird hauled himself up out of the deep seat he was sitting in and beckoned to the others. "Come on, let's eat. We've been up half the night again and need to keep our strength up.

Ladies first." He began to hand out plates to the bewildered and exhausted people in the room, and then helped himself to a large helping of cooked food, with a slice of the cake on the side.

"Mmm, this is delicious. Your cook must have been passed this wassail cake recipe down from her predecessor, as it is just as tasty as I remember it from the last time I was here. Or is it the same cook? I expect she'd be quite old by now."

Elsie pricked her ears up. "When were you last here Reverend? I was under the impression you hadn't been here before."

"Well, it's true I'd never been in the house before, however I've lived in and around the village most of my life, so came to a few wassails in my childhood. Always a lot of fun."

"Really?" Elsie screwed her eyes up as if to remember. "I don't recall seeing you."

"We were mere children, and I don't suppose we ever spoke, so that isn't surprising." Reverend Bird appeared to be slightly uncomfortable with the conversation but smiled his beatific smile as he inclined his head. "I remember coming up here a few times just to take in the view from the cliff, in actual fact. On more than one occasion I turned up and skirted the bushes in the garden to feast my eyes on the sea. No one ever saw me, not even the gardener. As a lad, I was extremely stealthy!"

Elsie turned to her brother. "Wills, do you remember Reverend Bird being here for any of our wassails in the past?"

"No, but there would have been loads of children here, we're hardly likely to have known them all."

"I remember you two very well," said the reverend. "I also remember your poor dear parents, such a terrible day when they died."

"You were here?" asked Elsie in surprise.

"No, no, not me. My father took the funeral though. I saw you as you passed by in the funeral procession, both with horribly sad faces. I'm surprised you weren't sent away to live with relatives."

"Yes, well we were old enough to be alone, but with a governess here to teach us, and all the servants. We refused to leave, and anyway it worked out fine."

"If Father and I had known, we would have been here for you," said Mary in a small voice. "I still don't know what our parents argued about, but I'm sure it would have been forgotten in an instant if we'd been aware. Why did they argue exactly?"

"We've an idea," said William at once. "But we're not certain."

Peter stepped forward, plate in hand. "I think I can tell you the answer to that one Mary."

The telephone was ringing as Inspector Thomas was trying to eat his breakfast. Sighing, he pushed his plate of half finished bacon and eggs to one side and dabbed at his mouth with his handkerchief.

"Police Inspector Thomas here, how can I help you?"

"It's me sir."

"Ah Turner, good morning."

"Morning sir. Quite an interesting thing happened at the Porter residence last night. The gardener and me had a good old catch up for one thing. I hadn't seen him in an age. He didn't have anything to say relevant to our investigation, but he took me into the kitchen for a cup of tea, which I appreciated as he had been just about to go home."

"Get to the point, Turner?" said the inspector impatiently.

"Well, we warmed our feet at the kitchen stove sir," said the constable, reluctant to cut short his anecdote. "He said all the servants were in a terrible state of shock when they found out about Mrs Porter. After a while, he went off home and I told him I'd pull the door shut behind me on my way out as I was just going to finish my tea. The servants had already gone up to their quarters by that time. I thought that was quite clever of me sir."

"Carry on," said Inspector Thomas. He began to fiddle with the telephone wire in irritation, and gazed back longingly at his breakfast that had begun to congeal on the plate.

"I hunted around, not really knowing what I was looking for, but two interesting things came to my attention." He cleared his throat, getting ready to share his news. "First of all I found a drawer in the writing desk, which was locked, so I looked until I found a key in the bottom of a pot, and it opened!"

"Turner, this is like pulling teeth, what was inside?"

"The newspaper clipping of the Percivals talking about the missing diamond."

"Is that so? Anything else?" The inspector sat forward expectantly, the telephone table he was perched on creaking with strain.

"Yes, a fiction novel."

"What kind of fiction novel?" The inspector realised he was clenching his jaw tightly and told himself to take a few deep breaths before saying anything further.

"Well that's the interesting thing sir. I recognised it at once, as the same book that we saw in the Percival library. The blurb on the back cover suggested that a solicitor turned into an amateur sleuth and solved the mystery of a missing jewel!"

"And the author's name, Turner?"

"You'll like this sir. It was a Mr Jonathan James."

"Who?"

"Jonathan James."

"Ah, I see what you're getting at now. This is one of the books written by Flora James's father. I think I need to take a little look at that book."

"Right you are sir."

"A solicitor, you say? Did this Jonathan James know the solicitor father of Peter Moore I wonder? Have you flicked through the book to get the gist of the story line?"

"Not yet, but I found another interesting thing. I saw Mr Porter's desk diary. On the day Miss Percival's house was burgled, there was a red dot in the entry."

"A red dot?"

"Yes sir, a red dot. He didn't want to write down what he was going to do presumably, so he put a secret mark down. Do you think he was the thief?"

Mary looked at Peter in surprise. "You can tell me the reason my father fell out with my uncle and aunt?"

"Yes. As I told you before, my father was the family solicitor before me, and I have read the notes, albeit cryptic ones, that are in the files."

Both Mary and her cousins put their plates down on the side table and gave the solicitor their full attention. Everyone else, apart from the reverend who was munching away at his extended breakfast like a cow chewing the cud, stopped eating and stared curiously at him.

"Your grandfather happened to be a very wealthy man and in his will, he bequeathed this house to your parents, William and Elsie. The Percival diamond he left to your father, Mary. However, not long after this was known, the diamond went missing and caused a big scandal. Suspicions and accusations were thrown around, but no one knew quite what had happened to it."

"It was left to Mary's father?" said Elsie sounding taken aback. "Why didn't you tell us this before?"

"I had no idea you were unaware of it. A lot of the notes I read came across as ambiguous to the extreme, but I knew what my father meant."

William got up and crossed the room, opening a cigarette box and carefully extracting one.

"Oh William, don't," pleaded Elsie. "You gave up smoking ages ago, please don't light it up."

"But I just don't understand it all," replied William, putting the cigarette behind his ear and exhaling loudly. "The diamond was meant for Mary's father? That would account for the angry letters."

"Yes, I'm sure of it," said Peter. "That much is in the will which I was sure you must have seen."

"No, we didn't see it, being mere children. We were led to believe that it belonged to us, and were only told that the jewel had gone missing when we were young. However, we recently found a receipt from Mary's father to our father for the thing."

"I'm guessing he found it somewhere here in the house, and that's what the falling out was about. He must have taken the diamond and given a receipt as proof, then never spoke to his family again. Well, they did do a bad thing to him I'm afraid, they stole his inheritance off him."

"So," said William, walking back to his chair and sitting down heavily in it. "My parents pretended the diamond had gone missing, and proceeded to claim insurance money for it, but still kept the thing, until Mary's father found it. How could they claim insurance if the diamond wasn't theirs?"

Peter cleared his throat. "I'll be honest with you, though you may not like what I have to say. It is your decision whether or not you want me to continue."

William once again reached for the cigarette behind his ear, and this time lit it. "Well, carry on then," he exhaled in a defeated fashion.

The smoke rose out of William's mouth and he began to pace up and down the hall, the smoke seeming to wrap him up like a cocoon. Reverend Bird stared at it mesmerised, munching away surreptitiously at his second slice of cake.

"Please carry on," pleaded Elsie whilst gazing at her brother with an anxious expression on her face.

"Well, I imagine your parents were somehow blackmailing my father. It's the only thing I can think of, though I have no idea what for. Perhaps it was a financial bribe, more than anything else."

"You mean he twisted the law to help them?" breathed Elsie, her face falling. "Oh, surely not."

"It would make perfect sense," sniffed Mary.

Elsie buried her face in her hands. "Oh, how dreadful! Why were your father's notes so veiled? Why not write down what he knew to be true?"

"I'm not entirely sure. All I know is that he was very interested in that diamond, and got me interested in it too. He wouldn't let me forget about it, in fact. I'm wondering now whether he was interesting me on purpose, as I'm assuming his hands must have been tied."

"Tied? What do you mean?" William's face looked like thunder and he puffed harder on his cigarette. "Are you suggesting my parents bribed your father into keeping quiet?"

"I'm not sure, but it's perfectly feasible. As I said, he got me interested, and I've followed any stories I've heard about it ever since."

"I'll tell you one thing, I don't much care for your suggestion. My parents are not here to defend themselves, and I don't appreciate you blackening their name." He stubbed his cigarette out in the ashtray angrily.

"I don't much like having to say this, however something evidently went on between them. Besides, my father's name is being blackened too."

Looking weary, Fred, who had refused any food, put the gun down on the shelf above the fireplace.

The maid came in with a fresh pot of tea, her wide eyes darting to and fro, and put it down on the sideboard. She began to gather up the dishes and went back with her tray laden, hurrying the last few steps as she got to the kitchen door.

Chapter 25

Inspector Thomas was sitting in the passenger seat as Constable Turner drove the car. He was flicking through Jonathan James's book, and kept exclaiming aloud.

"This is not fiction, Turner, no way. This is a factual account of what happened to the Percival diamond. Flora's father somehow found out the truth, and wrote about it. So, Terrence Porter read it. Who else do you think would have perused these pages?"

"Jonty Carshalton," piped up the constable at once. "It was one of the books in the Percival library."

"Exactly! Hey, watch out for that car."

Constable Turner yanked the steering wheel and swerved back to his side of the road waving an apology at the oncoming vehicle. The engine began to splutter and judder, and the car gently cruised along the side of a hedgerow and ground to a halt.

"What's happening with the engine, Turner? Quick, get it started again, we need to get to Oakmere Hall on the double."

Constable Turner pulled the choke out and began to pump his foot hard on the pedal but nothing happened apart from a small cough from under the bonnet.

"I've somethin' to say," said Jonty to William, who was sitting back next to his sister and looking shaken. "I reckon you've been good to me, an' I think I can help you out a bit."

"What is it Jonty," asked Elsie. She gave him a watery smile of encouragement.

"There's this book, see? It's in your library, written by a man named Jonathan James."

There was a sharp intake of breath. "But that's my father," breathed Flora. "He was an author. You have one of his books here?"

Elsie looked at her helplessly. "I really don't know Flora, I'm afraid I'm not big on reading, and neither is William."

There was a tense silence for a few seconds and Jonty swallowed hard, his moustache twitching.

"Do you want me to carry on talkin'?" he asked eventually, and Elsie nodded. Flora sat forward, her mouth slightly open.

"I read it not so long ago. The book was so interestin' like that I sat in your library all weekend until I'd finished it."

"Which book was it, and what was it about?" asked Flora. "My father's books are out of print, and there are some I haven't even seen."

Jonty shifted in his seat, not enjoying the attention. Reverend Bird was up on his feet stretching his legs and the others were moving about in their seats, suddenly aware that they'd been motionless with tension. No one noticed Terrence moving cat-like towards the fireplace.

"Well, I reckon it were about that diamond of yours," he said eventually. "The story tells a tale of a gem that was meant to have been passed down to a man on the death of the owner. However, the man's cousin and his wife stole it and bribed their solicitor into hushin' it up, and falsifyin' documents so that it looked as if the gem was meant for them."

Jonty paused and ran his hand through his thinning hair. It was as if he hadn't ever spoken so much before, or had so many people eager to hear what he had to say.

Terence, meanwhile, had continued to edge towards the fireplace and was now leaning against it; his elbow perched nonchalantly on the shelf above it, and his fingers edging towards the gun that Fred had left there.

"Do please continue," prompted Mary stiffly.

"Well, the story goes on, and the solicitor was unhappy with how he'd handled things, so he puzzled over what to do to make things better. In the end he made an appointment to meet an author and told his story of events to him. He left strict instructions for this author that the story wasn't to come out until after his death. So, the author writes it all down like, but then he decides to go one step further, and he approaches the cousin himself."

Flora and Elsie both gasped in unison. William rolled his eyes and crossed his arms.

"Well, the author goes to see the couple and tells them all he knows. They are obviously distraught, and try to bribe him into burnin' his material before it goes to publication. They offer him all manner of things to stop him talking but he flatly refuses to be told what to do."

"Well why did he tell them then? He must have wanted something," asked Fred looking confused. His freckles somehow seemed darker and he more sombre than before. Gone was the carefree Fred of the day before.

"He just wanted their side of the story to make his novel more rounded like," replied Jonty. "They try threatenin' him but he doesn't give in, and in the end they are so desperate that they tell him they will have him killed if he prints the book."

Flora went whiter than she had been a few minutes before. Her red lipstick, which she'd applied after her cup of tea, showed up strongly in her pale face, and she clutched the sides of her chair for support.

"My father died after using snuff that was sent to him as a gift…"

"Who was the gift from, Flora?" asked Fred at once. He went and stood behind her chair, resting his hands on her shoulders in a comforting way.

"Mother says he didn't know. It had been wrapped up beautifully, though, and looked really nice. Father was so happy, he thought it was a gift from an admiring reader of one of his books."

"Was there a post mortem?" asked Mary.

"No, the police weren't suspicious. The doctors said he must have been allergic to one of the ingredients, and had an extreme reaction, causing his heart to stop. But now, I'm wondering if…"

William laughed. "Come now, Flora," he said jovially. "Jonty is just sharing a story. It's fictional, made up. It isn't about your father."

"I think it is Wills," said Elsie in a quiet voice. She turned to Jonty again, who was looking decidedly ill at ease. "What happens in the end Jonty?"

"Well, the author, he gets fed up with bein' sent threatenin' letters from them, and so he decides to go and see them face to face to sort it out once and for all. He turns up in the middle of one of their lavish parties, and they go off down the garden to talk in private."

Reverend Bird, who had been looking rather ill for the past few minutes, clapped his hands together loudly. "I think we've all become rather too serious," he brayed. "As William says, this is all fictitious. I think we need to change the subject. Come on, the police will be here soon to continue conducting their enquiries. Let's stop talking for a bit, and get some fresh air into our lungs."

"But I want to know what happens in the story Reverend," said Elsie in annoyance. "We all do."

There was a murmur of agreement around the room.

"I think a brisk walk in the garden will do us the world of good," insisted the reverend. "Come now, let's get our outdoor things on."

No one moved.

"Do you know what I think," said Fred thoughtfully. "I think that you know more about this than meets the eye, Rev. It distinctly looks as if *you're* trying to change the subject."

All eyes turned again to the clergyman, and he seemed to wither in front of them. "I, er, I..." he stumbled. He sat down heavily on his chair and went silent.

Jonty continued talking. "As I were sayin' like, the author goes to visit in the middle of a party, and they go off to talk in the garden. He tells them to stop threatenin' him, and they refuse, saying he is goin' to be sorry for his writin'. There's a scuffle, the couple topple over the side of the cliff, and the author runs away in fright."

Reverend Bird whimpered in his seat.

"The novel is already in a finished state, but the author adds his final encounter and sends it off to his publisher the next day. The postman brings the snuff that has already been sent, and he takes it. He presumably died before the book came out." Jonty looked to Flora who nodded her assent.

"Yes, that's true. Father told Mother and I he had a story pending, but he wasn't sure when exactly it would be printed. We were surprised at that, I seem to recall, as he usually knew the date and time almost to the exact minute! William and Elsie's parents must have sent the snuff to him before he went to visit them: he would have got it on his return home. Presumably, if he'd agreed to destroy his story, they'd have told him not to touch the gift. Oh goodness, how awful." She began to sob uncontrollably, and Fred gave her his handkerchief, looking at her in concern.

"If there was a clause that it wasn't to be published until after my own father's death, if indeed this is about him, then we need to check dates," said Peter brusquely. "My father died a natural death before you ask, he was of a good age."

"But you said he kept talking to you about the diamond, didn't you?" said Elsie. "It looks as if he wanted you to find out the truth."

Peter nodded slowly, looking numb. "He did, that's why he got me intrigued and left those cryptic notes in the files. Poor Father, I hope he wasn't too traumatised about the three deaths. I know I would have been."

The sun was trying to get the attention of the group of people in the hall, and shone as hard as it could through the glass, bathing them in light. It seemed to laminate them all with its winter morning warmth.

"What is your take on this fiction, Rev?" asked William in a shaky voice.

"I'm afraid it isn't fiction." Reverend Bird's face crumpled up in pain, and he took a deep breath and exhaled loudly before continuing. "I told you earlier that I crept up here a few times as a child, I liked to watch the sea from up here. Well, one evening I came up, and saw something I wish I hadn't."

A flock of arguing seagulls suddenly swooped down to the garden for a tasty morsel they'd all seen, and a squabbling squawking sound echoed hollowly in the breeze.

"Come on Turner, what's wrong with this blasted thing? Get the car started," complained Inspector Thomas, looking at his constable disdainfully.

"Nearly there sir, it just needs speaking to nicely."

"Speaking to nicely?" replied the inspector in disgust. "Sometimes I really do question how you got into the force."

Reverend Bird forced himself to continue talking. It seemed as if all his bluster had gone out of the window, and was joining the seagulls as they flew away.

"There was a party going on, but I wanted to watch the sunset from up here. I wasn't snooping, just enjoying the wonderful creation that we've been given to enjoy. The sky was beautiful that night, a storm was brewing, and I wanted to watch it. I heard raised voices coming near me so I hid behind one of the hedges. Peeping out I saw three people, two men and a woman. I recognised Mr & Mrs Percival, but I didn't know who the other man was."

"Why were there raised voices? Did you hear what they were saying?" William wasn't sure if he even wanted to hear the answer.

"No, they passed by my hiding place and there was definitely an argument going on, but I didn't hear what it was about. Besides, I didn't want to eavesdrop. They went down to the cliff's edge and I could see that they were all still angry. I wanted to leave and go home, but I was scared that they'd see me if I came out from behind the hedge, so I stayed where I was." The reverend paused, his mind recalling memories he'd locked away in the past.

"What happened next?" urged William.

Reverend Bird swung round. He'd only been talking a second or two before, but William's voice startled him.

"Did the man push the couple over the cliff?" asked Flora tearfully.

"No, he didn't my dear. It was an accident, just as the book says. They were all way too near the edge, and I could see them gesturing at each other, all trying to get their own points across I should imagine. All of a sudden, the sun disappeared over the horizon and everything was cast into semi-darkness. The three figures stood facing each other, each resembling luminous statues, but a sudden gust of wind came and took two of them off. They returned to where they had come from, and the thunder roared over their memory." Reverend Bird's face was etched with pain.

There was a brief silence before he continued. "A few seconds passed and then the third person went running past my hiding place. I glanced at him, and he had a look of blind panic on his face. I'm so sorry I didn't say anything before." He glanced at William and Elsie guiltily. "I've never told a soul. I was so scared, I couldn't move from my spot for what seemed like hours. It was pitch black when I got the courage to go. How I got home on my wobbly legs I'll never know. I held that secret for many a year, and I even got into the church to dedicate my life to helping others, to make up for not coming forward before."

"But you couldn't have done anything, could you? It wasn't your fault." Elsie met his eyes briefly.

"No, but I could have said there was a third person there. I could have told what I saw. I should have come clean, and not been a weakling, but I thought I'd get in trouble for trespassing. When I saw your faces on your way to the funeral, I felt wretched. I'm such a coward."

"I don't put any blame on you, Reverend." Elsie turned to her brother. "I am so ashamed, I don't really know how to feel. This will take some time to come to terms with."

"All for a damned piece of rock," said Mary angrily. "Was it really worth it? That diamond's caused nothing but trouble. I want to find it just so I can smash it up and throw it into the sea."

"Why didn't you tell us about the book before, Jonty?" asked Elsie quietly.

"I had no proof it were about your folks like," replied Jonty in a small voice, his eyes sliding across to Terrence. "Thing is, I 'eard that someone else had read it and were also puttin' two an' two together."

"Who?"

"I expect he's talking about me," drawled Terrence from the

fireplace. He was holding the gun with one hand and fiddling with it with the other. "I must admit it was an illuminating read."

Mary stood up and faced him. "I wouldn't put it past you being the burglar in disguise that I passed in my road."

"Now, now," smirked Terrence. "Don't get yourself upset Miss Percival. I haven't admitted to that, but I do have to say that I really don't have much sympathy for those that leave their valuables lying around at home. You could have at least opted for a safe."

"You rascal! How did you know where to look?"

"I'm afraid you're not at liberty to ask me questions, and as I've already said, I've not admitted to anything," sneered Terrence. "However, just because I'm feeling generous today, I will tell you what I know. In return, I'd like to know where that diamond is."

William jumped to his feet. "Are you admitting to the theft?"

"SIT DOWN," shouted Terrence waving the gun about in abandon. "This thing is loaded and I will have no qualms in using it."

William sat down at once, and so did Mary. Elsie put her arm through her brother's firmly, to keep him in place. Flora, still with tears staining her cheeks, grasped hold of Fred's hands that were still resting lightly on her shoulders. He moved round and sat on the arm of her seat. The others were staring at Terrence with disbelief all over their faces, not really sure what was happening, or what might happen next.

Chapter 26

"So, which one of us here knows where the diamond is then?" Terrence began to slowly walk towards the little company, pointing first at one, then another.

"We don't know," said Mary. "I would have thought that was perfectly obvious."

"Ah, sarcasm, I see. I'm sure you wouldn't be quite so bold if you were on your own."

"Leave her alone," said Peter with a growl.

"Leave her alone?" laughed Terrence. He turned towards Peter and raised the gun towards his head. "Quite the gentleman, aren't you? I, myself, prefer to reserve judgment."

"What's that supposed to mean?"

"One might wonder why you should be buttering up an old spinster."

"How dare you!"

"Oh yes, forgive me. I meant to say 'buttering up a *rich* old spinster.'"

Mary sat up straighter in her chair and glared at Terrence.

Terrence laughed again, really looking as if he was enjoying himself for the first time that weekend. "You can sit there looking offended all you like," he said addressing Mary. "But don't you find it strange how he singled you out in your train carriage and proceeded to befriend you. He must have known who you were straight away, yet he didn't admit it. Remember, he had a vested interest in that jewel, and he had a score to settle on behalf of his father. Maybe he wanted it for himself. His father wasn't exactly honest when it came down to it, he allowed himself to be bribed. Like father like son?"

"I can assure you, Mary, he is talking nonsense," said Peter crossly.

Terrence continued talking. "Of course, you weren't the only one to seek her out, were you? Obviously, we have Fred Adams here, paid to look out for you. I bet he isn't adverse to a little double crossing himself, and where did Miss Percival find him? I bet he found her, just like he found William."

No one said anything, but their thoughts were whizzing about, trying to get a perspective on things.

"Then we have the budding journalist Flora James, out for a story on you and your diamond, she'd even stalked you in your own village, asking lots of questions about you. She befriended your cousin in order to get a story. How far was she willing to go? Can we really believe that she merely wanted a story for a newspaper? A likely story, I say! What she wanted was the diamond."

Flora's eyes narrowed and she pursed her lips up, not allowing herself to answer his accusations.

"Then we have the reverend. It turns out he was a witness to the deaths of the Percival's parents. What if he'd pushed them over himself, and his story is just a tissue of lies? I doubt the job of reverend pays that well. Surely he had some secret reason to be in that train carriage too. Maybe he even arranged my wife's poisoning in order to be asked up here."

"What you're saying is preposterous," blustered Reverend Bird. "I'm a man of God, not a common jewel thief. I wouldn't know how to begin to be as sneaky as you suggest."

Terrence ignored the reverend's outburst and continued to look at Mary. "So who exactly is it that you can trust, Miss Percival? It seems obvious your cousins are not to be trusted: they openly admit wanting a share in your riches was their intention. They only asked you here for their own selfish gain."

"I trust no one; never have, never will." Mary folded her arms and continued glaring at Terrence angrily.

The car engine leapt to life and Constable Turner let out a whoop of joy. "Here we go sir, let's be on our way."

They roared up the road, skidding round corners, the wheels kicking up the loose stones that were lying about.

"Faster Turner, faster. Something bad is going on up at the house, I can feel it."

The sun was shining its rays onto the floor, illuminating all the specs of dust that were floating about.

"You, Jonty, where is the diamond?" Terrence gripped the gun a bit tighter.

"How should I know?" whined Jonty.

"You have been threatening me for some time now, assuming I was the dastardly diamond defalcator." Terrence smiled to himself, pleased with his alliteration. "I don't have it, so how can I have been the thief?"

"I 'eard that you stole it, the word is all over the place."

"Amongst a den of thieves and liars, what would they know?"

"Enough to make you worry about what I might say," said Jonty triumphantly. "I thought you 'ad the jewel at first, but now I see you don't. I reckon you stole Miss Percival's box but that she'd actually hidden it elsewhere, some place no one would guess to look."

"I can assure you I did not, and that it was stolen," interposed Mary. "What a ridiculous thing to think. Where exactly are you imagining it could be?"

A sly look appeared across Jonty's face, making him appear even more weasel-like. "It ain't up to me to say," he said.

"No, but it is up to me," said Terrence. "Me and my friend the gun, that is. I suggest you tell me where you think it is."

Jonty gulped, and looked apologetically at William. "I'm sorry, Mr Percival. I 'ad hoped to have found the diamond for you and given it back to you and your sister. You've both been so good to me, and I wanted to repay you somehow."

"Stop wasting time," shouted Terrence. "Where is this hiding place?"

"It were only a guess, mind. I don't know for sure, but I thought it could be in Miss Percival's large knitting needle, the one she don't use. She said she used to hide things in it as a child, and that sprang to mind. I followed her outside as she 'ad her knittin' bag with her, and the night before I'd been in 'er room to try and have a look. But, in the centre of the maze she didn't have the large needles, she were just buryin' some actual knittin'. She were sleep walking." Jonty sat back frowning, but with a slight look of triumph aimed in Mary's direction.

Terrence aimed his gun at Mary and nodded at her to look in the knitting bag. "No funny business now, you know this thing is loaded."

Mary sighed in a resigned kind of way and reached down to pick up her knitting bag. "This is the most ridiculous thing I've ever heard of."

"Please humour us Miss Percival."

Unzipping it Mary took out her biggest needles. She shook them lightly to show the others that nothing was rattling around inside, then she undid the top of one and upended it but nothing came out. She did the same to the other one and, again, nothing came out.

"It seems I were wrong," muttered Jonty. His face went very red. "I was so sure..."

"Merely an excuse Mr Carshalton, merely an excuse. You went to my room to look for my diamond, for sure. However, I suggest to the others that it was you who broke in to my house to steal it. Being a regular here, you would have known all about it, I expect you had a good look in that trunk and found out about me."

"Then why was I in your room if I had already stolen it?"

Mary fixed a beady eye on Jonty, making him squirm. "Well, that's simple, you were in my room that night to plant that cyanide in my glass."

"But why would I?" squeaked Jonty in desperation.

"In case I recognised you in my road, despite your overly ridiculous disguise!"

"That weren't me," said Jonty in alarm. "That were Terrence Porter."

"If I were you, I would stop throwing accusations my way," said Terrence. He walked across the room and kicked the knitting bag under the table and then moved over to Jonty and held the gun up to his head.

"I 'ave another theory," said Jonty hurriedly. "Don't shoot."

"Another theory, ay? Let's hear it then."

"The letters D and I were written in the dust near Mrs Porter's body. Everyone seems to think it was the start of the word diamond, but what if she were tryin' to tell us who had harmed her?"

The atmosphere seemed to thicken with menace, and Terrence narrowed his eyes. "What do you mean exactly?"

"Miss Percival, her first name is Diane."

"Go, Turner, GO!" shouted Inspector Thomas over the roar of the engine as it turned the corner leaving the last of the little cottages behind in a cloud of fumes and dust from the road. Constable Turner put his foot down hard on the pedal, took a deep breath, and accelerated up the long hill road to the top.

Chapter 27

The cook, maid and butler were standing on the inside of the kitchen door listening hard.

"Someone needs to telephone for the police," said the maid in a low voice. "Mr Jenkins, why don't you go up the back stairs and go along to the west wing? You could use the extension in Mr Percival's bedroom."

"I don't dare to," replied the butler looking terrified. "What if they were to hear me from downstairs? I'd get myself peppered with bullets."

"You need to do something. Why don't you go and get help instead, Mr Jenkins," whispered the cook in a panic. "Something bad is going to happen. Nip out of the back door and tell the gardener's lad to hop it down that drive quick smart and summon the police."

"Right you are," said the butler, regaining his professional stiff upper lip for a second. "I'll tell him to go straight away. He's a fast runner, I've seen him zipping about in the garden." He tiptoed to the door and opened it, conscious of the squeaking hinges, and reminding himself to oil them as soon as he got the chance, if he got the chance. He held his breath for a second, almost expecting someone to come flying through the kitchen door, but no one did. He stepped outside.

Bessie, the maid, was all of a flutter, and began to fan herself with her apron. "I can't go out there into that hall, I simply can't. They'll have to call if they want a drink or anything. Oh, don't make me go out there again."

"Don't you worry," replied cook who was a bit wobbly-legged herself. She sat herself down on a stool. "We've done our bit, let's just sit here and peel the potatoes as if nothing had happened."

"I'd call that slander," Mary was saying to Jonty in disgust. "In fact, it is the most preposterous thing I've ever heard. I was introduced to Mrs Porter as Mary Percival; she'd hardly be likely to write the down the name that no one calls me. I won't dignify myself with answering your ridiculous accusation."

Everyone was looking warily at Mary, feeling confused and suspicious.

Terrence began to roar with laughter. "Your faces are all too funny. I didn't realise I was so good at this, I could get you to believe it's any one of you miserable lot."

"Terrence, you're acting like a mad man," said William in a quiet and controlled voice. "What exactly is going on, and why are you pointing the gun at us?"

'I tell you what; I'll put you out of your misery and let you in on a little secret," sneered Terrence, his gun pressed to Jonty's temple again. "I've nothing to lose. My wife's gone and I shall soon be out of here myself, off to sunnier climes."

Mary clicked her tongue in disapproval.

Terrence looked at her in disdain. "Think you're better than me do you Miss Percival? Think you're cleverer?"

"It's more clever, not cleverer," said Mary. "So in that respect, yes I do think I'm more clever than you."

"Well, how's this for intelligence? You've pushed me to say this, but I *was* your disguised burglar! You might have briefly suspected me, but you didn't see that coming did you?" Terrence strolled about the room vainly, catching his reflection in the mirror on the wall and smirking.

Elsie gasped and squeezed William's arm.

"Actually I did," retorted Mary. "I knew Mr Carshalton wasn't guilty. Despite your fake beard, I did notice part of your scar, and recognised it at once when I met you. It took me a little while to remember who I'd seen it on, but it dawned on me earlier."

Terrence seemed a bit taken aback. "Why, clever old you," he managed at last, a sarcastic tone entering his voice. "And there was me thinking that the fake beard had covered that scar. Let me tell you all about it, unless you reckon you know everything else too. Sit tight everyone. Well, I found out about the diamond's possible whereabouts from that trunk. It seems I wasn't the only one." He nodded at Flora and jabbed the gun a bit harder at Jonty's head. "I did a bit of detective work and found out where you resided Miss P, or should I call you Diane? It didn't take much to find out when you were in and when you were out. You're a creature of habit aren't you? I took my chance as soon as you had left the house that day. I rummaged about, looking at everything; then opened the hatch to the attic, and there it was! A box of letters and precious memories."

"Did you find the diamond in there?" asked Mary, despite herself.

"Indeed I did!" Terrence looked proud, and examined his manicured fingernails critically.

"Then where is it? What did you do with my property?"

"I can only guess that either yourself or Mr Carshalton here can answer that question, as it was taken from my house."

"The burglar was burgled?' said Mary. "How's that for retribution? Perhaps I took my property back."

"I wouldn't put it past you to have tracked me down and taken the thing yourself Miss P," retorted Terrence. "But, having been in the game for a very long time, I can sense whether people are telling the truth or not. Also, much as I'd like to believe D and I stand for Diane, I don't. You're as straight as they come. Straighter, in fact, and you don't know where it is. Jonty, you're the one that can tell us its whereabouts."

"I can't!" gulped Jonty. "I never saw it, never. If, as you say, you can tell if someone is telling the truth or not, you'll know that I am."

"You repeatedly sent threats in my direction, Mr Carshalton. If I didn't give you the diamond, you were going to inform the police."

"Exactly, the police. I didn't want it for myself, I wanted to give it to the Percivals." Jonty looked imploringly at William and Elsie.

"You are the only one who knew that I had taken it, well apart from my wife of course." As he said the words, a startled look crossed his face as if a truth were dawning on him.

"Your wife," said Jonty carefully.

The under-gardener had listened wide-eyed as Jenkins the butler had told him about the hold-up in the hall. He tipped his cap and put a brave expression on his face.

"You can trust me sir, I'll go and fetch the police. That Constable Turner, sir, he's a bit of a strange one, but I'm sure he'll know what to do. I'll go now sir."

Jenkins watched as the lad hared off around the side of the house, keeping low so he wouldn't be seen from any of the windows of the hall, and then returned quietly to the kitchen to observe the potatoes being peeled.

"Helen! Did Helen know about it too?" demanded William. "You two have been our friends for a long time."

"And what of it?" snarled Terrence. "There ain't no friends when riches are involved."

"But you are rich," protested Elsie. "What on earth did you need our diamond for?"

"My diamond," interrupted Mary.

"Sorry Mary, your diamond." Elsie looked sternly at her cousin.

"Everyone, stop talking," shouted Terrence. "Did I give you permission to speak?"

The room relapsed into silence at once. "Helen, she found out I was still thieving. I never stopped, to be honest."

"That's the first time you have been honest," said Mary under her breath.

"She told me to stop or she'd leave me. Leave me! I placated her for a time, and then someone slipped her the word that I was still up to my old ways."

Jonty cleared his throat.

"It was you, was it Jonty? You're going to regret ever having met me."

Reverend Bird slowly began to edge himself towards the front of his seat and manoeuvred himself to a more upright position, his hands grasping the arms. No one seemed to notice, and he carefully stretched his legs into a position where he could get up quickly if need be.

"So," Terrence was saying in a furious voice. "You told my wife did you?"

Elsie tried to calm the situation down a bit. "Terrence, Helen loved you. She would have forgiven you. Why, you were here for a social evening together, weren't you?" She gave him an encouraging smile. "You ended up staying the night."

"Helen was going to throw me out. My bags had been packed, and this party was to be our last time together. Not only had she found out about my little indiscretions, but she also found out about the diamond. Angry wasn't the word, and she wanted me to give it back. Give it back? I laughed in her face. Did she expect me to be left with nothing? Nothing! I refused to give it back." He stared angrily at everyone in the mirror, his back to the room.

Reverend Bird, feigning invisibility, suddenly stood up. Hearing no opposition to his movements, he began to tiptoe on surprisingly nimble feet to the side of the room.

"How did Helen find out about the diamond?" queried William in a loud voice, trying to throw the scent off the creeping reverend.

"I should imagine someone tipped her off and she hunted about the house for it. She found it in the desk drawer. It was with an article about the diamond, and had the picture of it there in black and white. I thought about laughing it off and proclaiming costume jewellery, but I think it would have been a waste of my breath. She knew alright."

"So why are you asking Jonty here where the diamond is?"

"He heard a rumour that I'd taken it, and I reckon he broke into my house and removed it. All this bluster he's coming out with is pure lies." He turned again to face Jonty, a cruel smile crossing his thin lips. "So, for the last time, where is it then?"

"I reckon it were your wife that removed it," said Jonty, looking decidedly pleased, despite his position. "She must've decided to give it back 'erself."

Reverend Bird was skirting the sofa, getting closer to the furious Terrence.

"I gave you your chance," shouted Terrence in a strangled voice and removed the safety catch from the gun. "Haven't I been trying to pay you back for being a tittle tattle? If it hadn't been for you taking a different bedroom from usual, you would've drunk that cyanide and died when you were supposed to. Helen shouldn't have been hurt."

"That poison were meant for me?" said Jonty in a small voice.

"Oh yes, and Miss Percival took it away and my poor Helen drank it instead."

Mary's hands flew to her face in horror.

"Then you had another lucky escape at the wassail, and little Miss Journalist got hurt instead."

Flora gave a strangled cry. Without thinking, she jumped up out of her chair, leapt over and slapped him hard across the face, making him flinch. He continued holding the gun in Jonty's direction but stared at Flora in fury. "I'll take that this time, but any more of your nonsense and you'll be sorry, very sorry."

Fred tentatively got up and took Flora's good arm, leading her gently back to her chair, where she sat down shaking, shocked at what she'd done.

Smirking, Terrence continued. "Where was I? Oh yes, I was saying that you were extremely lucky to get away with your life Jonty. Third time lucky now. Little Miss Journalist bought you a few extra minutes. Well, lucky for me anyhow. I don't know where the diamond is, but getting even with you will make me a happy man." His face was red where Flora had hit him, the finger marks showing on his cheek. "Say your goodbyes, it is time to meet your maker."

Just as he was about to pull the trigger and fire at Jonty, Reverend Bird took his chance and leapt liked a hunted gazelle straight onto Terrence's back, knocking the gun out of his hand and slamming him onto the rug with a shout of triumph. The gun went off with a loud bang as it spun around and slid off across the floor.

"Think you'd befriend me for nothing did you? Thought you'd use the services of a man of the church did you? You forget I have the heavenly host on my side." Reverend Bird sat heavily on Terrence, forcing the breath out of him, and pinning his arms behind his back. Muttering threats and swearing, Terrence wriggled and squirmed trying to free himself, but to no avail.

Meanwhile, the under-gardener had raced off round to the front of the house, zigzagging between the larger hedges and ornamental grasses. Once clear of the house, he'd sprinted down the driveway, keeping to the sides and dodging behind each tree, kicking up his heels in terror.

"What on earth is that person doing at the top of the driveway there, Turner?" asked Inspector Thomas, pointing. "Has he gone completely mad? Stop here a minute and let's see what he's up to. We may need to detain him."

Constable Turner drew the car to the side of the grassy verge and turned the engine off. He wound down his window and poked his head out, shielding his eyes from the sun with his hands. The under gardener was running towards them, darting and weaving between any foliage he passed.

"Sir, sir, stop sir," shouted the young lad, coming towards the police car, his arms waving in the air.

"We have stopped," said the constable. "What's his problem?"

"I think something must've happened up at the house," said Inspector Thomas sharply. He got out of the car and waited, leaning on the bonnet. Constable Turner joined him, staring in fascination at the antics of the young man. Eventually he reached them, panting and desperately trying to catch his breath back.

"Now calm down," said the inspector gently. "Take a deep breath and tell us what's wrong. Has something happened at Oakmere Hall?"

The stray bullet had ripped through the woodwork at the foot of the sideboard, leaving a gaping jagged hole, but thankfully not hitting anyone. In the kitchen the cook and maid had squealed in shock when they heard the bang, and clamped their hands over their mouths to try and stop the sound escaping. Jenkins jumped about like a hare, uncertain where the safest place to be was.

"Is anyone hurt?" asked William. "Are you all okay?"

Everyone nodded gingerly, their rapid heartbeats thumping loudly in their chests.

"Give me back that gun," shrieked Terrence, desperately trying to drag his arms loose from the vice like grip of the reverend.

"Not likely." William got up and picked up the weapon that had sped across the floor and landed near his chair just as Inspector Thomas and Constable Turner came bursting through the front door.

"Put that weapon down at once," shouted the inspector in a commanding voice, pointing his own gun at the man.

"Inspector, this has nothing to do with me," said William holding the gun out towards the policemen for them to take. "It's Terrence Porter you need to arrest. He's confessed to stealing the diamond and planting the cyanide in Mary's glass. He meant it for Jonty, who usually sleeps in that room."

"What?" Momentarily stumped, the inspector lowered his gun and stared at Terrence who was still bucking underneath the reverend and looking as if he were auditioning for a role in a western play. "We heard a man was yielding a weapon, but we didn't know it was Mr Porter! Reverend, get up please. Turner, arrest that man."

Chapter 28

As Constable Turner was leading Terrence out of the front door and towards the car, a blaze of sunlight flared out from behind a passing cloud and dazzled him. Without thinking, he let go of Terrence's arm to shield his eyes from the glare.

In an instant, Terrence took his chance and sprinted off around the side of the house.

"Stop, hey stop," shouted the policeman, taking his whistle out of his pocket and giving it a shrill blow.

Inspector Thomas, who had been saying a few words to the others, whirled round and saw Terrence disappearing off into the back garden. "Quick, after him."

The inspector, followed by William and Fred, gave chase, the others following at a slower pace.

Round the corner of the house they went, catching up with Constable Turner, and overtaking him.

"There he is, look!"

Terrence was dashing through the orchard, running from one tree to another as if unsure of where to go.

Orson, the under gardener who had got a lift back up the drive in the police car, was in the orchard untying the blue ribbon from the largest apple tree. He was feeling quite giddy with pride at having been the one to alert the police of the strange goings on in the house. He smiled at the apple tree, and then looked round, scared, as he heard shouts coming closer and saw the men running in his direction. Terrence, who hadn't spotted him, was running his way, red in the face and panting hard.

Putting two and two together, Orson realised that something needed to be done, and in a hurry. Quick as a flash, he dodged behind the tree and then put his foot out as Terrence ran past, and the man went crashing to the ground, giving Inspector Thomas a few valuable seconds to gain some ground.

"Stop him, stop him."

Orson hesitated, knowing he was no match for the strength of a grown man, and Terrence scrambled to his feet and whizzed off towards the back of the orchard and sprang over the fence.

William, Fred and Inspector Thomas, with Constable Turner lumbering a few yards behind them, spread out a bit to give themselves a better chance of catching their prey.

"He's making for the maze," panted Fred, making Inspector Thomas groan. He really didn't want to end up in that nightmare of a maze again. Getting lost in there had been one of his darker moments, and he wasn't about to repeat the experience in a hurry.

At the last second, as if he was thinking the same thing, Terrence veered away from the maze entrance and, darting worried looks behind him, zigzagged across the grass, making for the cliff. The others pounded after him.

At the cliff's edge, the old gardener was banging nails into the fence with his hammer, securing the new pieces of wood to the rickety posts. It wasn't perfect, he thought to himself, but at least it would hold until that whole section could be replaced. His gnarly old hands made slow progress of the job, but he was in no hurry. The sun was out, and the view was beautiful. Hearing shouting, he stopped his hammering and looked round to see what was going on. Mr Porter was running towards him as if he was taking part in a race, and Mr Percival and Mr Adams, Inspector Thomas and that strange constable were all on his tail.

"Be careful," he bleated, looking concerned. "This fence ain't secure yet."

Terrence took one look at him and vaulted right over the top of the fence, his eyes darting backwards and forwards, looking for the old steps that led down the cliff face to the sea below.

"Stop, you can't go down there," screeched the gardener. "It ain't safe. No one uses them there steps. You'll fall to your death."

Terrence didn't appear to be listening and began to climb stealthily down, holding on to the sides of the cliff with both hands, as the others ran up panting hard.

Inspector Thomas took one look at the steps and faltered, wondering if he had to follow. He knew he should, but it really did look dangerous. "Stop Mr Porter, where do you think you're going," he shouted. "There's no escape down there, only the sea."

Terrence was making slow progress, picking his way slowly over the bumpy and uneven steps. He looked up at the men who were leaning over the side and grinned. "I'm going to get out of here," he said. "I've nothing to lose. My wife's dead, and she's already written me out of her will. The diamond's gone, and I'm not going to prison for it. As to the cyanide, that was nothing to do with me, though I know you won't believe me."

William called down. "But you confessed to trying to poison Jonty."

"I was trying to frighten the man," shouted Terrence. He continued moving slowly downwards, his hands gripping the sides of the cliff face as he moved. "There's someone else here you could ask about it if you cared to."

"He's just trying to stall for time," said Inspector Thomas in disgust.

The gardener shuffled up, his blue eyes watery, and peered over the side. "Where does he think he's going?" he asked. "That old row boat was dashed to pieces in the last storm, there's nowhere for him to go."

"Old row boat?" queried the inspector.

"It's been there donkey's years," said William. "We weren't even allowed down to it as children. Those steps have been out of bounds for generations, I shouldn't wonder. We used to lie on our stomachs sometimes and wriggle close to the edge just to peer down and see if that old boat was still there. It always was, like a faithful puppy waiting for us to go and take it out!"

"So what's he doing, then?" The gardener was scratching his head looking puzzled. "He'll kill himself."

"I think maybe that is what he wants to do," said Fred.

Reverend Bird, Peter, Elsie, Flora and Mary were gathered near the orchard looking down the long length of the lawn towards the others. Peter told them not to go any further. "I would advise leaving the police to their work. We've had enough excitement as it is for one weekend."

"I certainly agree," said Reverend Bird. "Perhaps we should go back inside. Come on ladies."

They all turned tail and filed back inside, wondering how much more drama they were going to be subject to before the weekend had finished.

Terrence's foot had slipped and he began to slide down the steps, a stricken expression on his face. He grappled at the sides, trying to find something solid to grab hold of.

"For goodness' sake, come back up," shouted the inspector. "We'll help you up. Just take your time and shuffle your way back up the steps."

"I can't!"

As he had done as a child, William threw himself down on the ground, stomach first, and edged forward. Fred followed suit. They stretched their arms down, but Terrence wasn't within touching distance.

"Hold on to my legs," panted William. "I'll wriggle forward a bit more and see if he can catch hold of my hands.

Fred, with unhappy memories of doing the same for Flora, immediately moved back and grabbed hold of William's legs, the inspector following suit.

"Terrence, take my hands, come on you can do it."

Terrence shouted back. "There's nothing really left for me up there to be honest. I'd rather take my chances and try to swim out to the old lighthouse."

"Don't be ridiculous, man, you know you'd never make it. Besides, even if you did, you wouldn't be able to climb the cliff over there. Come back up, you have your life to live."

"I'll hang anyway for a murder I didn't commit."

"You may be acquitted if, as you say, there's no proof against you. Well, not for the cyanide, and you won't hang for theft. Come on, stretch your arms up to mine."

Terrence tentatively reached up, cringing and trying not to look down at the rocks below. The sea was quite gentle at that moment, and was lapping over the tops of the rocks in quite a friendly fashion, making them gleam in the sunlight.

"I tell you, I didn't plant that cyanide," said Terrence obstinately.

"Well who did then?" shouted Inspector Thomas, still holding on tight to William's legs.

"If I tell you, will I get a lesser sentence?"

The inspector shook his head and shrugged, not saying anything.

William made a swipe with his right hand and caught at the tips of Terrence's fingers. "That's it, one more time. Reach a bit higher."

"Careful there," shouted Inspector Thomas as William's legs began to shuffle further towards the cliff's edge. "Don't go forwards any further."

William swiped again and caught hold of Terrence's wrist. "Right, let's go. I've got him. Pull me back."

Terrence was dangling over the edge of the steps, his curly hair blowing back and his eyes wide with fright. "Pull me up, pull me up."

As they heaved, Terrence's hands began to slip out of William's.

With a shriek of fear, he fell, plunging down to meet his fate, the rocks grinning up at him wickedly.

Chapter 29

Later on that afternoon, once the inhabitants of Oakmere Hall had managed to calm down from the shock and get some much needed rest, Inspector Thomas and Constable Turner drove up the long tree-lined driveway again and drew the car up outside the front door. The gardener was at the front, tying up the fallen wisteria, which was desperately clinging to the wall, hesitant to let go, and he raised his hat politely at the two men as if he'd never met them before.

"Don't much like those peacock hedges, do you sir? Fair give me the creeps they do." Constable Turner gave an involuntary shudder.

"Topiary," commented the inspector looking at the garden.

"Topiary sir?" said Constable Turner in a puzzled voice. "What's that?"

"Never mind Turner, never mind. Let's get inside and tie up the loose ends of this case."

The two men walked up the steps to the front door and rapped smartly at it, and were admitted to the house by Jenkins, who gave them an almost imperceptible wink. "Come in gentlemen," he said, and stood back to let them walk in front of him.

"Ah, Inspector," said William, walking towards the policemen with his arm outstretched. "Come in. We're all pretty much rested up now, and ready to answer any questions you need answering. I'm finding it hard to believe Terrence has gone, I tried so hard to save him you know."

"We know that sir, you have nothing to reproach yourself for," said the inspector. "Before he fell we had a full confession: well actually only half a confession."

Elsie looked wary. "Half, you say? What do you mean by that?"

"Well Miss Percival, as he was hanging on to the rocks out there he confessed to stealing the diamond from Miss Percival's house, but he denies having put the cyanide in that glass."

"Well he admitted it to us," said Elsie. "I suppose he was just trying to get away with a charge of theft, and not one of murder. He thought he'd escape the hangman's noose."

The inspector nodded his head in agreement. "And he may have escaped it, too. Don't forget, his fingerprints weren't on that glass. The thing that's mainly troubling us now is where the diamond could have been put. If he knew, he wasn't going to tell us. He was adamant that it was stolen from his house. A team has been in the Porter's house for hours now, but nothing seems to have been hidden there that looks like a diamond. Plenty of other stolen things mind, including Miss Percival's box. The poor servants there are in a state of shock."

"My box!" said Mary. "When can I have it back?"

"Soon enough, Miss Percival. Soon enough."

"Perhaps Helen threw the diamond down somewhere when they were on their way here?" suggested Flora from her chair by the window. Everyone was sitting in the hall drinking cups of hot sweet tea and munching on the last of the wassail cake, feeling more relaxed, now that the nightmare was well and truly over.

"That wouldn't make sense, Flora," said Fred, who was sitting next to her. "She had wanted to return it, not get rid of it."

"Well, the marks in the dust definitely suggest that she was trying to tell us where it was hidden."

"I'm glad you don't believe she was trying to write my name," said Mary.

"As if I would believe that! Fred, are you suggesting it is here?" said Elsie. "Someone needs to search the Porter's bedroom."

"Up you go Turner," said Inspector Thomas, nodding his head in the direction of the stairs. The constable disappeared, treading heavily on the stairs, and feeling crestfallen at missing out on the discussion.

The inspector accepted a cup of tea from Elsie, and took it over to the fireplace where he placed it on the shelf and looked round at the people in the room. They all looked at him expectantly, as if waiting for the opening line of a play.

He cleared his throat. "A couple of questions. Firstly I'll come to you, Mr Carshalton. Why did you write that note for Jenkins to summon Peter Moore at an earlier date?"

Jonty's eyes darted from one side of the room to the other and back and he licked his lips, drawing attention to his unattractive moustache. "I 'eard the rumour that Terrence had stolen Miss Percival's diamond. I'm clean, but I still 'ave me ear to the ground. I remembered Terrence bein' here when the Percivals found that old trunk, and I soon heard he was plottin' to find Miss Percival's house. When William invited me for this weekend and said who else would be comin', I got worried and sensed trouble. Terrence was going to be 'ere and so was Miss Percival. I couldn't very well call the police could I? For starters, they wouldn't believe anything I were to say, then what exactly did I have to tell 'em anyway? No proof of nothin'. Instead, I thought the solicitor would be the next best thing, so I scribbled that note down and left it in the kitchen."

"And how did you know about the solicitor coming after the weekend anyway?"

"William told me that him and his sister were going to see if he could give them some advice about how to track down the diamond, and also pick his brains about the time it disappeared, seein' as his father had been solicitor beforehand."

"Yes, that is true, I did tell him that," said William.

"I still don't understand why you are friends," said Inspector Thomas looking perplexed. "From different walks of life and with different interests. Explain that to me please."

"How can you explain friendship?" drawled William. "Jonty and I help each other out, that's all. Plus, we like each other."

"Now that's interesting. You help each other out do you?"

William frowned. "Yes, we do. What's the problem?"

"Simply that Jonty has had a couple of alibis from you over the years, when accused of certain, shall we say, indiscrepancies."

"Inspector!" said William. "Are you suggesting we cover up for Jonty's supposed criminal activities? Why on earth would we do that? Frankly, that's quite offensive."

"Yes, it is," said Elsie, her green eyes flashing in the sunlight. She removed the hair tie that was sliding out of her hair, and redid the bun at the nape of her neck.

The inspector altered tack, sensing a change in atmosphere. "Well, how would you describe 'helping each other out' to me then?"

"Look 'ere," piped up Jonty. "I left that underworld behind me years ago. I'm now a reformed man, I keep me nose clean and I have educated myself at the library 'ere. I make up numbers when needed at the Percivals' parties, and they let me spend time readin'. There is nothin' more to it than that."

"It takes all sorts I suppose," mused the inspector, picking up his teacup and taking a sip. He was grateful to see Constable Turner tripping lightly down the staircase.

"Nothing there, I'm afraid," he said shaking his head sadly. "I've searched for that jewel with a fine tooth comb." He had envisaged himself holding it aloft like King Arthur holding up the mythical sword Excalibur. "I can look elsewhere, where else did Mrs Porter go?"

"Well, she could have gone anywhere really," said Elsie. "Downstairs, we were in here, the dining room and the drawing room. She may even have gone into the long gallery, as I know she liked looking at the pictures. However, wouldn't she be returning the diamond to Mary, and not to us?"

Mary, who was sitting next to Peter, looked at her cousin. "I can assure you she didn't give it to me. Whether or not she hid it in my room I couldn't say, and to be honest I don't think I care too much. That diamond has not brought happiness to anyone has it?"

"Do I have permission to search your room, Miss Percival? The police search team will be up here later on but if I can have a head start it could save them the trouble." Constable Turner stood very upright, his head inclined slightly towards the spinster.

"Well, yes, I suppose there wouldn't be any harm in you having a look, though I daresay you won't find anything of interest."

"Thank you. I'll just have a quick look in the long gallery on my way." The constable walked across the hallway, his shoes squeaking, and disappeared into the gallery happily. He'd been longing to have a look at the sea pictures, and he had always had a bit of a thing about oil paintings. Walking down the room slowly, making sure to keep a sharp eye out for any possible hiding place for a diamond, Constable Turner paused at each picture, staring intently at the canvasses. He was transfixed by one of them, noting the massive waves and tiny boat being rocked about in the stormy waters. Just looking at it made him feel a bit nauseous. The vivid blues and greens were stunning, and he made up his mind to brush up on his own painting skills when he got some time off.

The next painting he got to had a red boat sailing through calmer waters. The name on the side of it was The Percival. Was this the boat that used to be moored at the foot of the cliff? Shame it wasn't still there, it would be the perfect hiding place for a jewel.

William poked his head round the door. "Enjoying our paintings?"

"Yes I am. They're wonderful. Who painted them?"

"Various members of the Percival family over the years," said William, coming further into the room and standing looking at the pictures with his hands in his pockets. "Sadly, neither Elsie nor myself have an artistic bone in our bodies. We don't care much for art either, so this is yet another room we rarely frequent."

"What a shame sir, what a shame. You should put them in a gallery, where people would pay to look at them."

William raised his eyebrows in surprise. "People would pay to look at them? Not a bad idea if I may pay you the compliment. My sister and I are always after ways to boost our income." He walked out, looking thoughtful.

After a while, not finding the jewel anywhere, the constable reluctantly decided he had better go back upstairs and look at Mary's room. Letting himself out of the gallery door he went to the stairs and held onto the banisters as he went up, his knees creaking.

Elsie got up and walked over to Mary. "Look Mary, I want to say on behalf of both William and myself that we are really and truly sorry about everything. How about we forget about the diamond and start again as cousins with no hidden agenda? Our parents fell out, but there's no reason for history to keep repeating itself."

"I agree," said William with a smile. "We coped before that jewel and we will continue to cope. It's true, we don't have much in the way of finances but I'm sure we can think of something to raise some funds. It isn't your problem. Let's be friends again, please, you're the only family we've got."

Inspector Thomas gave a smile. He loved a happy ending. He inadvertently nudged the reverend, who was beaming with pleasure, and he nudged back, albeit a bit rougher.

"Well, I suppose it would be nice to have some family again," said Mary, thawing a little.

"Good for you, Mary," said Peter raising his teacup. "Blood's thicker than water at the end of the day."

"Yes, well I think the diamond has gone for good, so let's forget the thing and live our lives in peace." Mary gave a small smile.

"I shall come and visit you when you go back to your cottage, and take you out for dinner in celebration," said Peter with a wink.

Mary blushed. "I'd like that very much."

Fred and Flora, who were holding hands on the sofa, grinned at each other. "It looks like this house party has brought something better than riches. Love always wins out over everything else."

"And what are you two going to do from here on in?" asked the inspector, looking at them.

"Fred has ever such a lot of interesting stories from his work," said Flora, her eyes shining with excitement. "He's traced and tracked down all manner of crimes and criminals. I'm going to write them all down for him, and we may just get a fantastic book out of it, I'm going to get it published in honour of my father."

"Yes, but it's just a shame we couldn't complete this story by finding the whereabouts of the diamond," said Fred. "I'm sorry I wasn't of more help to you Miss Percival."

"You did just fine, Mr Adams. Just fine, and I shall pay you well for your help," replied Mary.

Flora looked at Elsie. "Else, are we still friends? I, too, am sorry if I hurt your feelings."

"Yes, of course we are. I was upset at first, but I'm over it. You're too good a friend to lose." The women smiled at each other.

Flora laughed. "I have an idea to boost your finances," she said suddenly, with a twinkle in her eye. "That wassail drink, its amazing! That entire vat was drunk by the villagers, and in record time too, I'll bet. Why not bottle it and sell it? Seems such a waste to only have it once a year, and your orchard is full of apple trees. I bet a lot get wasted."

William raised his eyebrows in surprise. "Do you know what, you're probably just joking, but that is actually a very good idea," he said. "We store a lot of the apples, but give an awful lot away to save them rotting on the ground. I really think that is not a bad idea at all. It could be a Percival enterprise! What do you think, Elsie?"

His sister was grinning from ear to ear. "I think it might just work," she said. "Thanks Flora, why we never thought of that before, I can't think. Just plain lazy I expect! Do you think we're maturing at last? Wills, we need to discuss it with the servants, there'd be more work for them."

"They'd love it, and it would mean them keeping their jobs," replied William. "Anyway, why just stop at wassail? You can do all manner of things with apples. We'll have to put our heads together and come up with some ideas. In fact, Mary, you could help us couldn't you? I remember your mother's apple jam, she used to make it when she was here, and it was a firm favourite in the family wasn't it?"

"Well, yes, it certainly is a good recipe. I make it myself from time to time and take it to the Women's Institute who love it. I could give you some pointers."

"I think you could do more than give us pointers," said Elsie taking her cousin's hand. "You could get involved, be a part of the fun, and spend more time here with us!"

"I think I'd like that."

"This calls for a celebration. Jenkins, please bring the decanter and some glasses." Elsie clapped her hands in delight at the thought of a happier and more stable future.

The butler appeared as if from nowhere, brandishing a silver tray. He took it to the sideboard and placed crystal cut glasses and a beautiful antique decanter onto it, before bringing it over to the small side table in front of his mistress.

"Thank you, Jenkins." Elsie began to pour out measures of the golden liquid into glasses. She passed them around happily.

"Not for me thank you Elsie," said Mary primly. "I'll stick with my cup of tea."

Elsie smiled. She got to the bottom of the decanter, and upended it to get the last of the drips out. Something rattled at the bottom, and she peered closely at it, wondering fleetingly if a shard of glass had broken inside. She gave a gasp.

"Wait a minute, what's this? Wills, look at this."

William stooped down and peered into the decanter, hardly daring to breathe. He took it from his sister's hands and turned it upside down, and a sparkling and multi faceted diamond tipped out and landed in his outstretched palm.

Time seemed to stand still for several seconds, and a silence fell upon everyone. The sun disappeared behind a cloud for a second and then came out again, as if it had winked. The inspector hurried across the room to have a look, before everyone else got up and began to crowd round William too, all exclaiming and talking at once.

"That's not glass is it?"

"I think it is the Percival diamond?"

"It must be!"

"What was it doing in there?"

"It really is the diamond, look at it."

"My goodness, how beautiful it is."

"Look how it sparkles!"

"I can't believe it, this really is the infamous Percival diamond."

Elsie took the jewel from her brother's hand and held it up to the light that was streaming in through the window. It was flawless, and the most brilliant rainbow of colours soared out of the facets, surprising them with its breath-taking beauty. "So this is you," she murmured. "What a lot of trouble you've caused."

She turned to Mary and held it out to her. "Here, I believe this belongs to you."

Mary hesitated before taking it and staring into its brilliance. She looked quite moved and said in a trembling voice, "I don't really know quite what to say. This was in Father's box for all that time, hidden up in my attic. It is stunning, and yet has been the cause of greed, blackmail, and more than one death. Some might say it was cursed. In its beauty all I can see is wickedness. What should I do with it?" She turned confused eyes to her cousins.

William shrugged and smiled sympathetically. "I don't think I believe in curses, but it is your diamond, Mary. You have to decide what to do with it."

"Well, it can't go back into the attic, can it? Call me superstitious but all the time it was in the box, its power was lying dormant. Now it has been let out, it's awakened the blackness of men's hearts."

The reverend gave a little cough. "The good book tells us that the love of money is a root of all evil. The diamond itself isn't evil, just the love of it."

"Well I don't love it, despite its beauty. Do you think I should put it in the bank?"

"Yes, that would be the safest place for it," said Elsie.

"However," continued Mary. "What would be the point of that? It would just stay there. I have no children to pass it on to."

"Then why don't you sell it?" William was staring mesmerised at the jewel in his cousin's hand.

"That wouldn't seem right either. If this diamond is cursed, the money I get from it will be cursed also. Besides, what if I passed the bad luck on to someone else with it?"

"I don't think it is cursed, Mary. Riches can bring out the worst in people's personalities, that's all. William and I are just as guilty; we were obsessed with finding it. Strangely, though, now I've seen it I feel detached and unmoved. It is an object, nothing more."

"Might I make a suggestion?" blustered Reverend Bird. "If you don't need the money, give it to those that do. The church restoration fund could do with a little help. That would be a good thing to help make up for all the bad."

"Don't make any rash decisions," said Peter. "Sleep on it, take a little time to decide."

"Yes, I think that's good advice," said Mary gratefully. "If I do decide to sell it, I should think it would raise an awful lot of money. I could do some wonderful things with it, couldn't I?" She took the diamond and placed it in Inspector Thomas's hand. "Could you possibly look after this for me? Consider it a piece of evidence for all that has been going on here."

"Right you are," said the inspector. He took out his handkerchief and wrapped the diamond carefully up in it before placing it in his inside pocket. "I'll write you out a receipt."

Just then Constable Turner tramped back down the stairs again. "No, it isn't in there," he said, catching his breath back. "I'm blessed if I can think where that diamond could be hiding." He looked around in surprise as everyone started to laugh.

"What, what's so funny?" he asked, going red in the face. "Have I said something wrong?"

Inspector Thomas looked at him and grinned. "Turner, get out your notepad. Write out a receipt for Miss Percival here for the diamond, please."

Constable Turner stared at his superior with eyes so large that the inspector half wondered whether they might fall out. "The diamond has been found, sir?"

"Yes, it was in this decanter." Inspector Thomas took his handkerchief out of his pocket, unwrapped it and held it up to show the policeman. "What do you think?"

Turner blinked several times and swallowed. "It is a thing of great beauty, sir. So the D and the I written in the dust was really for the word diamond then? Or was it for the word Diane?"

The inspector shrugged. "I doubt we'll ever know for sure."

"Mrs Porter hid it in the decanter in order to get it away from her husband, the poor woman," continued the constable. "She was trying to leave a message but couldn't complete it. I'll go and write out a receipt at once, my notebook's in the library." He disappeared quickly, trying to suppress the disappointment he was feeling about not having found it himself.

The inspector followed him in. "I wonder what Jonathan James would have made of this latest addition to his story. Shame he isn't alive to write it all down."

"A shame indeed but no doubt it'll appear in the book Miss James and Mr Adams are going to put together. I wonder what they'll call it? Now, if I were to write it down in a book, I'd give it a good title."

"Like what, Turner?"

The constable paused, his pen held poised over Mary's receipt. "Let me see. That diamond brought out the depravities of the human heart, causing five deaths. There were also five evils related to it. Envy, greed, anger, fear and revenge so I think I'd call it The Five Facets of Murder. Clever that, isn't it sir?"

"Yes Turner, very clever." Inspector Thomas wandered slowly around the library, ending up next to the table where Jenkins had piled the books up that had fallen on Helen when she'd collapsed. He picked up the top one with vague interest and gave a start. It was entitled '*The Mystery of the Stolen Diamond*' by Jonathan James.

"Look at this. I wonder if this was a coincidence, or if Mrs Porter was trying to tell us something." He picked up the book and placed it on the desk in front of his constable.

"I guess we'll never know for certain, sir. We'll simply never know."

Epilogue

A few weeks later, the twins were going through their trunk again, reading everything that was in there. The gardener was preparing for another bonfire, and the siblings wanted to get rid of the papers they didn't want to keep.

"Ah, look, this is a nice picture, Wills." Elsie held up an old photograph of her parents. "I feel as if I can forgive them now. They didn't understand the repercussions of what they were doing. I suppose they must have been desperate for money to have stolen the diamond like that. We were blinded by wanting it too."

"Yes, whatever they did, they were still our parents, weren't they? It's time to let it go and move on now."

"Mary's coming over again at the weekend with her apple recipes. I spoke to her on the telephone last night, and she seemed to be so much more relaxed. She told me that Peter Moore had arranged to take her to the theatre soon!"

William laughed. "I hope they'll be very happy together. It seems as if Fred and Flora have had a few outings together too. Right, have you finished with these papers? I'll take them outside to burn."

Elsie peered into the empty trunk. "Oh hang on a minute, what's that?" There was a hidden pocket inside, made with the same fabric as the rest of the trunk's interior, and the corner of a piece of paper was showing.

Reaching in, William put his hand in and pulled out an envelope. "Another letter from Mary's father."

"Oh don't bother reading it, Wills. All his letters are the same, long rants at how angry he was feeling. Just throw it on the pile over there."

"I'll just have a quick look." William took the piece of paper out of the envelope and read it noiselessly, his lips moving as he read the words. It wasn't long before a look of shock registered itself on his face.

"What is it William?" Elsie plucked the letter out of her brother's hand and began to read aloud.

"You must be mad to hush up the fact that your neighbour, Helen Paget, attempted to kill me. Why will you not believe me? I'm telling you, it was not an accident, as you suggested.

Once I'd found the diamond and figured out what you had done, everything went horribly wrong. You were in denial, I was angry, and that pernicious girl heard every word we said.

I went to sit on top of the cliff to contemplate what I should do, when she came along and asked to look at the diamond. As I handed it over I saw her eyes shining with greed and conceit, and a murderous heart unfurled itself and looked at me like a snake eyeing up its victim. She took it and pushed me with all her might, and if I hadn't managed to grab hold of that rock, I would have gone clean over the side. I heard her laugh as I was falling, and a more maniacal laugh I have never heard before or since. Hauling myself up, I snatched the diamond out of her pathetic grip and ran, fearful of a mere child!

Helen cannot be trusted. Her turpitude knows no bounds. Mark my words, that girl will not grow up to be a good person, she won't stop doing whatever it takes to get what she wants. If anything happens to anyone else at her hands, I will hold you personally responsible for wanting to keep this quiet.

My quality of life has changed since that visit, I suffer from my nerves and going out takes a huge effort of will. I am afflicted with night terrors and my poor daughter has to act as a constant companion to me. She has had to grow up too fast and watch her father deteriorating in front of her eyes. Nothing will ever be the same again. As I told you before, neither myself nor Mary will ever return to Oakmere Hall."

Elsie stared at her brother, her eyes reflecting the jolt of distress he was feeling.

William, who had stood up, sank back down onto the rug next to the trunk and put his head in his hands. "Oh no, this is awful. What does this mean exactly? Helen tried to kill Mary's father? Do you think that is true, or was the man delusional? Well, supposing she did try, but she was just a child, with a child's mentality. She grew up to be a lovely person. Helen can't have done anything wrong, she was returning the diamond to us wasn't she? She put it in the decanter."

"But what if she'd put it there to collect at a later date, once she'd got rid of Terrence?" Elsie realised she was wringing her hands together and consciously placed them on her lap, taking deep breaths to steady her nerves.

"You mean the poison was meant for him after all?"

"No, I didn't mean that. Terrence told us that Helen had told him the marriage was over, and he was going to leave once our party had finished. There was no point in planting cyanide in his drink."

William got up and began to pace the room, thinking hard. "This letter suggests that she wanted that diamond very much, and that she tried to kill Mary's father for it. What if Mary knew about it? Her father must have given her a reason as to why they weren't going to come back here again, and why he had then got so ill. Perhaps she knew, all along, about Helen trying to kill him."

"Are you suggesting that Mary poisoned Helen in revenge?"

"I don't know what I'm suggesting, to be honest. However, Terrence denied using the poison, didn't he? It could have been bravado that made him tell Jonty he'd tried to kill him. What if it had been Mary after all?"

Elsie began to think aloud. "Mary didn't want the diamond, did she? Wealth never interested her, that's obvious. What if she and Terrence somehow met, and they hatched a plan together? Remember how the maid thought she'd recognised Mary when she first saw her? That suggests she had been in Oakmere. If Terrence had told Mary that his marriage was over, and that his money was being cut off, they could have put their heads together. If he covered up for Mary's revenge on Helen, she'd let him burgle her house and take the diamond."

William shut his eyes. "What are we to do now?"

"Can we do anything? This is all just guesswork. The Inspector has already made Terrence the scapegoat for both crimes. Should we just let it go?"

"And let her get away with it?" William opened his eyes and stared at his sister in disbelief. "Our friends are dead, and not once has she offered us any financial help, though she knows we are in need."

"Did I say we'd let her get away with it? Oh no, brother dear. She'll not get away with a thing. We just need to put out heads together to come up with a suitable plan."

About Salema Nazzal

Reading, writing and the English language has always been a passion for Salema and so she trained to teach English as a foreign language and went to work in Beirut for a few years. She started off teaching adults at a language centre and then ended up at a school on the grounds of an orphanage.

Now back in England, she spends her time writing, looking after her two children, and cats (not necessarily in that order!).

In 2015 Salema's first 1930s style whodunit, The Folly Under the Lake, was published by Pneuma Springs. It outsold 'Girl on the Train' at the Haslemere Bookshop and finished the year being their overall bestseller, even selling out at the book launch. The interest has been overwhelming!

Inspiring authors include the queen of crime herself Agatha Christie and J Jefferson Farjeon because they write good old-fashioned crime stories that are gripping from start to finish. She also loves the writings of Naguib Mahfouz, an Egyptian writer, who won the 1988 Nobel Prize for Literature.

Connect with Salema Nazzal

www.facebook.com/authorsalemanazzal

or

PSP Featured author's page
http://www.pneumasprings.co.uk/Featuredauthors.htm#Salema Nazzal

Other Book(s) by Salema Nazzal

The Folly Under the Lake, ISBN 9781782284031

Multi-millionaire Walter Sinnet is crooked and ruthless. He builds an impressive underwater folly on his property. Wishing to show off, Walter welcomes a house party to his home, but an angry storm lashes down on the village and traps everyone inside the estate. A guest's jewellery goes missing and a dead body is found floating in the lake.

Lightning Source UK Ltd.
Milton Keynes UK
UKOW01f2049130217
294301UK00001B/1/P